A DEATH OF FRESH AIR

A RIGHT ROYAL COZY INVESTIGATION MYSTERY

HELEN GOLDEN

DREW BRADLEY PRESS

ALSO BY HELEN GOLDEN

ISBN (P) 978-1-915747-23-5

Edited by Marina Grout at Writing Evolution

Published by Drew Bradley Press

Cover design by Helen Drew-Bradley

First edition September 2024

To my Ab Fab girls: Helen, Helen, and Cathy.

For the friends who turn ordinary moments into extraordinary memories.

Thank you for your fabulous friendship through the years and, I hope, for many years to come…

NOTE FROM THE AUTHOR

I am a British author and this book has been written using British English. So if you are from somewhere other than the UK, you may find some words spelt differently to how you would spell them. In most cases this is British English, not a spelling mistake. We also have different punctuation rules in the UK.

However if you find any other errors, I would be grateful if you would please contact me helen@helengoldenauthor. co.uk and let me know so I can correct them. Thank you.

For your reference I have included a list of characters in the order they appear, and you can find this at the back of the book.

1

3 YEARS, 5 MONTHS EARLIER. WITH THE KILLER...

Thwack!

A metallic taste filled my mouth as I bit down on my bottom lip, the force of the blow having caused me to clench my jaw. I flinched as the impact of the rubber cosh reverberated through my shoulders, sending a shockwave into my arms and down into my hands. I'd never hit anything that hard before.

The man on the receiving end of the blow crumpled to the ground.

Dropping my wobbly arms, I didn't move, my heart pounding in my chest. *Did I really do that?* A wave of nausea washed over me as I looked down at the cosh hanging loosely by my side. This wasn't how I'd wanted things to go. Why hadn't he just taken the offer? Hadn't he realised that by refusing to cooperate, he was signing his own death warrant?

I took a big gulp of air, then slowly let it out, breaking the eerie silence that had settled on the room. My heart rate was coming under control as I took another deep breath. *It's done now.*

I looked down at the man's body, memories of the heated

argument replaying in my mind. I'd given him a way out. All he'd had to do was take the money and disappear. No one would have ever known. But he'd refused.

"What you're doing is wrong," he'd said.

Like anything was ever that simple.

"I don't want to be part of this," he'd said.

Well, it was all very well having principles, but if it was going to cost you your life…

I shook my head as I leaned in closer. The rise and fall of the man's chest was just perceptible if you looked close enough. *Right, time for action.*

I swiftly returned the cosh to my pocket, and checking my gloves were still firmly in place, I bent down and rummaged in his pockets. *Ha, keys!* I retrieved the bunch and examined them. *Perfect.* I pocketed them, then grabbed the unconscious man's legs. Dragging him along the kitchen floor wasn't too difficult. The heavy cotton of his chef's whites slid easily across the shiny resin flooring. I stopped a few metres in front of the walk-in freezer and slowly lowered the man's legs to the floor. Reaching up, I pulled the steel handle, and the door eased open.

The cold air hit me immediately, almost taking my breath away and sending a shiver down my spine. *I need to speed this up…*

Scampering back to the body, I lifted the man's legs up again and pulled him across the threshold. The container was filled with the sharp, crisp scent of frozen foods and the musty smell of aged metal and frost.

I deposited the body at the far end of the icy container as the harsh chill in the air nipped at my exposed skin, hitting my lungs and causing me to cough. A cloud of icy breath hung just in front of my face. I needed to get out of here before I froze to death.

As I turned, my eyes quickly darted past the shelves displaying lumps of meat, plastic containers of liquids, and bags of chopped vegetables and rested on a white circular handle on the side of the container just to the right of the open door. 'Use in case of emergency,' it said. I shivered. *Shall I just leave him and go? But what if he wakes up and uses the emergency handle? I'd better not risk it.* I retrieved a roll of gaffer tape from my other pocket, congratulating myself on the foresight I'd had to bring it, the cosh, and some gloves. Working quickly as the cold set into my bones, I secured his hands at the wrists with the tape. *Just in case...*

Keen to get out of the deadly ice-box as soon as possible, I took a last glance at the man, then turned and hurried out of the freezer before pivoting back around. Gripping the handle tightly, I yanked it down, sealing the icy container shut with a resounding clunk. I looked up and checked the temperature on the display above it. Minus eighteen degrees. It shouldn't take long. I reached up and hit the red button marked 'locked' and it lit up.

I gave a deep sigh as I rubbed my hands together, the gloves causing a friction that heated them up. I stared at the closed door of the freezer, a knot pulling in my stomach. I'd crossed a line that could never be uncrossed. I winced. *It was the only way.*

It's too late for regrets.

Right! *The most important thing now is not to get caught. I need a plan...*

3 YEARS, 5 MONTHS LATER, FRIDAY
4 JUNE

T*he Society Page* online article:

<u>Ryan Hawley and Simon Lattimore Announce the Name of Their New Venture</u>

Fenshire will soon have a new restaurant in the charming seaside town of Windstanton. Ryan Hawley, renowned chef and Bake Off Wars *judge, and crime writer Simon Lattimore, winner of* Celebrity Elitechef *two years ago, have today announced their restaurant, due to open on 10 July, will be called SaltAir.*

The pair recently purchased the building Clary House, which was built in 1857 by the wealthy Victorian landowner Marmaduke Clary. Talking on Fenshire FM this morning, Ryan told the radio station, they wanted to offer both a casual dining space and an opportunity for people to experience occasional fine dining. He said, "We hope SaltAir will appeal to both visitors to Windstanton and the people who live in the area. We will offer a relaxed dining experience downstairs in the SaltAir restaurant, where food will be seasonal and local.

Upstairs will be available for private dining and our monthly supper club, SaltAir Fine, which will be a fine dining experience with a different themed eight-course tasting menu on offer at each supper club event."

Lady Beatrice, the Countess of Rossex, who lives at The Dower House in nearby Francis Court, and her business partner, Perry Juke, who is also Simon Lattimore's husband, have been overseeing the redesign and refurbishment of the property, working with local company Hallshall Building Renovations. In his interview, Ryan said, *"We're going for a relaxed vibe downstairs that compliments the views of the sea, with a more formal feeling upstairs, reflecting, in a modern way, the history of Clary House."*

The building was previously owned by local entrepreneur and chair of the Windstanton Rejuvenation Council, Julian Thornton. He opened The Seaside Lounge six years ago, a popular and successful restaurant headed up by innovative chef Victor Blackwell. Shortly after Chef Blackwell left in January three years ago to take up an opportunity in the Antipodes, Mr Thornton closed The Seaside Lounge, and apart from the temporary letting of two apartments on the third floor, Clary House has remained empty ever since.

A grand opening is due to take place on Thursday 8 July, where selected guests, including fellow chefs and food critics, will get a taste of what is to come. Online bookings to dine at SaltAir from Saturday 10 July opened yesterday, and there is already a three-week wait for a reservation. The SaltAir Fine supper club will begin on Sunday 25 July, and bookings will be open from Thursday 8 July.

THREE DAYS LATER, MORNING, MONDAY 7 JUNE

"**D**o you think we've got everyone?" Ryan Hawley asked as he took a sip of his coffee.

Lady Beatrice, the Countess of Rossex, half closed her eyes. Getting together the guest list for the grand opening of SaltAir was turning out to be much harder than she'd expected. *Have we got the right people?* As she mulled over the question, her gaze swept around the Breakfast Room at Francis Court. The morning sun filtered through the floor-to-ceiling windows, casting a glimmering mist that danced on the tiled floor. The aroma of rich coffee mingled with the buttery scent of pastries, creating a warm, inviting atmosphere. It was mid-morning, and the restaurant was filling up with visitors and staff ready for their morning coffee and cake. Daisy, her little West Highland terrier, was huddled by Perry Juke's feet, ever hopeful that a stray morsel would fall from the table above.

"We've got the local who's who," Perry replied as he subtly tore off a small chunk of cheese scone and, without looking down, lowered his hand and popped it into Daisy's waiting mouth.

Perry! Bea gave him a look that said, "I'm not stupid. I saw that!"

He ignored her and carried on, "But we need a few more names who will create a buzz."

Simon Lattimore tipped his head to one side. "Like?"

"Like influencers and people the press will be interested in," Perry replied. "You need to balance good publicity with good food. It's all about the right mix of people."

"Okay," Ryan said. "Let's see." He referred to the list in his hands. "Finn Gilligan and Mike Jacob will be there."

The attendance of Finn, Ryan's fellow chef and co-presenter of the popular TV show *Two Chefs in a Camper,* along with Mike, the other *Bake Off Wars* judge, who was also a well-liked chef, would generate a lot of interest.

"And of course we've got Lord Fred and Summer, who will be a massive draw for the press," he continued.

Bea suppressed a sigh. The press were still obsessed with her elder brother, Lord Frederick Astley, and his girl-friend of the last four months, TV presenter Summer York. It had been over a month now since they'd gone public with their relationship, and yet they still dominated the headlines in the popular press most days. "They wouldn't miss it for the world," Bea assured Ryan, twirling the rings on her right hand. "Sarah and John are looking forward to it too. Sarah has a lot of influence locally." Bea's sister and Fred's twin, Lady Sarah Rosdale, managed the events at Francis Court. She had an extensive network of local suppliers, some of whom she'd already introduced to Ryan and Simon. "Ma and Pa would come, but they'll be away in Ireland. So you'll have to make do with me, Sam, and Archie." Bea's fifteen-year-old son, Sam, and his best friend, Archie Tellis, could hardly contain themselves. Huge foodies and massive fans of Ryan, they'd even offered to help prep food during the day and act as servers on the night.

"Archie and I can hand out canapés," Sam had suggested to Simon and Ryan when he'd been home from boarding school the previous weekend. "And we can tell people exactly what's in them and everything." A smile tugged at Bea's lips as she recalled his enthusiasm to be a part of the project. With his love of cooking, she knew she was going to have problems keeping him away from SaltAir's kitchen over the coming school summer holidays.

"Speaking of guests," Perry interjected, his tone playful and teasing. "Will the dashing Fitzwilliam be gracing us with his presence?"

A blush tinged Bea's cheeks. She swallowed. "Yes, he'll be there," she confirmed, tucking a strand of her thick red hair behind her ear. "But we'll be arriving separately... you know, with the press and everything."

The heat in her cheeks was burning now. Her relationship with former Protection and Investigations (Royal) Services (PaIRS for short) Detective Chief Inspector Richard Fitzwilliam was still very new, and they were slowly learning to navigate their circumstances *and* their feelings for each other. *It still feels fragile*, she admitted to herself. She worried that if their romance came under too much scrutiny, it might not survive.

At least since his appointment to Superintendent at City Police, which had him heading up the Capital Security Liaison Team, Rich no longer worked for the organisation responsible for her and her family's safety. That personal-work conflict wasn't an issue anymore, and that made things easier. However, apart from Perry, Simon, Fred, and Ryan, no one knew about their burgeoning relationship, and for the moment, Bea was happy to keep it that way. "Enough about my love life," she deflected, her gaze shifting from Perry to Simon. "What about Isla? Will she be able to come?"

Simon's newly discovered teenage daughter, Isla Scott, had left to return to Scotland three weeks ago to stay with her late mother's relatives.

"I hope so," Simon said, his expression softening. "She may even spend a few months here afterwards before she goes to Spain. When I video-called her last night, she seemed open to the idea."

Bea smiled at her friend. It would be good for father and daughter to have some time together before Isla went off to study at university in Barcelona. But her smile faded as she caught Perry's sullen expression out of the corner of her eye. She stifled a sigh. She knew from their conversations that Perry was still wary of the girl who had suddenly turned up a month ago and dropped the bombshell that Simon was her father, due to a brief holiday fling he'd had with a Scottish waitress working in Spain almost twenty years ago. Looking at Perry's slightly petulant pout, Bea's heart twisted. *I hope given time he will embrace the situation.*

"Well," Simon said cheerily, clearly wanting to defuse the tension that had descended. "Short of the King and Queen turning up, I don't think we can get much more press attention."

Perry, seeming to pull himself together, nodded. "Yes. But" —he turned to Bea with a sly smile— "no offence, Bea, having so many members of the royal family coming will get the press there, but they'll only be interested in taking pictures of everyone arriving and leaving. We also need people who will go back to their own audience and tell them how great the place looks and, most importantly, how amazing the food is."

"I think you're right," Bea said, her mind briefly

wandering to the guests they'd already considered. She took a sip of her coffee, savouring its boldness, then added, "We need a few more local influencers who know what they're talking about when it comes to food."

"Okay," Ryan said. "Let's see." He referred to the list in his hands. "Perhaps we should invite Rob Rivers. He's got considerable clout in the local culinary scene and could bring in some good publicity."

"Rob Rivers?" Bea raised an eyebrow. Rob Rivers, the chef-patron of the bistro Rivers by the Sea in Windstanton, was well-known locally, often doing food slots on Fenshire radio and local TV news shows. He'd even appeared as a guest on a couple of national cooking shows. *But...* "Isn't that like inviting the competition to your doorstep?"

"Sometimes," Perry chimed in, waggling his eyebrows, "you have to keep your friends close and your rivals closer."

Ryan grinned. "His reputation relies on him being open and honest. If he says bad or untrue things about us, it will reflect poorly on him."

Bea tipped her head. *That makes sense.* "Then yes, we should invite him."

"We should probably add Marco Rossi to the list too," Simon added, pointing to the guest list. "He's got that Italian charm people love—"

"And he has a huge following on social media," Perry jumped in.

"He's the food critic, isn't he?" Bea asked.

"A local one," Perry told her. "He rarely goes outside of Fenshire."

"Which is exactly why we need him," Simon explained. "His perspective is unique. Plus, he's quite the character."

"Added," Ryan said as he scribbled on the list.

"Is Bella DeMarco on there?" Perry asked, reaching for a

blueberry scone from a plate in the middle of the table. Underneath it Daisy stirred. Bea gave Perry a warning look.

Ryan consulted the list. "Er…no. Who's she?"

Simon frowned and turned to his husband. "Wasn't she the head chef at The Fawstead Inn a few years back?"

"Ah," Perry said, a gleam in his eye. "She was indeed. But since she went on the TV show *Love Resort*, she's given that up. She's now a full-time influencer and food blogger."

Bea grinned. No one knew more about reality TV and its stars than Perry. "She sounds like a must-have to me." Simon and Ryan gave a nod of agreement. "I assume you have Julian Thornton on your list?"

"The previous owner of Clary House?" Ryan asked "No. He couldn't wait to get rid of the place, so I didn't think he'd be interested in coming back anytime soon."

Bea had forgotten Ryan wasn't local. He wouldn't understand that Julian Thornton was Windstanton's answer to the Duke of Westminster. Bea had met the older man on several occasions when she'd attended charity events in the seaside town. "He owns a lot of other buildings in Windstanton, including The Parade shops, the new cinema complex, the retirement village, the bingo hall, the theatre, a business park, and the amusement arcade on the pier. He's also chair of the Windstanton Rejuvenation Council and very active in the town's rotary club."

"He's a big player in this town," Perry added with a flourish, his blond hair catching glints of sunlight as he bobbed his head. "I think he'll feel slighted if you don't ask him."

"He's on the list now," Ryan said. "Anyone else?"

"Liv Belmont?" Perry suggested, wiping his mouth of crumbs. "You can't not invite the drama queen of Windstanton Theatre."

"She's the manager of the Theatre Royal here," Simon

explained to Ryan. "Olivia's got style," he said as he gave Perry a sly grin. "And influence. She'll bring in the arts crowd if she likes the place."

"All right then," Ryan said decisively, writing the last name down and then surveying the list. "Looks like we've got a guest list that will turn any restaurateur green with envy."

4

SOON AFTER, MONDAY 7 JUNE

Daisy jumped up from her position curled up by Perry's feet and gave a short *yap* as two women walked into the Breakfast Room.

"So I said to him, 'If it's covered in mould, it can hardly be called fresh, can it?'!" a woman's voice cut through the room's quiet chatter. Bea turned and watched Ellie Gunn, Francis Court's catering manager, and Claire Beck, Francis Court's HR manager, amble through the sunlit space. Ellie spotted them and waved as she and Claire made their way over to the group where they greeted an excited Daisy.

"You look like you're up to no good…" Ellie said as she straightened up and gestured to the strewn papers in front of Ryan.

"We're knee-deep in guest lists," Perry told them.

"Oh, for the opening of your new restaurant?" Ellie beamed at Ryan, who inclined his head.

Claire, her red glasses perched jauntily on her nose, beamed at him too. "Ah, The Seaside Lounge reborn! Maisey spent her evenings weaving between those tables," she said, her full lips curving into a nostalgic smile.

Ryan frowned and looked at Perry.

"Claire's sister, Maisey, worked there before it closed down." Perry rose and pulled out chairs for Ellie and Claire.

"Yes," Claire said, eyeing up the plate of uneaten scones in the middle of the table. Perry pushed it towards her and Ellie, who was now sitting next to him. "When Victor Blackwell was the chef there." She leaned in, her voice dropping into a conspiratorial whisper. "Before he left." Her curls bounced as she nodded before picking up a fruit scone and tearing it in two.

"I heard he went abroad, following his dreams or some such thing, to Australia?" Perry said, arching his brow.

"Maybe. Maybe not," Claire confided, tapping the side of her red frames. "He went on holiday and never came back. No warning. No farewell—just poof!" She flung her hands out, almost taking Perry's eye out with the knife she had in her hand, ready to butter her scone.

Bea's nose twitched. Was Claire suggesting there had been something suspicious about Victor's leaving? She racked her memory. She remembered little about The Seaside Lounge other than it had done a great ice cream sundae that she and Sarah had sometimes treated Sam and her nephew Robbie to during their trips to the beach when the boys had been young.

"We don't really know much about the previous restaurant, just that it closed down a few years ago and has been empty since then," Simon told them.

"Well," Claire said, putting down her half-eaten scone. "The Seaside Lounge, as it was then, was a real Windstanton draw. It was doing great until the chef, Victor Blackwell, walked out about three-and-a-half years ago during a four-week closure while they were having the dining room and toilets refurbished. Then, when Vic left, Julian Thornton, who owned the building, decided to close it down." She shook her head sadly. "Without Vic, the heart of the place just…well, just stopped beating."

"Julian held on to it, trying to get planning permission to turn it into luxury flats, but the council repeatedly turned him down for a change of use. He finally gave up earlier this year," Ellie added.

"Luckily for us," Simon said with a grin.

Putting down her coffee cup, Bea asked, "Why did Vic leave?"

Claire shrugged. "Had a better offer supposedly. He went on holiday to Australia and never returned. He sent Julian an email saying an amazing opportunity had come up there, so he was staying. And that's the last anyone ever heard of him…" Her voice trailed off.

They all looked at Claire. She let out a sigh. "Maisey was really surprised he didn't come back to say goodbye or get in contact to explain. She felt they were like a family — her, Vic, and the others who worked there. She said it was unlike him to just leave like that."

"But come on, Claire," Ellie chimed in. "You have to admit he was a funny bloke was Vic. He was a talented chef, a real innovator. But he had a touch of arrogance about him… No one was *really* surprised he just upped and left to pursue something bigger and better." She gave a wry smile. "I keep expecting to see him crop up fronting one of those cooking shows on TV from Down Under." She cocked her head with a small shrug. "But then again, he wasn't really a people person."

Bea let out a slow sigh. So it wasn't really a mystery after all. Just Claire's sister being annoyed that a slightly big-headed chef had left for greener grass without saying goodbye.

"As far as I'm concerned," Perry said, picking up his coffee. "As long as we don't find him buried under the terrace, I don't really care where he's gone!"

5

A WEEK LATER, MORNING, MONDAY 14 JUNE

Bea unwound the backseat window slightly and peered out as the Bentley rolled into Windstanton, which was the very picture of quaint seaside charm. *It looks like a vintage postcard*, Bea thought as they drove through the bustling main street.

Beside her, the gentle snoring that had been coming from Daisy stopped, and Bea felt the little dog's paws on her lap as Daisy climbed up to get a better view. They turned right at the bottom of the wide street, onto the road that ran along the side of the promenade.

Perry took in a deep breath of fresh air. "I love the smell of the sea."

Bea glanced over at him sitting on the other side of the backseat. His eyes were closed, a dreamy look on his face. His blond hair caught the sun's rays streaming through the car window, giving him an almost ethereal glow.

Smiling, Bea returned her gaze to the window and beyond. On the sweeping walkway, a group of children chased the receding tide in the shadow of the looming wooden planks of the pier, which seemed to stretch endlessly towards the horizon. *There's definitely something relaxing about being by the sea.*

Daisy's ears suddenly pricked up at the sound of seagulls flying overhead, their cries a soundtrack to the waves lapping in the distance. She scrambled on Bea's lap and stuck her nose out of the top of the window.

"I think seagulls may have overtaken squirrels as Daisy's new obsession," Perry said, his voice laced with amusement.

"Indeed," Bea said with a grin as she grabbed her little dog's harness, not one hundred percent sure the terrier wouldn't launch herself through the partly open window to get a closer look at the squawking birds.

As the car slowed down to turn onto a side street, Bea straightened and shifted Daisy off her knees, returning the little dog to the space in-between her and Perry. The Bentley rolled to a gentle stop before Clary House, and Bea's heart skipped a beat as she gazed at the majestic Victorian building standing tall and proud, its ornate architecture drawing her eyes upwards to its intricately carved stone details in the weathered red-brick walls and beyond that to the towering turrets on top that reached up towards the heavens. As Fraser opened the door, Bea clipped on Daisy's lead, and they followed Perry out of the car.

Perry walked past the wrought-iron gates adorned with swirling patterns that stood between two massive stone columns that would soon welcome visitors into SaltAir and headed straight for the side entrance. But Bea paused, and giving Daisy a gentle tug on her lead, she led her to the edge of the building, past the iron railings that surrounded the terrace, and up to the top of the road where she could over-look the breathtaking expanse of the sea. The surface of the water in the distance shimmered under the morning sun. The salty breeze carried with it the distinct scent of the ocean, and Bea closed her eyes for a moment, taking in a deep breath.

When she opened them again, her gaze was drawn towards SaltAir's empty terrace to her right. In her mind's eye, the sundeck was transformed into a vibrant scene, bustling with customers. Chairs faced towards the sea, inviting diners to soak in the panoramic views as they savoured their food. She could almost hear the clanking cutlery and murmured conversations filling the air, intermingling with bursts of joyous laughter.

She smiled to herself, her heart swelling with excitement and determination. This was Simon and Ryan's dream, and she was determined to help them make it a reality.

———

"I think it's the first time I've been in here and been able to talk at a normal level," Perry said as they reached the last few steps of the grand staircase, Daisy at their heels, as it met the spacious first floor landing.

While the plaster in the kitchen in the basement dried, ready for the countertop installation, the builders were taking a well-deserved long weekend off. "Indeed," she agreed, her hand trailing off the end of the banister. Bea had to admit the quietness was slightly unnerving. "You can imagine this place really *is* haunted when it's this—"

Daisy gave a sharp bark and, turning on her heels, scampered up the stairs towards the second floor. Bea looked at Perry, her heart thumping in her ears. *What's Daisy heard?*

"Is something or someone up there?" Perry whispered, his eyes wide as he stared up into the darkness.

They both froze as they heard footsteps thudding on the

stairs above them. Bea swallowed. *Yikes!* She wanted to move, but her feet were like lead.

Relief washed over her when she heard a familiar voice say, "Hello, Daisy."

Ryan! The renowned chef, TV baking judge, and co-owner of SaltAir, came bounding down the stairs with his signature exuberance. He sported a goatee and a cleanly shaved head. His brown eyes twinkled as he caught sight of Bea and Perry. His large mouth curved into a huge smile, revealing a set of perfect teeth. "Surprise!" he said as he stopped in front of them. "I moved into the apartment this weekend," he told them excitedly.

One of the advantages of having bought the whole of Clary House was that it came with two large flats on the second floor. Ryan, who lived in London, where he was executive chef at Nonnina, a fine dining restaurant in Knightsbridge, was keen to also have a base in Fenshire to allow him to spend as much time as he needed in Windstanton to make SaltAir a success. And as the production company that made *Bake off Wars* had just confirmed him for the ninth series of their popular baking show and a celebrity special, both of which were being filmed at Francis Court again, having one of the flats to use had seemed like the perfect solution. The other flat had been offered to the newly appointed head chef of SaltAir to entice him to leave his previous position at a five-star country hotel in the Cotswolds.

"I saw you coming in on the camera on the front door," Ryan continued as Daisy sped past him and ran back to Bea. "It's very handy. I'll show you both how to access it from your phones later when we've finished wiring up the whole place. They're doing the rest of downstairs and the back car park next."

They both nodded.

"We wanted to see what the supper room looks like now it's been emptied and repaired," Bea told him as she moved across the wide landing, Daisy at her heels.

"Yes," Perry added, following her. "We want to make sure the vision we had still works now it's been cleaned up."

"I'll confess," Ryan said as he fell into step beside them. "I had a sneaky peek inside when I arrived yesterday. You won't be disappointed." He grinned, and Bea couldn't help smiling back. Ryan's good energy was infectious. She knew from previous projects that the few weeks before completion were the most stressful for the owners — everything was empty, so it was hard for them to envision how the bare spaces were going to be transformed into the rooms of their dreams. She, on the other hand, loved this step in the process — when all the knocking about, reconfiguring, and clearing up had been done, and she stood there before a blank canvas, ready to create the environment that would bring the atmosphere she imagined.

Pushing open the heavy wooden door of the supper room, Perry walked in. Bea heard him gasp as she tailgated him into the room.

Wow! Bea stopped still. The Victorian room was a sight to behold.

Ornate chandeliers hung from the high ceiling, their crystal prisms refracting the sunlight into a dazzling display of colours. Elaborate mouldings, now repaired, adorned the ceiling, depicting intricate floral patterns that seemed to come alive under the soft light. The floor, once covered in dust and debris, now gleamed with fresh polish and matched the dark oak panelling that crept half-way up the walls above, which had been freshly plastered. The room exuded a sense of grandeur and elegance that sent shivers down Bea's spine. As she stepped further into the room, she could imagine it filled with people dressed in their finest attire, enjoying the exquisite food amidst the opulent ambiance.

Perry's voice snapped her out of her daydreaming. "Do you see it, Bea? The potential?" His words were filled with excitement, mirroring her own anticipation.

Smiling at him, she dipped her chin slowly. All the ideas she and Perry had discussed would work perfectly in this room.

"Imagine this," Perry said to Ryan, gesturing around the room with his arm. "Walls painted deep, dark red. Tables dressed in linens as white as snow, and there" —he pointed towards the bay window— "a grand piano with gentle tunes mingling with the tinkle of cutlery and low conversation." He turned to Ryan. "What do you think?"

Ryan raised his eyebrows. "Music to dine by," he mused. "I like it."

Bea beamed. "We want an ambiance of elegance but with the warmth of a home. I want diners to feel special but at the same time, relaxed and comfortable."

A soft rustle drew their attention to Daisy, who had found a patch of sunlight and was circling inside it. Once she was sure she had exactly the right spot, she dropped and curled up with a heavy sigh.

"Daisy certainly seems at home," Perry said with a grin.

"I trust you both to make it work," Ryan said. "I still find it hard to believe we're already booked out in the restaurant downstairs for the first four weeks solid. And SaltAir Fine inquiries are through the roof."

Bea's stomach fluttered. Windstanton had embraced the new venture with open arms. *I just hope we can live up to the town's expectations.*

6

A FEW MINUTES LATER, MONDAY
14 JUNE

As Bea, Perry, and Ryan made their way downstairs to the ground floor at Clary House, the echo of footsteps in the foyer heralded the arrival of Simon. Daisy gave a low *woof* and sped off ahead of them to greet one of her favourite people.

"Sorry I'm a bit late. The call to my editor went on longer than I expected," Simon said as they reached the spread of geometric tiles that made up the floor of the lobby. "Honestly, I've rewritten this chapter three times already, and she's still not satisfied," he huffed.

Perry placed a hand on his husband's arm. "I'm so sorry, love. Will it take long?"

Simon shook his head. "No, not really. I just want to get these edits agreed so I can concentrate on this place."

Bea dipped her chin sympathetically. She knew how hard Simon had been working over the last few weeks to get his latest crime novel into a final version for his publishers.

"Is upstairs looking good?" Simon asked as they moved through the hallway. The other three nodded. "So it's just—"

"The restaurant!" Perry finished as they entered the room

at the end. Bea stared at the vast space before them, the remnants of its former grandeur still visible. The wallpaper, once opulent and adorned with delicate patterns of blooming flowers and intricate vines, was faded, with its edges curling.

The air hung heavy with dust, somewhat obscuring the sunlight that filtered through the grimy floor-to-ceiling windows, highlighting the debris-laden, unpolished floor. The glass panes had cracks in places that added an eerie touch to the already dilapidated atmosphere. Cobwebs stretched across the corners of the room, and the view of the sea was disguised by grubby lace curtains in front of dusty plastic that had been placed over the windows to keep out prying eyes. The elaborate iron-clad doors stood tarnished with blacked-out panes of glass in the centre.

Simon sighed, scanning the room. "It's still such a mess in here."

"Oh, don't worry too much about that," Perry said, reassuring him. "We have it all in hand with Charles. The glaziers are here early next week, and all the repairs are scheduled once the kitchen has gone in. The issue we wanted to discuss is—"

"This," Bea interjected, pointing to a thick false wall on her left that jutted out into the room like a colossal wooden whale; it partially blocked the windows, casting a shadow over that side of the room. She walked around it and gestured at the bulky dark-wood bar behind it. "And this."

"We think it all needs to go," Perry said, rubbing his hands together as they followed Bea.

"Knock it down?" Simon mused, his finger tapping against his chin.

"Why?" Ryan asked, eyeing the structure with a critical gaze.

"It blocks the flow as you come in," Bea said, demonstrating with her arms. "Without it, guests will arrive and immediately see the views as they step through the door rather than being distracted by that eyesore."

"So move it?" Ryan pondered aloud.

"Well, replace it," Bea said. "We'll build something less intrusive and more modern. Something slick. The question is, do you want to make it a focal point or not?"

Ryan and Simon looked at each other.

"I want nothing to distract from the view," Simon said eventually.

"I agree," Ryan said.

"How about over along the far wall then?" she suggested. "It will be easy for the staff to get to, and it will look good as you come through the door, but once you turn towards the windows, you won't see it."

Everyone agreed. "Great. We'll get it all knocked down later this week, after the kitchen has gone in and before we start all the repair work. I already mentioned the possibility to Charles, and he says it's not a big job. It's just a stud wall that went up when this room was redone just before it closed. It shouldn't take long."

"Oh," Perry said to Bea, clapping his hands together. "I love a good demolition. Can we come and watch?"

Bea shrugged. "If you want. But I doubt it will be very exciting."

7

LATER THAT WEEK, MORNING,
FRIDAY 18 JUNE

"Morning, you two!" The voice was rich with enthusiasm and unmistakably that of Charles Hallshall, the contractor's manager. He emerged from the kitchen, wiping his hands on a cloth as Bea and Perry walked into the foyer of Clary House.

"Morning, Charles." Perry extended a hand, greeting the contractor with a firm shake. "How's the dining room coming along?"

"We're about to knock down the old bar and remove the false wall. Once that's done, we'll build the new bar, re-plaster the walls and ceiling, then repair and polish the floor. After that, it's up to you two. Do you want to watch us do the demo?"

They nodded. Charles handed them both a hard hat, goggles, and a hi vis vest, and they followed him along the hallway. Bea's stomach fluttered with excitement as she put the waistcoat on. She couldn't wait to see how much extra space they were going to gain with the removal of the bar and stud wall. *And that view…*

The faintest tang of sea salt lingered in the air from the

partly opened doors leading onto the terrace as Bea stepped over the threshold and into the once grand dining room. Beneath their feet, the wooden floorboards creaked as they made their way across the majestic room. Her eye was drawn to the two boarded-up windows in the corner. She pointed at them. "Did you ever find out if anything was taken, Charles?" she asked, referring to the break-in that had occurred three nights ago. The two windows had been smashed from the outside late on Tuesday night.

He shook his head. "Not that we can see, although it is all a bit of a mess in here. All my lads have done a check of their power tools and equipment, but nothing seems to be missing. They were the only things of any value that we can think of that were in here."

That seemed consistent with Simon's theory that it had just been some local lads who'd done it for a dare, and as soon as the alarm had gone off, they'd fled.

"What did the police say?" Perry asked.

"Actually, it turns out the alarm that went off wasn't in this room as we'd assumed. That circuit hasn't been wired to the new system yet, apparently. It was the one in the hallway that leads to the back door. The uniform guys who came to investigate think whoever it was had a van out the back in the car park and planned on opening that door to get tools they needed or to let someone else in, then they were going to steal things from the rooms upstairs. Possibly even Ryan's flat. Of course, they couldn't have known we were in the process of having a state-of-the-art security system installed. It's just a shame the car park wasn't done by then, or we'd be able to see who was there."

"Seems like we had a lucky escape then?" Perry said.

"And it just goes to show that investing in the alarm system has paid off already. It won't take long for the news to get back to anyone with criminal intent that this place is well protected," Charles added, rubbing his hands together. "Anyway, let's get on, shall we?" he said, his voice echoing slightly in the cavernous space. He led them across the room, then stopped when they reached the middle of it. He pivoted his sturdy frame, clad in a tweed jacket and fawn-coloured chinos. "This used to be an old ballroom back in the day. It was built in the mid-eighteen hundreds," he continued, a hint of pride lacing his words as his blue eyes met Bea's. "Back when Windstanton was all corsets and parasols."

"Imagine the conversations these walls have absorbed over the years," Perry said, grinning. Bea dipped her head, her imagination conjuring up images of Victorian gentry sipping tea amongst the clinking of china and rustling of silk skirts.

"It used to be the main social hub of the town back then," Charles said.

"So what happened?" Bea asked.

"As transport links improved, people went further afield for their holidays. Most small seaside towns like this saw a decline in the number of visitors. That, in turn, led to a reduction in investment in the area. Everything got rundown, and eventually hotels and restaurants were forced to close. The final straw was when the train station closed in the 1980s. The place just died."

Bea wrinkled her nose. The thriving town she knew today, with its combination of boutique hotels, modern rental apartments, exquisite tea shops, and unique artisan shops was hard to reconcile with the place Charles was describing.

"But that all changed recently?" Perry said.

"Yes. Over the last few years, these Victorian seaside towns have become popular again. Partly because they offer a nostalgic charm that people are drawn to. You can't find that in modern beach resorts. People want to escape the hustle and bustle of city life and immerse themselves in a place where time seems to stand still. And partly because of the revitalisation efforts that have happened. Simon and Ryan were very lucky to get this place," Charles said, raising an eyebrow. "It's almost the last empty building of any significance remaining here that hasn't already been snapped up." He suddenly clapped his hands together. "Anyway, back to the present. Shall we see what we have over in that corner?" He gestured to the corner by the door where two workmen were assembling some temporary scaffolding in front of the wall on this side of the bar.

"Here's a thought," Perry said to Bea, stepping closer to a swath of faded floral-patterned wallpaper beginning to peel on the wall next to the bar. "What do you think about going vintage? Nothing too cheesy, just a subtle nod to the building's glory days?" His hand went to his chest. "Oh, what about that verdure tapestry silk wallpaper depicting afternoon tea in a Victorian orangery we saw the other day?" He gestured to the side wall. "It could go on there."

"I love it," Bea said, smiling, her mind already rifling through antique markets and vintage shops. "That could be charming if we can source the right items to go with it in time."

Donning their hats and goggles, they moved to stand next to Charles. They watched as one of the men ascended a ladder, stepped onto the scaffolding platform, and began to pummel the wall with a sledgehammer. The first strike reverberated through the room, sending a cloud of dust billowing into the air. Bea automatically put a hand up to shield her eyes even though she was wearing safety goggles, a thrill of anticipation coursing through her veins. *Once this goes, we'll have a clear view to the water.*

As the builder continued his relentless assault on the wall, piece by piece, flakes of aged paint and plaster rained down like confetti. Then suddenly the man paused. He kneeled down on the wooden planks that made up the platform and peered into the widening crevice in the wall. He plucked a torch out of his top pocket and turned it on.

"I've got something here, boss," he shouted down in a gruff voice.

"Probably just an old rat's nest," Charles said to Bea and Perry as they moved towards the wall. "We've already found a few of them around the back of the offices."

Bea shivered at the thought of rats scurrying around the place. As she looked up at the workman, who had carefully pulled away another piece of plaster, a look of confusion spread across his face. *What is it?* Her pulse quickened, intuition telling her he'd found something more than a rodent's ex-home.

With a final tug from the builder, a large shard of dry wall collapsed, revealing a large cavity. As dust billowed around them, Bea coughed, waving a hand in front of her face. She lifted the goggles onto the top of her hard hat and peered through the settling haze as the man shone his torch into the hole—then recoiled. *Crikey!*

"Blimey," he muttered, the word hanging in the air like a shroud.

Indeed! A musty smell of decay seeped into the room. Bea instinctively put her hand up to her nose and moved to get a better look.

There, nestled within the hollowed-out wall, was a large roll of heavy-duty plastic sheeting. *What the?* As she leaned closer, her arm knocked Perry's, and they both jumped.

Giving her a nervous smile, he whispered, "I don't have a good feeling about this…"

Me neither.

The worker, his face pale, retreated down the ladder and stood behind them as Charles stepped forward gingerly, his face solemn as he stared into the gaping hole. "Good Lord," he mumbled. He looked around and grabbed a large pair of scissors.

Bea's heart skipped a beat. *What's in there?* She lowered her hand, the smell having dissipated, but held her breath as Charles began to carefully cut through the plastic.

As the blades sliced through the sheeting, she noted clumps of chalky crystals attached in patches to the inside. As the fragile layers fell back the sheeting was stained dark.

She couldn't help herself. She inched forward.

As she gazed into the cavity, her breath hitched. *Oh my goodness!*

"Oh my giddy aunt," Perry gasped, his face only inches from hers.

Silence swaddled the room as they stood frozen in time for a few minutes, gawking at the mass of bones.

8

A FEW SECONDS LATER, FRIDAY 18 JUNE

Bea's heart raced as her eyes fixed on the newly uncovered compartment. *Is it human?*

Perry leaned in, his expression sombre yet undeniably captivated by the grim tableau before them. "It looks like human bones to me. Look. There's a skull."

Charles stood stock-still, his usually composed demeanour replaced by a look of stunned disbelief. He removed his hard hat and safety glasses, then ran a hand through his neat blond-grey hair as he peered into the cavity. His Adam's apple bobbed up and down. "I think so too."

Oh my goodness! Bea's stomach did a somersault. *Who?*

"Remember what Claire's sister said about the previous chef here?" Perry murmured, his voice a low thrum against the silence.

"Victor Blackwell?" Bea swallowed hard.

"She told Claire he would have been in contact to at least say goodbye. Maybe she was onto something—"

"And he never went in the first place?" Bea finished for him, her mind a whirl of possibilities. *How did he end up inside a false wall?* She let out a long breath through her nose. *Someone must have put him in here...*

"It could be Vic all right," Charles said, his eyes narrowing as he surveyed the remains. "But then, I guess it could be anyone."

Bea felt the chill of the room seep into her body as she stepped backwards. "We should call the police," she said in a slightly wobbly voice.

"Absolutely," Charles agreed, already reaching for his phone. "No more work today, boys," he called out to his crew. "Don't touch anything. Go down to the staff room, and I'll join you in a minute." The workmen left as Charles wandered off, his mobile phone glued to his ear.

Perry had already whipped out his camera and was snapping photos from every angle. Bea shot him a look that was mixed with horror and admiration—it had been useful in the past when Perry had taken photos of the crime scene, but it still felt tasteless to her. "Must you?" she asked, arching an eyebrow.

"You never know; they might come in handy when we start our investigation," he replied, clicking away.

What? Bea's shoulders tensed. *No! No more investigations.* "Perry, we're not investigating this. Surely, the police will—"

"Bea. We open in three weeks, remember? We can't have this room tied up as a crime scene. We need to get it finished."

Bea's heart sank. Perry was right. They were on a tight schedule as it was. A delay like this could jeopardise the opening. She ran her hand through her long hair. "Can we at least see who the police send? If it's someone like Mike, then he'll understand the urgency."

Mike Ainsley of Fenshire CID was well known to both of

them. They'd worked with him before to solve a time-sensitive case. He was discreet and—

Perry made a squeak-like noise. "What if they send Saunders from PaIRS?" he asked in dismay.

Bea felt lightheaded. *Oh no, not Saunders!* Newly promoted Detective Chief Inspector Hayden Saunders from PaIRS had been sent to Francis Court two months ago to investigate a murder that had taken place on the set of *Bake Off Wars*. Not only had he been rude and dismissive of their help, but he was inexperienced with serious crimes. She shivered. If Saunders got involved with this, it could take ages to close. She mentally shook herself. *Come on, Bea, get a grip.* There's no reason PaIRS will need to be part of this. She shook her head. "We're not in a royal home, and I can't see how a skeleton could be considered a threat to me. I think it's unlikely PaIRS will need to take charge of this." *I hope I'm right!*

"Well," Perry said. "Let's hope it's Mike. Because if it's not, then I don't see how we'll have a choice but to—"

"The police are on their way." Charles' booming voice interrupted Perry. He walked over to them, pocketing his mobile.

Noting his furrowed brow and the way his eyes darted around the space, Bea's heart went out to Charles. *He won't want delays to the refurbishment either.* He had another job starting in mid-July. He'd only agreed to squeeze the refurbishment of Clary House into his schedule as a favour to her and because it was straightforward. He'd been confident he could get it completed before his long-standing commitment commenced. *But now....* "Thank you, Charles," Bea said, offering him a reassuring smile. "Why don't you grab a coffee and join your men? We'll deal with the police when they arrive."

The contracts manager nodded gratefully and lumbered towards the door that led to the hallway, his shoulders slumped. *Poor Charles.* It had all been going so well... *Oh my goodness! We'll have to tell Simon and Ryan.* Her stomach dropped. How would she break the news to them that a possible three-year-old murder might scupper their plans to open SaltAir on time? She turned hopefully to Perry. "Have you told Simon yet?"

"Yes, of course. He and Ryan are on their way."

Bea let out a deep breath in relief.

"Have you told Fitzwilliam?" Perry asked in return.

Bea rubbed her forehead, the headband of the hard hat making her skin itch. Her mind churned. She wanted to tell Fitzwilliam the boyfriend, but Fitzwilliam the senior police officer? That was more complicated.

Perry raised an eyebrow at her. "You *are* going to tell him, aren't you?"

"I don't know," Bea said honestly, her hands twisting together. "You know what he's like about us getting involved in police investigations." A knot tightened in her stomach. Could she trust him to handle the news without it bleeding into their relationship? If he asked her not to get involved, which he was bound to do, would she agree because he'd asked her to and let her friends down? Or would she go ahead and ignore his request, upsetting him and perhaps ruining things between them? When they'd finally admitted their feelings for each other seven weeks ago, she'd learnt his repeated warnings not to get involved in his cases had been driven by an overriding desire to protect her from danger rather than his disapproval. Because he cared about her. It was hard to argue against that. *So how do I tell him I might need to do the one thing I know will worry and stress him out?*

The sound of sirens getting closer dragged her from her dilemma. The piercing blue and red lights of police cars as they came haring along the promenade sliced through the blackened windows and temporarily painted the inside of the dining room in a garish light show.

"That's them then," Perry said, his eyes dancing with excitement. "Let's hope it's someone we know," he added, holding up one hand with his fingers crossed.

Bea gnawed on her bottom lip. In her head, she was already rehearsing her words for Fitzwilliam, wondering how to navigate the fine line between their personal life and his professional one. She'd been aware that at some stage they would face a test such as this, but she hadn't expected it to be so soon...

9

SHORTLY AFTER, FRIDAY 18 JUNE

"Here we go then…" Bea said to Perry as, now divested of their safety paraphernalia, they walked towards the hallway door. They passed through the main doorway just as the last of the police cars rolled to a stop outside Clary House, their pulsing lights dancing over the facade of the building. They stepped out on to the pavement and waited.

"What's wrong with us, Perry? How do we always find ourselves with a dead body?" Bea asked.

"Just lucky, I guess," he replied lightly as they watched three uniformed police officers jump out of the lead vehicle, one of them unfurling a strip of yellow tape with the words 'crime scene' splashed on it. Great! *Just the sort of publicity we* don't *need right now.*

As the door of the car in the middle of the three vehicles opened, Bea held her breath. *Please be Mike Ainsley.* A lofty man stepped out from the passenger side. His short greying hair and well-trimmed beard gave him an air of experience and authority. He took an object out of his pocket and brought it up to his mouth. His face temporarily grew hazy behind a cloud of mist. Bea pushed her breath through her teeth. It wasn't Mike Ainsley. *Rats!*

"Who is it?" Perry whispered in her ear. She shrugged. She didn't recognise the man either.

"He looks like an old bloodhound," Perry mumbled, not unkindly, as they watched the police officer's lanky build move with surprising grace towards them. Bea suppressed a giggle as she noted his down-turned mouth and slightly droopy eyes. *He does!*

"Let's just hope he can *sniff out* what happened here quickly," Bea said, smirking.

Perry rolled his eyes. "That was terrible."

"Thank you," she replied with a grin, then her face cleared. "Look, Perry. Our focus needs to be on getting SaltAir opened on time. We can't get distracted by a police investigation. Agreed?"

Perry tilted his head to one side. "But surely if we help, then they're more likely to get this wrapped up before…" He trailed off when he saw her face. He let out a deep sigh. "Okay. Agreed," he said reluctantly.

Bea caught a whiff of something fruity as the man stopped in front of them, his fingers wrapped around an electronic cigarette. "Detective Inspector Albert Finch, Fenshire CID." His voice was deep and slow. "I don't think we've met before, my lady." He gave a curt bow, but didn't offer his hand. Close up, he looked younger than she'd originally thought. *Early fifties possibly?* Bea gave an awkward smile in return. Finch's watery eyes turned to Perry. "And you are?"

"Er, Perry Juke, inspector. I work with Lady Beatrice. We're overseeing the refurbishment of the building."

"And it was you two who made the discovery, was it?"

"Well…" Perry hesitated and glanced at Bea. "We were there when it happened."

A much younger, dark-haired woman stopped next to Finch. He didn't introduce her.

"So assuming this is murder, do you think the body belongs to Victor Blackwell?" Perry asked.

What?! Why was Perry asking that when they'd just agreed not to get involved? She turned and stared at him. He sheepishly mouthed, "Sorry."

The woman quickly typed something into her phone while Finch's thick grey eyebrows shot up into his hairline. "Victor Blackwell? The chef? Why do you think it's him?"

Perry coloured. "Er, well…I heard he'd upped and gone to Australia three years ago and never came back, and this is where he worked at the time. So I thought maybe he didn't go after all…" He looked down at his feet.

"Let's not get ahead of ourselves, Mr Juke." His calm voice did little to hide a hint of irritation in his eyes. "For now, just know we're on the case, and you don't need to worry about it." He turned to the woman. "Sergeant, take a couple of uniforms and secure the scene. Hopefully, Forensics will be here in the next few hours." The DS gestured to two officers who were standing by the wall, and they followed her inside.

Hours? Bea frowned. In her now unfortunately rather extensive experience, the forensic squad was normally close on the tails of the investigating team. She glanced at Perry, who gave a quick shrug.

"We've stopped work, inspector, as you would expect. Everyone who was on-site when the discovery was made is waiting in a room upstairs. Just to let you know, we're up against a tight deadline. The restaurant opens in three weeks, and the dining room, where the…er, remains were found is the last major space we need to transform. Any delay is going to jeopardise our timeframe, so we need to regain access to that room as soon as possible."

Finch, who'd been listening patiently to her, nodded slowly, then tipped his head to one side. "Unfortunately, countess, that's not how it works." He shifted slightly. "Cold cases can take time. They don't have the same level of urgency—"

"But this one does to us, inspector." Bea tried to keep calm, but her frustration was mounting. It seemed like Finch was all too content to go at the slow pace of these investigations. The sound of hurried footsteps halted her next words as Simon and Ryan rushed towards them. Their faces were a mixture of shock and disbelief at the sight of police cars outside their restaurant.

"We came as soon as we could," Simon said, addressing Perry and Bea. "Can we—"

"Lattimore?" Finch's voice rose in surprise.

Simon turned around and stared at the man who'd called his name. He froze. "Finch?"

They know each other? This was good. If Simon knew the man who was investigating the case, then they should get the inside track on how it was progressing and perhaps even get it sped up. *Oh...* The look on the men's faces stopped her in her tracks. Simon was still staring at Finch, his mouth slightly open, while Finch was giving him daggers. *Oh, this doesn't look very hopeful...*

"I'd read somewhere that you were trying your hand at being a restaurateur," Finch said, an undercurrent of disapproval in his voice.

Simon said nothing.

Bea coughed.

Still nothing.

Perry gently nudged Simon in the ribs.

Simon finally seemed to come out of his trance. "Yes… er…I own this place," he stammered.

What's going on? Simon was normally the calm and collected one among them. She caught Perry's eyes, but he seemed as confused as she did.

"Along with me," Ryan added, clearly sensing Simon wasn't functioning at full capability. "Ryan Hawley." He offered the inspector his hand.

Finch took it as he pressed his lips together. "I see," he said quickly. "Well, gentlemen, I haven't anything to report as of yet." He cleared his throat. "I'm off to look at the scene, but I'd like to talk to you all once I've done that." He turned to Bea. "Is there somewhere you can wait?"

Ryan spoke up. "We'll be in my flat, inspector. Second floor. Please come up when you're ready."

Finch gave a short sharp nod, then heading to the door, he took a puff from his vape pen and disappeared in a fog of smoke.

Bea, Perry, and Ryan immediately turned to Simon. "What was that all about?" Perry asked. Simon, his posture still somewhat rigid, shook his head slowly. "What's he doing here?" he mumbled to himself.

"Simon!" Perry's voice had a sharp quality to it that was rare for him. "Talk to us."

"Sorry," Simon said as he pushed his hand through his short-brown hair. "We worked together when I was in CID."

"And you didn't get on?" Bea said, trying to hide her disappointment. *This is going to make things awkward…*

"Not really. We had a clash of styles, shall we say? Then I

left the police force and never saw him again. I heard he'd transferred to another department."

Perry stared at him for a few seconds. "There's more, isn't there?" he asked, resting his hand on Simon's arm.

Simon gave a big sigh, then looked at his husband. "I filed a complaint against him six months before I left."

10

NOT LONG AFTER, FRIDAY 18 JUNE

"Here you go." Ryan handed Bea a mug of steaming black coffee and returned to the kitchen area of his flat on the top floor of Clary House. Bea took a welcome sip of the aromatic liquid as her eyes quickly scanned the room. Filled with warm colours and comfortable furniture, the two-bedroom flat looked much cosier now that Ryan had settled in. *I bet Fay helped him furnish this.* Fay Mayer was Ryan's girlfriend. A sassy blonde, she was a food journalist based in London but was planning to join him in Windstanton as soon as the building works were complete.

When Bea had first met Fay during a local food festival the previous year, she hadn't been too sure about the smart, ambitious woman, but as she'd got to know her, she'd learned to appreciate that Fay was much softer and more fun when she came out from behind her tough food-critic persona. *It will be lovely to have her around more.*

Ryan returned from the kitchen, holding a plate of chocolate-covered biscuits. "Fay and I made these over the weekend. We've been experimenting with making vegan treats for a tasting menu I'm thinking of introducing at Nonnina."

Perry's face looked like a squeezed lemon as he gingerly took one from the plate Ryan offered him and examined it. Simon had experimented making non-animal based food in the past, but Perry had rejected all his attempts to, as he put it, "jump on the vegan band waggon", so Simon had given up.

"It won't kill you, Perry, I promise," Ryan said with a grin.

Bea watched in amusement as Perry nibbled a corner of the biscuit. His face cleared, and his eyebrows rose. "It's actually okay," he said in a surprised voice as he took another bite.

Bea glanced over at Simon, who was sitting on the other side of the dining table, gazing at Perry, his face a mixture of astonishment and amusement. "Well, Ryan, for Perry to say that about something vegan is high praise indeed," he said.

Ryan grinned as he sat down next to him and placed the plate in the middle of the table. "Now that they have Perry's seal of approval, tuck in."

Bea declined. She wasn't in the mood for anything sweet, but Simon helped himself. *Is he all right?* He seemed to have recovered from his encounter with Finch, but he hadn't really expanded on his bombshell revelation that he'd made a formal complaint against the man while he'd still been in the police force. She was keen to know more, so the only way to find out was to ask... "So how do you feel seeing Finch again after what I presume has been a long time?"

Simon, his mouth full, shook his head, then swallowed. "I'm fine. Just surprised, that's all." His brows furrowed. "I haven't heard much about him since I left." He shrugged casually.

"And are there still bad feelings between you?" Ryan asked.

Simon let out a sigh. "Not on my part, although I'll

confess I don't like the man. But no disciplinary action was taken against him in the end, so there's no reason why he should hold a grudge." Simon tilted his head, and giving a wry smile, he shrugged. "Anyway, it was a long time ago now. It's water under the bridge."

Bea frowned. Simon might think that, but the look on Finch's face had said a lot more. *Is Simon downplaying all of this?*

"Anyway, enough of me. Let's talk about our dead body."

"We think it could be Vic Blackwell," Perry told him.

"Hold on," Ryan interrupted. "I thought he went to Australia? Isn't that what you said?"

"Yes, but then Claire's sister, Maisey, said it was unlike him to not say goodbye. All I'm saying is perhaps he didn't…" Perry trailed off.

Bea racked her brains. *Didn't someone say there was an email?* "But there was an email from him saying he was staying there, wasn't there?"

Perry shrugged. "That's what Ellie said, but…" He trailed off.

Simon rose. "Why don't I give Steve a ring?"

Steve, affectionately known by them as CID Steve, was an inspector in Fenshire CID and a good friend of Simon's. He'd been their very useful 'inside man' during other local cases. "I'll see if he can shed any light on what CID's approach is and if they know anything about Vic's so-called disappearance."

Bea watched Simon vanish through the door leading into the hallway to make his call as Ryan let out a noisy sigh. She turned to meet his troubled eyes.

"What about the restaurant opening?" he asked. "If we can't get access to the dining room, then we'll never be ready to open on time. Plus, the negative publicity once this gets out will hurt us. We might draw a few curious people, but the majority won't want to eat next to a spot where someone was murdered." He ran his hands up and down the side of his face.

Poor Ryan. Bea had never seen him this flustered. He was normally upbeat and calm. But then, this was an enormous investment for him. It had to work. "We'll do everything we can to keep the details of the exact location out of the press," she reassured him while making a mental note to talk to her mother. Bea still found it a bit alien that her mother, Her Royal Highness Princess Helen, the king's sister, was in fact the owner of the online gossip rag *The Society Page*. With the attitude of 'if you can't beat them, join them', her mother had secretly been in control of the news outlet since she'd been in her early twenties. She argued it allowed her, and through her, her family, to have an element of control over what was said about them, and Bea had to admit it had come in handy in the past when untrue rumours had needed quashing. *She should be able to help.*

"And don't worry," Perry said. "If we have to, we'll get to the bottom of this ourselves. After all…"

Will we? Bea thought as he carried on. She wasn't so sure she wanted to. She could already imagine Rich's reaction if she told him she was getting involved in *another* murder investigation, especially one where he wouldn't be around to look out for her. Heat prickled her cheeks. She liked how protective he was of her. She smiled. It was so sweet the way—

Wait! Hold on. Pull yourself together, Bea. You don't need protecting. You're an independent, strong woman with a useful knowledge of self-defence. (This was courtesy of a 'how to avoid getting kidnapped' course she and her sister, Sarah, had been on a few years ago). She raised her chin slightly. *You can hold your own. You don't need a man to protect you.* In previous encounters with unsavoury sorts, she'd managed to get herself out of some pretty hairy situations. *But,* a little voice in her head said, *maybe next time you won't be so lucky...*

"Bea? Are you okay?" Perry turned to face her.

"Er, yes. Sorry. What were you saying?" She'd have to put her concerns about Rich's reaction to one side for the moment. She needed time to think.

"I said we have more motivation than anyone else to get this resolved quickly."

"Indeed." *He's right.* They didn't want this hanging over the opening of the restaurant and distracting everyone from their dining experience.

The door to the sitting room swung open, and Simon reappeared, a mixture of relief and concern etched on his face. He joined them at the table. "I got hold of Steve," he began as they all leaned in. "Mike Ainsley's on holiday, and DS Hines' on paternity leave. So no chance of either of them getting involved, I'm afraid."

Bea's stomach dropped. So they'd have no one who would be sympathetic to their need for discretion and speed to help chivvy things along.

"So it's down to Finch, is it?" Ryan asked.

"Yes, I'm afraid so. He's a cold case expert, which is why he's been assigned to the case. Steve says he's thorough but slow. There's no urgency with cold cases."

Bea exchanged a worried glance with Perry. Time wasn't on their side with the opening looming. They couldn't afford for Finch to leisurely plod along at his own tortoise-like pace. She clenched her fists. Perry was right. They would have to get involved if they wanted this done in time.

"Then we'll need to investigate ourselves," Perry said firmly.

Simon let out a deep sigh. "I don't—"

"Are you sure about this?" Ryan interrupted, his eyes darting between Bea and Simon. "We could get into trouble. That could be even worse for the future of this place."

"Ryan, we're already in trouble," Perry said. "There's a dead body in your restaurant. Is that what you want people talking about?"

"No, of course not."

"Then we need to get this put to bed before the opening so that it's not."

Simon rubbed one of his eyebrows. "He has a point, Ryan. Once this gets out, everything we're doing here will be overshadowed by the skeleton in our wall."

"Right." Ryan sighed. "So what do we do now?"

The back of Bea's neck prickled. *We have no choice.* They were going to have to find out what had happened for the sake of the restaurant and its future. But how on earth was she going to break it to Rich that she was, once again, sticking her royal nose into a police investigation?

11

EARLY AFTERNOON, FRIDAY 18 JUNE

Stirring her Earl Grey tea, Bea tried to relax back into her chair and ignore her churning stomach. The Breakfast Room was bathed in the afternoon sun, but the warmth couldn't chase away the cold in her fingertips. She had to let Rich know about them finding a body. *Again*! She stifled a groan. It had only been seven weeks since they'd wrapped up the investigation into the murder on the set of *Bake Off Wars*. *How can this be happening again so soon?*

A gentle snore from Daisy, who was under their table with her head resting in her paws, caught her attention. She looked down at the dozing little white terrier. *Can I swap places with you, Daisy? Will you tell Rich? He adores you. He might take it better coming from you...*

"Hello?" Perry's voice cut through her imaginary conversation with her dog. "Are you okay, Bea?"

"Sorry," she said, forcing a tight-lipped smile. "I was just wondering how to break the news of our find to Rich."

"You haven't told him yet?" Simon asked, unable to hide the disbelief in his voice.

Bea dropped the teaspoon on the table and crossed her

arms. "It's only been a few hours. We've been busy." She lifted her chin, heat prickling her cheeks. "And anyway, he's at a conference…"

Simon, a slight grin tugging at the corners of his mouth, slowly dipped his chin. "Of course."

She blew out a noisy breath and uncrossed her arms. She leaned over and patted Simon's hand. "Sorry. I just don't know how he's going to react, and it's worrying me."

Simon placed his hand over hers. "It'll be fine, Bea. Just tell him the truth."

"Yes," Perry jumped in, amusement in his voice. "It's hardly your fault you keep stumbling over dead bodies, is it?"

She pulled her hand away from under Simon's and glared at Perry. "Me? It's you too, you know!"

He winked at her. "I know."

Perry enjoyed the drama of a murder case more than she did. Yes, she wanted to see justice done. And yes, she wanted to help and protect those she cared about. But as a reality TV devotee, Perry got much more pleasure from delving into the lives of others and digging up their secrets than she did. The corners of Bea's mouth twitched upwards. He was very good at it. Whereas she nearly always ended up upsetting someone!

"Bea," Simon said, his brown eyes holding hers in a gaze. "Seriously, you can't be with someone you're afraid to talk to."

But it's not like that… "I'm not…" She trailed off. How could she explain to them that it wasn't that she was afraid he would ask her to stay out of the investigation. What she was really afraid of was that she would agree. Because she didn't want to worry him. Because she didn't want to cause him stress. Because she loved him… *Oh my goodness! Am I going to turn into one of those soppy women who only wants to make the man in her life happy?*

No! She raised her chin. She would call him and tell him they were going to investigate this case whether he liked it or not! She picked up her cup of half-full tea and took a sip. *I'll just finish my tea first...* "So we need to start thinking about suspects. Who wanted Vic dead three years ago and why?"

Perry and Simon exchanged glances, then Perry looked back at Bea, a resigned look on his face. "All right. I think the first thing to do is to talk to Maisey, Claire's sister. She worked at The Seaside Lounge, so will know all of his work colleagues. She got on great with Vic from what Claire said. She might even know about any friends he had outside of work."

Bea dipped her head. "That's a good idea. We should give Claire a ring and—"

"Hold your horses, Turner and Hooch." Simon waved his tea cup at them. "We don't know for sure the bones you found are actually Vic's."

Bea raised an eyebrow. "But we're fairly sure—"

"You can't go around asking questions about Vic and implying he's dead. What if it's not him?"

She suppressed a sigh. Simon had a point. It would be irresponsible of them to say anything at this point. "How will they identify the body?"

Simon shrugged. "It depends what they have to work on. They can tell gender, height, and estimated age just from the bones. They will use dental records or DNA matching to get a definitive answer if they can."

"But how long will it take?" They didn't have time to wait. They opened in three weeks.

"It all depends. If he had a local dentist, then they may be able to match the records quite quickly. If they have his DNA on file, it could be even quicker, but unless he's been in custody at some stage and had his DNA taken, then it's unlikely he'll be on the National DNA Database."

Perry, who'd been studying his phone, looked up. "What if they found something with the body?"

Simon shrugged. "If they can match something as belonging to a specific person, then that will obviously help."

"So like this?" Perry held up his mobile phone with a photo on the screen, then using his fingers, he zoomed in.

Well, that might help... A tarnished badge was nestled in-between two chalky ribs and some scraps of mouldy fabric. Bea and Simon leaned in closer. There was no doubt; what was written on the name badge in fancy font was still legible. *Victor Blackwell — Head Chef.*

"So it must be him then?" Perry asked.

"It certainly could be him, and it will be enough for them to focus on matching his identity. But in itself, it's not enough."

"But—" Perry began.

"Perry, someone could have put it there deliberately to make us think that it's him," Simon pointed out.

"I suppose so," Perry said, pouting.

"Look," Simon said in a softer tone. "Why don't I give Roisin a ring and ask if she knows what's happening?" Perry brightened up.

Roisin was Simon's best friend and also, handily for them, quite senior in the Forensics Department at Fenshire Police. Maybe she could even get their skeleton's examination bumped up the list.

Beep! The screen on the phone in front of Bea burst into life. A name flashed up. *Rich.* A smile automatically split her face, then her breath caught in her throat as she saw the text message.

. . .

Rich: *I've just heard body remains have been found in Windstanton. Is it too much to hope that it wasn't you and Perry who found them? xx*

She swallowed. *Of course, he still has his contacts…* She should've known he would find out sooner or later. She reached over and picked up her mobile.

"Fitzwilliam?" Simon asked. She nodded.

Bea: *Yes, sorry! I would have told you earlier, but it's all been a little crazy, as you can imagine. xx*

The heat crept up her neck. *It's not a lie really… I have been busy.* Working out how to break the news to him…

Rich: *Are you okay? xx*

Aw, that's nice that he's asked…

Bea: *Yes, I'm fine. It was a shock of course, they were in the wall we were having knocked down at Clary House. xx*

Rich: *We'll be taking a break in about 15 mins. Can I call you then? xx*

. . .

Bea rose. She didn't want to have a conversation with Rich in The Breakfast Room, which was now beginning to fill up with visitors eagerly awaiting their award-winning afternoon tea.

Daisy lifted her head and stared up at her mistress. "Come on, Daisy. I'm going to the office to talk to Rich," she told Perry and Simon. "Let me know if there are any new developments."

"Will do," Simon agreed as Bea clipped Daisy's lead on. "Good luck!" Simon added.

She smiled gratefully at him. *I think I'm going to need it...*

———

Ten minutes later, Bea sat behind her desk in her and Perry's office in the Old Stable Block at Francis Court staring at her phone.

Come on, Bea. He won't bite.

She glanced over at Daisy, who was now curled up in her bed on a chair in the corner of the office. "Are you sure you won't take this call for me, little girl?" she asked. Daisy ignored her. Bea took a deep breath as Rich's name flashed up on the screen. She accepted the call with a shaky finger.

"Hello, trouble." Her stomach fluttered. His voice was deep and slightly husky. His mild northern accent sent a shiver up her spine. In a good way. *Oh my goodness, I've got it bad!*

"Hey, you," she replied. *Did that sound a bit drippy?* She cleared her throat. "So how's your conference going?"

"Dreadful. It's death by PowerPoint. More than once today, I've seriously considered breaking the glass on the fire alarm just to bring a bit of excitement to the whole thing."

She stifled a snort of laughter.

She knew he was finding his move from PaIRS to City Police and the promotion from chief inspector to superintendent that had come with it, involved a lot more meetings, conferences, and admin than he'd expected. But, he'd assured her, he would get used to it. On the positive side, he was enjoying collaborating with the various intelligence services who worked alongside the police to protect the capital city, London.

"And it's only day one of three," Rich added with a heavy sigh. "I'm hoping for a minor crisis back in the office, something I can use as an excuse to leave early."

Bea suppressed a giggle. She'd never seen this side of him until recently, and she loved the little insights into his life that he now shared with her.

"Anyway, enough about this drudgery. Tell me about your discovery at the restaurant," he said.

Bea told him about the contractors having found the skeleton when they'd knocked down the wall as she and Perry had watched and about Perry's belief that it was Victor Blackwell, the chef who'd worked at the previous restaurant at Clary House.

"So is Mike in charge of the case?"

"No. He's on leave. But anyway, it's been passed over to the Fenshire Cold Case Unit." She told him about Finch and what they knew about him.

"So what happens now?" His tone was even. No mention of her keeping her nose out. *Yet...*

She pinched her lips together. "As Simon has pointed out, we don't even know for sure it *is* Victor's body. But the opening of SaltAir is looming, and most of the building is a crime scene."

"Um…" Rich exhaled softly. "I hate to say it, but Simon's right. It could take days, even weeks to ID the body."

"But we don't have weeks, Rich. We open on the eighth of July. If the case isn't solved before then, it's going to ruin the opening and overshadow everything Simon and Ryan are trying to do at Clary House."

"I'm sorry. Perhaps this Finch chap will catch a break and have it wrapped up in no time."

Not at the pace he works, according to Simon and CID Steve. But she appreciated Rich was trying to make her feel better.

There was what sounded like a bell ringing at the other end of the line. "That's the five-minute warning that the next session is starting. I'd better go as I need to grab a large coffee to take in with me, or I'll have no chance of staying conscious for the rest of the afternoon."

"Don't resort to setting fire alarms off. Promise?" Bea said, smiling.

"I'll try," Rich replied with a chuckle. "We'll talk later. Stay…er safe, Bea."

"And you stay…er awake, Rich." His laughter echoed down the line as she cut the call. For a moment she stared at her phone screen. "Thank you for not saying it," she murmured. *Not yet, anyway,* a little voice in her head added.

12

EVENING, SATURDAY 19 JUNE

T*he Society Page* online article:

BREAKING NEWS Body of Chef Found Three Years After He Had Left to go to Australia

Human remains found in a wall inside a disused building sparked a major investigation yesterday and have now been identified as those of Victor Blackwell, who was head chef at Windstanton's The Seaside Lounge.

Officers were called to a property in Windstanton in Fenshire yesterday by building contractors who had found the skeleton when removing a false wall. The pathologist and detectives on the scene confirmed they were human remains, but at the time were unable to identify the deceased. A murder investigation has now been launched, according to a police spokesperson. Detective Inspector Albert Finch from Fenshire's Cold Case Unit said, "I want to assure the local community that although this is a disturbing and unsettling find, we have a presence in the area to complete inquires, provide reassurance, and to listen to any concerns." The building, which is closed to the public, "is likely to remain a crime scene for some time, while we unravel what exactly happened here."

Victor Blackwell was assumed to have left Windstanton during the temporary closure for refurbishment of The Seaside Lounge three years ago, having been offered a job in Australia. Now police believe he may never have left as planned. Fenshire police are asking for anyone who has information about Victor Blackwell's movements after Friday 3 January three years ago to come forward.

———

Bea lounged on a blue velvet sofa in the sitting room of The Dower House, Daisy curled up beside her and fast asleep. One of Bea's hands was absently stroking the little terrier's ear, while her other hand was holding her tablet horizontally, so she had the best view of her son, Sam, who was currently at his desk in his bedroom at his boarding school, Wilton College.

Daisy emitted a loud snore that caused Sam to laugh. "Does Daisy do anything other than sleep, Mum?" he asked, still grinning.

"I'll have you know she's just been with me on my run this evening. We did five miles. So she has every right to be asleep. I'll be joining her soon."

Through the open sitting room door, the noise of the grandfather clock in the hall chiming nine times signalled an end to their chat. "It's time for you to get ready for bed, darling," Bea said reluctantly, hating having to say goodbye to her precious boy. "But only two weeks, and you'll be done and coming home."

"I can't wait, Mum," Sam replied in his new deeper tone.

It had been a shock to her when, after months of his up-and-down croaky voice that she'd thought would never break, it had finally given way to something that sounded remarkably like his father. Bea's husband, James Wiltshire, the Earl of Rossex, had died in a car crash fifteen years ago, before Sam had been born, but now her tall and handsome son was growing up into a replica of him.

"Me neither. But first you need to get this sports competition out of the way. I hope the it goes well tomorrow, darling. You've got this."

"I know!" Sam rolled his eyes, then grinned.

"Now get some sleep!"

"I will. Night, Mum. I love you."

Bea's heart swelled. "Goodnight, darling. I love you more."

She waved and blew him a kiss, then the screen went blank. She let out a deep sigh. She couldn't help worry about her son. Sam was sporty and creative, and like his father, he was also charming and personable. All great qualities that Bea was very proud of. But he wasn't academic, finding the classic subjects "boring", as he put it. At her last teacher-parent conference, his teachers had been confident that Sam had done enough to pass all of the exams he'd recently taken, with top grades predicted in art, design and technology, physical education, and drama *I just hope they're right.* She knew how much he wanted to stay on to do his A-levels in the sixth form at Wilton, but he needed to pass all his core subjects along with at least four others to be accepted. She sighed again, and Daisy woke, turning to nudge Bea's hand with her wet nose. "Oh, Daisy. Will he be all right, do you think?" Daisy licked her hand. Daisy clearly thought so. *Well, that's good enough for me...*

The sudden buzz of her mobile phone grabbed her attention, and she looked to see Perry's name flashing up on the screen. She accepted the call.

"Have you seen the news?" Perry asked as soon as the line connected. Without waiting for her to answer, he continued, "They've confirmed it was Victor Blackwell in the wall at Clary House!"

"Already?" Bea's brows furrowed. "I thought it would take days, possibly weeks."

"Here, I'll let Simon explain." The line crackled slightly as the call switched to speaker.

"Hey, Bea." Simon's deeper, more measured voice filled her sitting room. "We got lucky. Victor was pulled over for a drink-driving offence six months before he died. He refused to give a roadside breath test, claiming if he was seen, it would impact his career. So they took him into custody. The good news is that while they had him, they also took a sample of his DNA along with his blood. It's fairly standard these days."

"And was he over the limit?"

"No. When the results came through five weeks later, he was quite a way below it. There were no charges. But his DNA had already been entered on the national database, so when Forensics put his name in the police system yesterday, it came up, and they were able to compare it to a sample they took from the remains. It was a perfect match."

"So we can start investigating straight away!" Perry chimed in. "Shall we meet in The Breakfast Room at Francis Court at eight-thirty in the morning?"

"Sure. See you there." She cut the call and went to her favourites list. She'd have to call Rich. When she'd spoken to him a few hours ago, she'd promised she would update him if anything changed. As she reached her finger out to select his name, a ring coming from the main door startled her. *Who's that at this time of night?*

She heard a door in the hall open, and with relief, she caught the sound of the steady footsteps of Mr Fraser as he made his way to the front door to answer it. Just as well he and his wife, who lived in the house and looked after her and Sam, hadn't turned in for the night yet.

As muffled voices seeped through the hallway, Daisy's eyes shot open. Within seconds she'd jumped off the sofa and had darted through the sliver of open door, into the hall, barking excitedly. It was clearly someone Daisy was pleased to see. Maybe her brother, Fred? She rose and smoothed down her thin jumper.

There was a tentative knock on the sitting room door, and a familiar face poked around the door frame.

Her stomach flipped. *Rich!*

13

SHORTLY AFTER, SATURDAY 19 JUNE

"Surprise!" Rich said, his voice betraying a little trepidation as his brown eyes met hers. A warmth stirred in her chest as her face broke into a huge grin, and she moved towards him.

"Hey, you," she managed to get out as he strode across the room to meet her. He swept her into his arms, pulling her close. Bea let herself sink into the comfort of his embrace before lifting her face to his. They shared a lingering kiss that was both a greeting and a promise of more to come. Daisy, not wanting to be left out of this enthusiastic reunion, circled around them with excited whines, her nose nudging at Bea's legs. Bea laughed but made no move to pull away from Rich's embrace.

"I've missed you," he murmured into her hair before planting another kiss on her lips.

She looked up into his face and tilted her head to one side. "Are you sure it's not just that you were bored to death at your conference, and you'd be pleased to see almost anyone right now?" she asked cheekily.

He gave an exaggerated frown, then said, "Yes, that's probably it."

She laughed as she wiggled in his arms and tried to hit him on the chest. Daisy barked as if to remind them she was still here, and they broke apart, both laughing. Rich bent down and gave Daisy a scratch behind the ears. "Of course I've missed you the most, little girl."

He looked up at Bea with a smile that made her knees go weak. She reached her hand out and took his. "I *have* missed you," she said in a soft voice.

"Glad to hear it," he replied, his eyes crinkling with a familiarity she'd grown to love.

As they stood grinning at each other like a couple of Cheshire cats, there was a short sharp knock on the door. They dropped each other's hands as Fraser entered, carrying a tray containing a large silver coffee pot, two cups, a small milk jug, and a bowl of brown sugar cubes. "Coffee, my lady."

"Thank you, Fraser," Bea said, her voice laced with genuine appreciation. She glanced at Rich, and he winked at her. He was still getting used to having the Frasers around when he was at The Dower House, but as with everything that was different in their lives now, he was slowly coming around. It didn't stop him from teasingly apologising to her when she was at his flat in Richmond about the lack of staff and how she would have to load the dishwasher herself.

They walked over to the sitting area by the fireplace where Fraser was laying the coffee things on the low table between the two large sofas. Daisy jumped onto one of them as Fraser straightened up, and tucking the tray under his arm, asked, "Can I get you anything else, my lady?"

"No, thank you, Fraser. That will be all this evening. Have a good day off tomorrow, and I'll see you on Monday."

"Thank you, my lady. Good night, Superintendent." He offered them a curt bow and glided out of the room.

"I wish he wouldn't call me Superintendent," Rich said when the door had closed behind him. He threw himself down on one of the sofas, and Daisy immediately curled up by his side. "I feel like I'm at work."

Smiling, Bea took the sofa opposite him and, perching on the edge, picked up the coffee pot. "Fraser is a stickler for proper protocol even when it's just us. Using your title is the correct form of address, I'm afraid."

Rich huffed as he accepted a cup of steaming coffee from her. "It makes me feel old!"

She grinned as she cradled her own cup between her hands. "Try and see it as him having professional pride in his job."

"I'm not sure he likes me," Rich said, a hint of petulance in his voice.

Aw, so that's what this is about... "That's not true. He has a tone he uses just for those he doesn't approve of. I promise you if Fraser didn't like you, I would know."

Rich nodded slowly. "Okay, I'll trust you on that."

"And if it helps, I know Mrs Fraser is very taken with you. After you left the other weekend, she asked me for a list of your favourite foods so she could get them in for the next time you were here. She even referred to you as 'that handsome man of yours'." A prickle of heat hit Bea's cheeks as she recalled the cheeky grin on Mrs Fraser's face when she'd said that. *Was he her man now?*

Rich grinned. "Handsome, heh?"

Bea frowned. "Although I'm not sure her eyesight is what it used to be."

He laughed out loud, and she smugly took a sip of her coffee. She loved making him laugh like that. "So how did you manage to get away from your conference? I thought it still had two more days to go."

"It does. And what I'm about to tell you may make you question my integrity, but in my defence, I reached the point where I was suffocating in all the hot air coming out of the presenters and ready to resign if it would get me out of there. So when my boss, the chief superintendent, got called away, I made an excuse and left too." He gave her a rather sheepish look. "I may have given the impression I was involved in the same incident."

Bea suppressed a giggle and arranged her face into a disapproving look. "Frankly, I'm shocked you could be so deceptive, and...and—" It was no good; she couldn't keep it up. She laughed.

Relief washed over Rich's face, his eyes twinkling. "I'm not convinced the boss didn't make it all up to get away too."

They both relaxed back into their sofas as a comfortable silence fell around them, broken only by the gentle snores coming from Daisy, her head now resting on Rich's thigh.

"So I saw they've identified your old bones," Rich said a few minutes later, trying to sound casual but failing.

Bea tilted her head to one side and studied his expression. *Is that why he's here? Has he come to warn me off the case in person?* Her shoulders stiffened. She leaned forward and placed her cup on the table. "Yes, as we suspected, they belong to Victor Blackwell."

"I thought it would take them a lot longer..." Rich sounded cautious now.

Bea crossed her arms, and leaning back, she told him what Simon had told her earlier about Vic's DNA already being on file.

"That was lucky then." Their easy conversation had turned into something awkward and stilted. Silence fell.

Why doesn't he just come out and say it? Then the voice in her head said, *Why don't* you *say something?* What had Simon told her the other day? *You can't be with someone you're afraid to talk to.*

"Did you come here to warn me off this investigation, Rich?" She held her breath.

"No!" His denial was emphatic and sincere.

She blew out the air she'd been holding in.

He raked his fingers through his grey-speckled brown hair and continued, "The truth is that although I'm enjoying my new job, I miss the excitement and challenge of investigating a case." He let out a deep sigh. "And I miss working with you. We're a good team."

Bea's hands tingled as heat radiated through her chest. A giddiness overcame her. *He misses working with me!* Then her chest tightened. Not for the first time, she'd misjudged him. *I really must stop jumping to conclusions about him.* She beamed. "I miss working with you too, but how can you get involved? Surely this is out of your remit now?"

A grin tugged at the corners of his mouth. "Officially, yes. But in this new job, my team works mainly from home or Cheltenham, so I now have the flexibility to work from anywhere I choose. I can pop up to London for the odd day when I'm needed there."

Her stomach flipped. *So he could work from here?*

"So I was thinking I could work from here. That way I can help you guys if you need me, and I'm there for—" He stopped and bit his lip.

"For what?"

"Erm, for backup. You know. If you needed it..." He trailed off, rubbing his nose.

"Backup?" Bea stifled a grin and feigned indignation. She

rather liked the idea of him being nearby. Not that she intended to admit that to him.

"Look, Bea." He swallowed noisily. "I wouldn't dream of asking you not to get involved. I know how important it is to you to get this resolved before the opening. I also know it would be pointless, and as it's not my case, I have no right to do so. But I can't help worry about you being in danger." He ran his fingers through his hair again. "Now I've found you, I don't want to lose you, Bea."

She could barely breathe. A huge smile split her face. "Neither do I. I mean…I don't want to lose you either."

"So can I stay?"

"Yes," she said softly, a rush of excitement coursing through her. She shot up from the sofa. "I think the library will be the best place for you to work from." She held out a hand to him. "Do you want to have a look and see if it will be okay?"

He grinned as he took her hand and stood, a mischievous glint lighting his eyes. "You know, sharing a house for a few weeks will be the ultimate test of our relationship," he said, a corner of his mouth twitching upward. "We might end up hating the sight of each other."

Bea arched an eyebrow. "Don't worry. We've plenty of rooms here I can escape to if I want to get away from you."

"Fair point." He chuckled as, hand-in-hand and with Daisy following, they headed out into the hall.

14

BREAKFAST, SUNDAY 20 JUNE

The early sun streamed through the grand windows of The Breakfast Room at Francis Court, casting a warm haze over the mostly empty tables. Not open to the public until ten, it serviced only staff at this time in the morning. One of the advantages of being an employee of the estate was the free meals available in the restaurant or The Old Stable Block cafe throughout the working day. It was still too early for the retail staff, but a smattering of estate workers were tucking into a hearty breakfast before their day ahead.

Bea was grateful for the anonymity of the quiet restaurant. She'd been unsure about coming to a public place with Rich, even one that was in the grounds of her own home. Bea's chest tightened. *Is it just a matter of time before someone spots us and puts two and two together?* Her gaze swept the room discreetly, but the diners were too engrossed in their food to be paying any attention to her and Rich.

Were they safe for the moment? She twisted the rings on her right hand. *Am I worrying about nothing?* After all, Rich was a well-known face around Francis Court, having been based here with his team from PaIRS during several investigations over the past eighteen months. And, of course, more recently, he'd lived in one of the cottages on the estate for several months while recovering from being injured in the line of duty earlier in the year. As part of his recovery, he'd frequently walked around the estate gardens, often accompanied by a combination of her, Simon, Perry, her brother, Fred, and even her son, Sam. *No one will bat an eyelid about seeing him here*, she reassured herself.

"Bea?" She looked over to Rich, who was sitting opposite her at the table of four, leaning forward, a look of concern on his face. "Are you all right?"

"Yes, sorry, I was just wondering" —she leaned in— "if we're safe here, do you think?"

"Safe?" He frowned.

"I mean, from anyone realising, we're…um…you know, together," she whispered.

His face cleared. "We've been in here dozens of times together before, Bea. Why should anyone suddenly take any notice?"

Is he right? But… "Things are…well, different now."

He grinned. "I know that, and you know that—"

But how long before someone picks up on the change in the dynamic of our relationship?

"—but unless I suddenly leap across the table, take you in my arms, and kiss you thoroughly, I don't think anyone else will guess." He winked at her. Heat rose up her neck. He leaned over the table and whispered, "However tempted I might be right now…"

Awful man! She tried to give him a stern look but failed miserably, a smile tugging at the edges of her mouth. He grinned back. *You wait. I'll—*

Daisy, who'd been curled up by Rich's feet, suddenly jumped up, her tail wagging as a woman in her mid-forties approached their table.

"Superintendent, how nice to see you again." Nicky, a regular server in The Breakfast Room, beamed at Rich as she stopped by their table. She leaned down and made a short fuss of Daisy.

"Thank you, Nicky. It's great to be back," he said, smiling. Nicky had been particularly attentive to Rich when he'd been staying at Francis Court during his rehabilitation. There was no doubt she was a big fan.

"You can't beat the healthy Fenshire air. Isn't that true, Lady Rossex?" She turned and beamed at Bea.

"Absolutely, Nicky."

"Now what can I get you both?"

Bea ordered just coffee for herself. She wasn't a breakfast person. "Mr Juke and Mr Lattimore are joining us shortly, so can I order two bacon rolls and a full English, please, both with coffee?"

"Make that two full English breakfasts, will you, Nicky? And coffee for me too."

Nicky made a note of their order. "I'll get the chef to do some extra bacon for Daisy," she said. Before Bea could point out that Daisy didn't need any extra bacon as Perry would give her half of his, the server was already hurrying towards the kitchen, notepad in hand.

About to settle herself back down next to Rich, Daisy gave a low *woof* and bolted across the room as Simon and Perry strolled in through the large glass doors leading in from the terrace. They stopped to say hello to Daisy, then noticing Rich for the first time, they both smiled broadly and waved.

Simon was the first to reach them. "Fitzwilliam, this is a

surprise. I thought you were stuck at the conference from hell?"

"Did you sneak out?" Perry asked, joining them.

Rich stood up and greeted both men, then explained about his recent escape. "So I'm going to stick around for a while and work from The Dower House."

Perry, now sitting next to Rich, glanced at Bea and smirked. She stifled an urge to stick her tongue out at him.

"And if I can assist with the, er…issue at Clary House, then I'm more than happy to do what I can." Rich held up his hands. "Although just to be clear, I don't want to interfere or step on anyone's toes. Officially, I'm not involved, of course."

Simon, sitting next to Bea, held his palms open. "The more help, the better, Fitzwilliam. We open in less than three weeks, and the local papers are already having a field day speculating about Victor's death. It's threatening to over-shadow the whole thing. Ryan will be back tomorrow and, of course, he's keen to help too."

"Yes, it's great you're going to be around for a while," Perry said, his gaze flickering back to Bea.

Okay, I'll fill you in later…

"What we really need now is a plan," he continued, then seeing Nicky heading towards them with their drinks, followed by another server carrying a tray laden with hot food, he added, "After breakfast, that is."

———

"So I suggest the first person we should speak to is Maisey," Perry said, slipping the last piece of bacon from his plate under the table and into Daisy's waiting open mouth.

Perry! Bea gave him a look. He held his hands up. "All gone," he muttered.

"Who's Maisey?" Rich asked, wiping his mouth with a napkin as he pushed his empty plate away.

"You know Claire, our HR manager here?" Bea replied. Rich nodded. "Maisey is her younger sister, and she used to waitress at The Seaside Lounge—"

"That's the name of the restaurant that was downstairs at Clary House until just over three years ago—" Simon clarified as he cut his last sausage into three pieces.

"And so she worked with Victor," Perry continued. "They got on well, according to Claire. Maisey will give us all the gossip about Vic and the people who worked there with him. She might even know who his friends were."

"So you can compile a possible suspects list?" Rich sounded impressed.

"Exactly!" Perry agreed, picking up his mobile phone. "In fact. I'll text her now and see when she's free."

"Meanwhile, I thought I'd try to find out who the builders were that did the refurbishment of the dining room," Simon said, picking up the last morsel of sausage. "They're the ones who built the bar and false wall where Victor was found. I have all the documentation from the sale of Clary House, so hopefully the details of exactly what they did and when will be in there somewhere." He dipped his sausage-ladened hand under the table, and before Bea could cry, "No!" Daisy had gobbled it up.

"Simon!" she admonished.

"Oh, sorry. I forgot we weren't supposed to be feeding her extras."

A likely story! Daisy was due her six-month checkup this week, and Bea seemed to be the only one who was concerned she was the same round shape she'd been at the end of last year when the vet had called her, "still a bit on the chunky side".

"Would it help if I did some digging into the previous restaurant? The Seaside Lounge, I think you called it," Rich offered, getting them back on track. "I should be able to get access to financial records and shareholders' information. Money could be a motive. It often is."

"Great idea," Simon said. "I'll also keep in touch with my mate Steve and see how the police investigation is going."

"Talking of the police, what do we know about this Finch fellow?" Rich asked him.

"Inspector Albert Finch. In his mid-fifties, I guess. He's been with CID since before I joined. I worked with him on a couple of cases in this area when they were short of staff, although I was based in King's Town. I'm not sure how long he's been with the Cold Case Unit, but from what I can remember of him, I can imagine it would suit his personality. He's slow and methodical, and he's lived in Windstanton all his life. He knows the area like the back of his hand."

"And Simon lodged an official complaint against him before he left!" Perry added with a flourish.

Rich's eyebrow shot up, and he looked at Bea.

Oh, I forgot to tell him about that! She gave him an apologetic look and mouthed, "Sorry."

"Is it a problem?" Rich asked.

Simon shook his head. "I don't think I'm on his Christmas list, but it was a long time ago, and we've moved on."

Perry's phone buzzed. He picked it up. "Brilliant. Maisey will see us first thing in the morning," he told Bea as she took the last sip of her now cold drink.

"That's all sorted then," Simon said, putting his empty

cup on the table. He rose. "Why don't we all meet tomorrow evening when Ryan's back?"

"Great. Why not come over to The Dower House? I'll cook dinner," Rich suggested.

Bea nearly choked on her coffee. "Really?" she spluttered as her eyes darted to his face. He flashed that easy smile of his that suggested he had everything under control.

"Sure, why not?" He shrugged nonchalantly. "As long as you think Mrs Fraser will relinquish control of the kitchen for a short while?"

"She'll no doubt be delighted to have the evening off," Bea said, still not sure if he was being serious.

Perry stood to join his husband. "Well, that sounds like a plan," he said, his eyes twinkling with amusement. They bid farewell, leaving a still rather stunned-looking Bea staring at the man in her life with a mixture of confusion and pride.

———

"Rich," Bea began, unable to contain her curiosity as they arrived home later and made their way down to the kitchen to check on supplies. "Er, about this dinner. You do realise who you've offered to cook for, right?" She leaned against the work surface, her arms resting on the top. "The winner of *Celebrity Elitechef* and the executive head chef of a Michelin-starred fine dining restaurant in London."

Rich merely chuckled, unfazed as he filled a bowl with water for Daisy and put it down on the floor in front of her.

Bea had to admire his brazen self-assurance, but did he really know what he was doing? Yes, he had prepared a couple of meals for them before in his flat, but they'd mainly comprised of precooked food from the local Waitrose that he'd heated up in the oven. Did he have a hidden culinary talent she wasn't aware of yet?

"Why do you think Perry and I never dare to cook?" Bea added when he didn't seem to react. *Is he not at all daunted by cooking for these experienced chefs?*

He straightened up. "Bea," he replied, turning to face her with a confidence that bordered on audacity. "Don't worry. I make a mean spaghetti bolognaise."

15

EARLY MORNING, MONDAY 21 JUNE

Bea pulled her thick knit cardigan around her, glad she'd picked it up at the last minute as she'd left the house this morning. It was early, and although the day promised to be another warm and sunny one, right now it was chilly in the back of the Bentley. She reached out and pulled a sleeping Daisy, who'd been curled up on the seat between her and Perry, a little closer, then grabbed a thermos of black coffee from the holder by her side. Rich had made it for her while she'd been having a shower earlier. He'd handed it to her, accompanied by a kiss, as she'd left The Dower House. A tingle ran up her spine. *I could get used to that...*

Should she ask Fraser to put the heating on? She glanced over at Perry, but he seemed to be comfortable enough in his crisply-pressed long-sleeve shirt. She took a sip of the hot black liquid. She'd warm up soon enough. "It's good of Maisey to agree to see us so quickly, but why so early?"

"She's a nurse now and has to be on shift at nine. It was either this or wait until this evening." He looked down at the sleepy little dog beside him. "I'm sorry, Daisy. I know it's early, but Maisey loves dogs, so we need you to charm her for us so she'll talk." He ruffled the top of her head.

"If she's anything like Claire, I can't imagine she'll need much encouragement," Bea said, grinning. Claire Beck, Francis Court's human resources manager, was known for her outgoing and bubbly personality. She, like Perry, also loved a good gossip.

Perry grinned back. "That's fair."

As they reached the outskirts of Windstanton, Perry turned to Bea, a mischievous twinkle in his blue eyes. "So that was a bit of a surprise yesterday, Rich offering to cook tonight. It's very brave of him, considering the diners."

Bea couldn't help smiling as she recalled their conversation last night. "It gets worse," she said. "He's cooking pasta."

Perry raised an eyebrow. "Does he realise Simon's half-Italian and grew up working in his parent's Italian restaurant?"

She shrugged. "I don't know. But even if he did, I don't think it would daunt him. He told me not to worry. He said, and I quote, 'I make a mean spaghetti bolognaise.'"

Perry chuckled. "That's quite a claim."

"I know," she said, a warmth in her voice. "That's one of the things I love about him, his confidence."

"Love?" Perry arched an eyebrow playfully, leaning closer. "You said 'love', Bea! Oh my giddy aunt, you lurvvv him…"

Bea's cheeks burned. *I said love!* "You know, I think I do," she mumbled, fixing her gaze on Daisy to avoid Perry's knowing look.

Perry reached out his hand and grabbed hers. "That's brilliant, Bea! I'm so pleased for you."

She looked over as she gave his hand a squeeze. "It's a

little bit scary, but thanks. But not a word to anyone, okay? Especially not Rich." Her words were firm, yet there was a pleading note buried within them. "I can't have him know, not until I'm sure he feels the same."

"Bea, the man changed jobs so he could be with you." Perry chuckled, shaking his head. "If that's not love, I don't know what is."

Is he right? While she knew it had been a big deal when Rich had transferred from PaIRS back to City Police, it had also been a promotion. *Would he have made the move anyway?*

Before Bea could think about it anymore, Fraser brought the car to a gentle stop in front of a charming brick house adorned with hanging baskets full of vibrant blooms. The door swung open as they alighted from the car, and a woman wearing a dark-blue uniform with long curly hair bounded out, her arms outstretched in welcome. She enveloped Perry in a bear hug as Daisy jumped around barking. "Perry, it's been too long!" she cried, then released him and bent down to fuss Daisy. "And you're adorable. What's your name?"

"This is Daisy," Perry said, smoothing down his shirt. "And this is Lady Beatrice. Bea, this is Maisey Dixon."

Bea smiled as she stepped forward and held out her hand to the woman who had now straightened up. "Nice to meet you, Maisey."

Maisey gave a bob, then took Bea's hand, shaking it with gusto. "My lady, how good to meet you. Claire talks about you and your family a lot."

"Please call me Bea," Bea said, smiling. Observing Maisey's bright eyes and the eager tilt of her head, Bea realised just how much she resembled Claire. "Claire's a very valued member of the team at Francis Court," she told Maisey, scooping up a wriggling Daisy.

Maisey beamed at her, then ushered them through the door and led them through the hall and into a warm, inviting kitchen. She indicated for them to take a seat at the wooden table in the middle of the room as she turned to the counter by the sink and hit the button on the kettle. "Tea or coffee?" she asked.

Having opted for another coffee, Bea cast a quick look around the room as Daisy made herself comfortable on her lap. The yellow walls were adorned with charming photos in gold frames, and blue shelves dotted the walls, holding an assortment of knick-knacks, giving the room a cozy feel.

Maisey handed out the hot drinks and sat down. "I was beside myself when I heard," she began, her hands fluttering over her mug of tea with 'NURSE (n) The first person you see after saying, "Hold my beer and watch this!"' on the side. "You know, reading it was Vic's remains they'd found... It's just so shocking." She took a gulp of hot liquid.

"Did you suspect anything?" Perry asked gently.

She put her cup down and tilted her head to one side. "I thought it was odd when we were told Vic wasn't coming back just like that." Her eyes misted over. "I mean, I said at the time that Vic wouldn't have decided not to come back without saying something to me. We were friends." She took another gulp of tea and swallowed it loudly. "Now it seems I was right."

"Did you share your concerns with anyone?"

She shook her head, looking rather sheepish. "Only Claire. Everyone seemed convinced that he was in Australia. And, to be honest, it wasn't that much of a stretch to think that he might have stayed if the right opportunity arose. He'd seemed a bit distracted those last few weeks." She puffed out her cheeks. "But he would have told me. I tried to call him, and he never answered. I texted a couple of times too, but the messages weren't read. But then Claire pointed out that if he was in Australia, he'd have stopped using his UK mobile and would have got one out there." She shrugged. "It made sense, and I had no other way of contacting him." She sighed and dipped her head. "I suppose I should have…"

"Maisey, you weren't to know." Perry was firm, and she nodded slowly in return.

"When did you last see him?" Bea asked, taking a sip from her brimming cup of coffee.

Maisey's gaze drifted to a corner of the room as she conjured the memory. "Last time? It would have been that Friday. I think it was the third of January," she said, her voice tinged with a hint of sadness. "We'd closed on the Thursday, and we'd just finished a mammoth two-day deep clean of the kitchen. Everyone was ready for the time off, I can tell you."

"Go on," Bea encouraged, putting down her cup.

"I was the last to leave, just before five. I know because I was being picked up by a friend at the restaurant at five. Vic stayed behind. He said he had some paperwork to do. He wasn't leaving to fly to New Zealand until that Sunday morning, so he said he might as well get it done before he went."

Perry frowned. "New Zealand? I thought he was going to Australia?"

"He was, but he was going to New Zealand first for five days or so. He wanted to visit some famous glacier there and do some whale watching. He was really looking forward to it." She looked wistfully out of the window, then checked herself. "Then he was flying on to Australia for the remaining twelve days."

"Was he going alone?"

"Yeah. He'd booked it fairly last minute, I think."

"So you left…" Bea prompted gently.

"Oh, yeah. He locked up after me." She slowly shook her

head. "I never imagined that would be the last time I'd see him."

"Where did you go?" Perry asked.

"As I said, my friend came and got me." Maisey's voice brightened. "We headed to Luton and from there, we flew to Greece. We had such a laugh…" She trailed off, clearly lost in her memories.

Bea coughed. "So was there anyone who might have wanted to hurt Vic?"

"There must have been, I suppose, seeing how someone killed him." She paused and looked at Bea as if it was obvious.

"Er, yes. I suppose you're right. Any idea who that could've been?"

"Not at the time, no. Everyone at The Seaside Lounge got on fine—Rob, Marco, Bella. We were like family. But, of course, now that we know he never went to Australia or New Zealand, it can only have been one person, can't it?"

Bea froze for a second. *Maisey knows who killed Vic?* She glanced over at Perry, who was staring at Claire's sister, his mouth half open. Bea took a deep breath. "And who is that then, Maisey?"

"Well, it must be Julian Thornton."

16

BREAKFAST, SUNDAY 20 JUNE

B ea stifled a gasp. *Julian Thornton? The previous owner of Clary House and upstanding Windstanton business owner? Surely not.* "Er, what makes you say that, Maisey?"

"He's the one who told us Vic wasn't coming back because he'd taken up some post over on the other side of the world. He said Vic had, 'had an offer that he couldn't refuse'." She air quoted the phrase. "But he must have been making that up to cover up the fact he'd killed him."

Bea's eyes narrowed. She looked over at Perry. Was Maisey saying she knew that was what had happened or was she just making an assumption? Perry caught her eye and raised an eyebrow. "But there was an email from Vic, wasn't there?" he asked.

There was? Bea frowned as she tried to remember. *Oh, yes. Claire said that was how they knew he wasn't coming back..*

"So Julian said. But I didn't see it." She dipped her head to her chin as she gave him a knowing look. "I mean, if Vic was dead, then Julian could've just said that there was an email, couldn't he?"

She has a point, I suppose... Unless... "Someone could have written it to make it look like it'd come from Vic."

Maisey tilted her head to one side. "Only if they had access to Vic's email address. No. I don't think there ever was an email," she said firmly.

Is she right? Had Julian made it up? Or had the killer sent it from a false email address? It was certainly food for thought. "Tell us about the other people you worked with at The Seaside Lounge."

"Rob Rivers was the senior sous chef. Talented and competitive, he was Vic's right-hand man. Now he has his own place, Rivers By The Sea."

Bea nodded. She'd never been to the popular Windstanton restaurant but had heard good things about it.

"I like to go there for special occasions, you know. It reminds me of The Seaside Lounge. Rob's style is very like Vic's used to be. And you know he's on the TV and radio now?" She didn't wait for a reply but continued, "He's the local go-to man on all things food in the region. He's done very well for himself."

"And did he and Vic get on?" Bea asked.

Maisey took a sip of her tea. "Oh, you know what chefs are like. They argued, of course they did, but nothing serious. I think it was mainly because Rob was nipping at Vic's heels, and Vic wanted to keep him in his place. Other times, they would work on recipes together, happy as Larry."

Was Rob so ambitious, he'd killed Vic to get ahead? It's possible...

"And what about the others?" Perry nudged her.

"Then there was Marco Rossi."

The name rang a bell to Bea. "The food critic?"

"Yes. He was the maitre d back then, although I think they call them front of house managers these days." She smiled. "I like Marco. I stood in for him when he was off, and he was teaching me about wine. He's a bit of an expert, as you probably know; he writes articles about it for *The Sunday News* magazine and various local papers."

"How did he get on with Vic?" Perry asked.

"Well, Marco's Italian, so he could be fiery sometimes, but Vic knew how to handle him. They respected each other, I think." She put her cup down, a frown creasing her brows.

"But?"

"Now I come to think about it, Marco had been a bit off with Vic for a few months. Not unprofessional or anything, just not as much banter between them as usual. It felt like he was trying to avoid him, you know?"

"Any idea why?"

Maisey shook her head. "In fairness, as I said, Vic had been preoccupied, so could they have had a falling out? I don't know…" She trailed off, then shrugged. "It was probably nothing."

Or maybe it was *something…* They'd have to ask Marco about it when they got around to talking to him.

Perry took a final swig of his coffee and popped his cup on the table. "Anyone else?"

"The only other permanent member of staff was Bella DeMarco. She was the junior sous chef."

Perry's eyes lit up. "The reality TV star!"

"She's an influencer now and blogs about food and drink. But, yes, she was on *Love Resort*." Maisey couldn't quite hide her disapproval.

"How were she and Vic together?"

Maisey hesitated. "She was a bit of a diva even back then. In reality, she was the least senior person in the kitchen, and she didn't like that much. Rob was quite indulgent of her. She's young and pretty, you know."

Ah, I see…

"Rob tried to mentor her, although she seemed to think she didn't need it. But Vic found her hard work and left her to Rob. Again, I don't think she liked that. She wanted Vic's attention."

It doesn't sound like Bella would have had any reason to kill Vic. More likely the other way around….

"And is that everyone?" Perry asked.

Maisey shrugged. "I think so. We had some temps and part-time staff, but Vic left the management of them to me, Marco, and Rob." She smiled fondly. "He wasn't really good with people, you know. He kept mostly to himself. Not one for small talk, he wasn't." She straightened up. "The place could be dead quiet sometimes, but we had a laugh and that." She gave a grin. "Oh, and it paid great too."

"So you must have been gutted when the restaurant closed?" Bea suggested.

Maisey exhaled, her bubbly demeanour deflating. "Yes, I was at first. It was so unexpected," she said, her voice laced with disbelief. "We were due back on the Friday, and the restaurant was reopening on the Saturday, but on the Thursday night, I got a message from Julian telling me we were all to meet him at his office at The Parade the next morning. I was shocked when I got there, and he dropped the bombshell." Maisey shook her head slowly. "At first, he just told us Vic wasn't coming back. Rob offered to step in and run the kitchen, but Julian said that The Seaside Lounge wasn't reopening. So we were all laid off just like that." She snapped her fingers.

On Bea's lap, Daisy opened her eyes and looked around as if trying to find out what had wrenched her so suddenly from her slumber. Bea gave her a reassuring stroke on her head, and the little dog settled back down with a sigh. "How upsetting for you all," Bea said.

"I think at the time, I was so thrown by the news Vic wasn't returning that it didn't quite register that I'd lost my job too. Me and Rob tried to persuade Julian to reconsider, but he was adamant it was his only option."

Why didn't he want to keep it open? Surely he could have just got another chef?

"Marco's reaction was strange though. He actually seemed pleased. But then perhaps that was a reaction to Vic leaving. As I said, things had been cool between them at the time."

"And Bella?" Bea prodded gently.

"She didn't seem to be that bothered either." She shrugged. "But then it all worked out well for her, didn't it? She went off to become a big media star." She smoothed down her uniform. "And I went on to do my nurse's training, so I suppose it all worked out for the best in the end."

Actually, it had worked out well for *all* of them. Rob now had his own successful restaurant, and Marco was a much sought-after food critic and wine expert. Bea hesitated. All except Vic, of course; it hadn't worked out at all for him.

Maisey looked at her watch and rose, placing her empty cup in the sink. Bea was suddenly conscious they were close to outstaying their welcome. "We really appreciate you talking to us today, Maisey," she said, looking pointedly at Perry, but he seemed oblivious to Bea's subtle hint that they needed to go.

"Just one last thing, Maisey."

Really, Perry? The poor woman needs us to go!

"Did Vic have a family or a partner at all?"

Actually, that's a good question...

"No family that I know of. He certainly mentioned no one

to me. There was just Liv as far as I know. Before they split up, of course."

"Liv?" Perry asked.

"Yes. You know, Olivia Belmont."

"Liv was his girlfriend?" Perry seemed surprised.

Bea trawled her memory. Wasn't Olivia the manager at the Windstanton theatre who Perry had suggested should be invited to the SaltAir opening?

"Yes, they'd been on and off for about two years. But a month or so before Vic went away… I mean, er was killed, they split up. They had a huge argument, and that's when he booked the trip to New Zealand and Australia on his own." She shook her head sadly.

"And how was Liv when he didn't reappear?"

"I think she was upset he'd just left like that without saying anything to her…" She trailed off and rubbed her temple. "Although now, of course, we know he didn't."

Bea swept Daisy up in her arms and stood. "Indeed. We really must let you get on. Thank you again, Maisey, for your time."

Perry rose. "Yes, thanks, Maisey. It's been very enlightening."

They followed her along the hall as she said, "Oh, it's been no trouble. In fact it's been quite nice to reminisce a bit."

Maisey opened the door and beamed at Bea. "Claire said you weren't stuck up, and she was right! Who would've thought royalty could be so…down to earth?"

Perry snorted, then tried to cover it up with a cough as he headed out of the door.

Bea turned and smiled at her. "Er, thank you," she replied.

17

EVENING, MONDAY 21 JUNE

B ea leaned on the smooth granite of the breakfast bar, watching Rich as he finished feeding a long sheet of pale dough through a shiny silver contraption. *We have a pasta maker?* The resulting long thin strips of pasta curled up on a board in front of it. She couldn't help but be impressed.

When he finished, he moved over to the large American-style fridge and grabbed a cucumber, some tomatoes, radishes, spring onions, and a handful of herbs from the salad drawer. Dropping them onto the chopping board, he began to slice and dice, a faint frown of concentration creasing his brow. Not a domestic goddess by any stretch of the imagination, Bea was in awe of just how comfortable he was in the kitchen. Although, as he'd pointed out to her on a number of occasions, he was used to looking after himself, having lived alone for the last twelve years.

Even so, the ease at which he'd settled into life at The Dower House still astonished her. He'd already set up an impromptu office in the library with Fraser's assistance earlier today, his technology sprawling across the large mahogany desk by the window overlooking the rear gardens like a countrified mission control. And then there was Mrs Fraser, who had been fluttering around him all afternoon, assisting with dinner preparations as if she was his junior sous chef.

A juddering in her heart made Bea raise her hand to her chest as a wave of heat passed through her. *He just fits...*

At that moment, Rich glanced up at her, his eyes full of warmth as he tilted his head and gave her a lopsided grin. Was he happy here? *He certainly looks it...* Their eyes met. Her pulse sped up. *I could get lost in those brown eyes of his.* She instinctively smiled back.

She'd shocked herself earlier when she'd admitted to Perry she'd fallen in love with Rich already. But was Perry right? Were her feelings reciprocated? *Come on, Bea, say something. You're a strong, independent woman. Take control and tell him how you feel...* "Er, Rich—"

Over by the range, Daisy who had been snoring softly in her bed, sprung up with a low *woof.*

"Yes?"

"Um, I think that's them."

Coward!

Rich winked at her, then picking up the board, he tipped the salad into a large bowl and said, "Don't worry, Bea. I have it all under control." He wiped his hands on a nearby tea towel, then holding one out, added, "Come on. Let's go and greet our guests."

She hopped off the stool and, taking his hand, followed him out of the kitchen and up the stone stairs. They entered the hallway just as Fraser came out of a room off the corridor to their right.

"Your guests have arrived, my lady, Mister Richard. I've put them in the drawing room."

Rich had told her earlier that Mister Richard was the

compromise he'd managed to negotiate with the Frasers that afternoon after he'd asked them if there was something they could call him as an alternative to Superintendent. Something less formal. Their first suggestion had been Sir, which he'd pointed out was still very formal. Then they'd offered Mr Fitzwilliam. He'd asked them if they would call him Rich or Richard, and that was when they'd finally agreed on Mister Richard. *I wish I'd been a fly on the wall during that exchange!*

"Thank you, Fraser. We'll take them through to the dining room in a minute."

He dipped his head, then walking around them, headed for the basement.

———

As they entered the dining room, a smile flickered on Bea's face. She'd asked Fraser to keep it casual, and probably against his better instincts, he'd done just that. The soft glow of candlelight added warmth and ambiance to the room, the flickering lights dancing on the deep-green walls occasionally highlighting the paintings that adorned them. The long table that dominated the room had a large vase brimming with fresh flowers at the head, adding a touch of vibrant colour to the space. The table was set with the everyday crockery as opposed to the fine china that no doubt Fraser would have preferred to show off, although, she noted he'd not been prepared to scrimp when it had come to the silver cutlery, which was neatly set out for the five of them in the middle of the table.

As they settled down around the grand oak table, Fraser appeared with a large jug of water and then began expertly pouring the wine. When he left, Bea and Perry gave the others a brief summary of what Maisey had told them that morning.

"That gives us some names to start with," Rich said as he took a drink of his wine. Then he turned to Simon. "Did you find out anything about the builders who'd put up the wall?"

Simon shook his head. "A dead end at the moment, I'm afraid. I found out the company was called White and Son, but it ceased trading two years ago. The owner, Jack White, has moved away. There were no plans or any details of the work completed in our copy of the documentation for Clary House. I even rang up the solicitor who dealt with the sale to see if they were holding anything, but he's sunning himself in Majorca and not due back for a fortnight."

"Perhaps Charles can help with that?" Bea said, taking a sip of red wine. "Builders talk, don't they? And he's local; he might know something."

The door opened, and as Fraser stood to one side and held it, Mrs. Fraser pushed a trolley into the room. The aroma of tomato, herbs, and garlic filled the air. Bea licked her lips as the couple placed down in the middle of the table: one large serving dish of deep-red bolognaise sauce, another of perfectly twirled piles of pasta, a deep bowl of crisp salad, and a big oval plate laden with slices of golden focaccia glistening with olive oil.

"That looks and smells delicious, Mrs Fraser," Perry said, leaning forward.

"Ah, it's nothing to do with me this evening, Mr Juke," she said, glancing over at Rich. "Mister Richard here has to take all the credit."

"Now, now, Mrs Fraser," Rich protested. "It was a joint effort."

She shook her head. "I just cooked the pasta and put the bread in the oven. You made it all."

Bea suppressed a smile. *They're so sweet together!*

"Well, while you two argue over who did what, I can't wait any longer," Perry said, picking up a serving spoon and gingerly moving a mound of spaghetti onto his plate.

The Frasers left as they all helped themselves to the food.

"Ummm…this is really tasty," Simon said, balancing his fork in one hand as he gestured with his other at his plate.

The others mumbled their agreement through mouthfuls of food, and Bea's heart swelled with pride. They ate in silence for a while, then Ryan, scraping a spoonful of bolognaise onto a piece of focaccia, said, "Just following on from what you said before the food arrived, I'm seeing Charles tomorrow. The police have finally given us the green light that the building work can resume everywhere but the dining room, which is still a crime scene, so we're agreeing to a new plan. I was going to ask you to come too, Bea." He licked his lips, then popped the bread into his mouth.

"Of course. We can ask him what he knows about this Jack White and his company," she replied, wiping her mouth with her napkin. *That was delicious.* She glanced over at Rich, who was still eating. He momentarily paused and gave her a cheeky grin.

"Rich, that was very moreish," Ryan said, pushing his plate away. "I'm impressed. If you ever decide to give up policing, I could always find you a place in one of my restaurants."

"You can come and work at SaltAir," Simon said, grinning.

Rich held up his hands as he swallowed his last mouthful. "Look," he said. "Before you both get carried away… Full disclosure — I took the recipes from Simon's cookbook, *Simon Cooks*. The only change I made was to add a dash of dark chocolate to the sauce."

The revelation sparked a round of warm laughter. *No wonder he was so confident they would all like it!* Her cheeks glowing, she raised her glass to him.

"Dark chocolate? Why didn't I think of that?" Simon mumbled to himself, a grin still on his face.

Fraser slipped in, moving quietly among them to refill wineglasses and whisk away empty dishes. Rich cleared his throat. "So down to business," he said, his voice turning serious but still relaxed. "I've gone through the last few years of accounts of The Seaview Lounge before it closed down, and everything looked okay."

"Just okay?" Simon asked.

"The turnover was high —it must have been bustling back then— but so were costs."

"So low profit?" Ryan leaned back in his seat and crossed his arms. "Welcome to the world of hospitality."

"The staff were quite well paid, which I wasn't expecting. I thought they'd be on something closer to minimum wage, and they had a lot of temporary staff from what I could see."

"That would match with what Maisey told us," Perry piped in.

"Interestingly, Julian Thornton was the only one listed as a director, so Vic was a business partner in name only. Like everyone else, he was an employee."

The door cracked open, and Mrs Fraser appeared with dessert. A second before, Bea would have put money on the fact that she was too full to eat any more, but the sight of the large bowl brimming with crumbled meringue, vibrant red strawberries, fat purple blueberries, and dollops of whipped cream made her change her mind.

Perry's blue eyes lit up as the housekeeper-cum-cook placed the dish in the middle of the table and announced, "Eton Mess. Enjoy!"

"And let me say now," Rich chimed in. "This is all Mrs Fraser. I completely forgot to plan for dessert."

Bea caught the twinkle in his eye as he glanced at Mrs Fraser. She dipped her chin and smiled at him before silently withdrawing from the room.

With bowls passed and spoons diving in, conversation turned back to the matter at hand. "So do we know the time of death?" Ryan asked, raising a piled up spoon to his mouth.

"Maisey said she was the last to leave on Friday night, and that was at five in the evening. Vic locked up behind her," Perry said.

"And we know he was due to be flying to New Zealand on Sunday morning," Bea added.

"Well, we know he wasn't there three weeks later when Julian called the staff in and told them he was closing the restaurant down. It must have happened at some time between those two events. Most likely before he was due to fly on the Sunday, unless he went to New Zealand as planned and was killed when he came back?" Simon said.

"Maisey said he was spending twelve days in Australia, so with the five days in New Zealand and the one day of travelling" —Perry looked at his fingers as he counted— "he would have been due back on the Thursday. That's the day before Julian told them he was staying in Australia." He tilted his head to one side. "That seems unlikely, doesn't it?"

"Indeed," Bea agreed.

"If we can find out if he turned up for his flight or not, that will narrow it down to between the Friday evening and the Sunday morning," Rich pointed out.

"If he was home during that time, one of the neighbours might have seen him?" Ryan suggested.

"Maybe one of the others met up with him?" Bea said.

Rich dipped his chin. "We should talk to them as soon as we can."

Bea looked down at the side of her plate where a copy of the invitation to the exclusive opening of SaltAir sat. Ryan had picked them up in London while visiting the capital and had brought along copies to show them. An idea began to form in her mind. Weren't all of the names Maisey had given them also on their invitation list? "Why don't we hand deliver the invites? That way we have a legitimate excuse to talk to them tomorrow."

"That's a great idea, Bea," Simon said. "Perry, you should start with Liv Belmont. She has a soft spot for you, so you should be able to charm her into telling you more about her relationship with Vic."

"Ah, Liv." Perry grinned, running a hand through his strawberry-blond hair. "She's been nagging me to join the Windstanton Players for ages," he told the others, his blue eyes twinkling with mischief. "But she hasn't offered me the right part yet."

Bea stifled a snort of laughter. She could see her friend holding out for a leading role. No bit parts for Perry!

"Yes. I'll tackle Liv."

"Careful, she might just cast you in her next production," Simon warned, his smirk betraying his amusement.

"Not unless it's the lead, my dear!" Perry replied, raising his hand to his chest dramatically. They all laughed.

"I'd like to drop by on Julian Thornton," Bea said. "I've met him a few times before at civic events in the region, so I think he'll talk to me. I'd like to know more about the email Vic sent him, saying he wasn't coming back." She glanced at Perry. "If it exists, of course, which Maisey seriously doubts."

Rich cleared his throat, but Simon jumped in before he had time to comment. "I'll come with you. I can ask him about the missing plans. That will save me having to wait for the solicitor to get back."

Rich smiled at Simon. "Thank you, that would be great."

"I'll also give Roisin a call," Simon said. "And ask her if they have an idea on the time of death. That will save us a lot of time."

They all nodded.

The grandfather clock in the corner of the room struck nine, and Rich sighed. "I've got to catch an early train to London tomorrow," he told them. "But if there is anything else that comes up while I'm travelling, then let me know."

At that moment, Fraser entered the room. "Would you like coffee in the drawing room, my lady?" he asked with his usual impeccable timing.

"Yes, please, Fraser." Bea could imagine Daisy patiently waiting for them in her bed on the window seat, having been banned from the dining room. Bea couldn't trust Perry, Simon, *or* Rich not to sneakily try to feed her under the table. *But she'll be missing us by now.* She stood and turned to the others. "Shall we?" She indicated towards the door, and they all rose. As they left the room, Bea gave a satisfied smile to herself. *Dinner was a great success, and now we're moving forward with the investigation.* Overall, it had been an excellent evening.

18

MORNING, TUESDAY 22 JUNE

Perry lounged back in a red velvet chair in the Windstanton Theatre cafe, his slim figure aimed towards his companion, who was reading the embossed invitation he'd just handed her.

"This is lovely," Olivia Belmont said as she flipped the thick card over on the round wooden table between them. "Thank you for hand delivering it, Perry." She flicked her straight black hair away from her face as she leaned down and picked up her phone and began to type. "Right, SaltAir's opening night is now firmly in my calendar." She returned her mobile to the table, her eyes shimmering with excitement. "Everyone's buzzing about the place. I can't wait."

Perry took a sip of his coffee. *She seems very calm about it. And she's not mentioned Vic yet at all. My turn then...* "Won't it be strange for you to go back to Clary House after all this time?"

"Strange?" Liv's blue eyes clouded over in mock confusion, the corners of her mouth dipping in a frown. "I wasn't exactly a regular at The Seaside Lounge, Perry."

So she's going to play that game, is she? "Really?" Perry

shifted in his seat and leaned forward. "Because I'd have thought as Vic's girlfriend, you would've spent quite a bit of time there."

Liv's poise faltered, her eyes widening just enough for him to know that he'd scored a direct hit. Then, with a graceful tilt of her head, she recovered. "Oh, that was all a long time ago," she said with a dismissive flick of her wrist, her voice a little too airy.

Perry noted the slight tremble in her hands. His knowledge of her past relationship with Vic seemed to have thrown her.

"So when are you going to join the players, Perry? I think I have just the right part for you in my next production."

Is she trying to distract me? He tilted his head to one side. *I wonder what the part is...*

"We're doing The Importance of Being Ernest." Liv tapped a manicured nail on the table. "I think you'd be the perfect Algernon."

Would I? Yes. I probably would. And it's one of the main characters... He set his cup down with a clatter. *But you won't put me off from my questioning that easily.* "I'll have a think about it." A smile split Liv's face. He continued, "So I can't help wonder, how did you feel when you found out Vic's body had been discovered?"

Her smile faltered, and she glanced away. "I was shocked, naturally," she replied, her voice a touch unsteady. "I thought he was over in Australia."

Although clearly reluctant to talk about it, she'd seemed sincere when she'd said she'd thought he was still abroad. Perry's gaze softened. "You were close, once upon a time. It must be upsetting to know he's dead."

She took a deep breath, her chest rising and falling beneath her silk blouse. "Yes, we were close. But it was over between us long before he…" She trailed off, looking up and out through the small window just over Perry's shoulder, then her eyes met his. "But I didn't want him dead, Perry, so yes… I am…er, sad, I guess."

"Who ended things between you two?"

Expecting her to say Vic, he was surprised when she replied, "Me." He raised an eyebrow, and she continued, "Vic always put his cooking above everything else, including me." She gave a short, sharp laugh. "I grew tired of being second to a soufflé."

He believed her. So if she'd been the one to call time on their affair, then she'd had little reason to want him dead. But maybe she knew who might have. "So who do you think would have wanted to harm him?"

Liv stirred her cup of tea and lifted it to her lips. She took a sip, then tilted her head to one side. "I'll confess I have given it a little thought since I found out about…well, you know. And the only person I think who may have wanted Vic out of the way was Rob Rivers."

Interesting…

"He was always so ambitious. He thought Vic was holding him back."

"Did Vic ever feel threatened by Rob?"

"Vic?" Liv smiled wryly, finally meeting Perry's gaze. "Vic was confident to the point of arrogance about his cooking. He didn't think Rob had enough creativity to fill a pastry case, let alone take over as head chef."

So had Vic been secretly worried Rob would threaten his position as head chef but had just put on a front to Liv? Or had Rob been delusional about his abilities? Either way, it gave Rob a motive for having wanted to get rid of Vic. *On to the next…*

"Marco Rossi and Vic," Perry continued, watching Liv closely. "How did they get along?"

"Fine as far as I know." Liv's voice was clipped, her body language suddenly guarded.

Oh. What's she hiding? Did she know something about Marco and Vic's relationship she wasn't prepared to divulge? Perry filed that under 'to be continued' and asked, "What about Bella DeMarco?"

Liv's lips pursed. "Ah, Bella. Yes, she's done well. But then when you look like that…" She trailed off with a sigh, then shrugged. "Vic didn't think she had what it took to tough it out in a working kitchen." She glanced at her watch. "Well, I have to—"

Oh no, I haven't found out if she had an alibi yet.

"Did you see Vic at all after the restaurant closed for its refurb?" Perry blurted out.

Liv looked slightly taken aback. "Er…no, I was busy with *The Wizard of Oz* script," she replied briskly, not meeting his eyes. "And why would I? Vic and I were over by then."

She's lying. But about what she was doing or about not seeing Vic that weekend?

Liv stood abruptly, her chair scraping sharply against the floor. "Anyway, it's been great to see you, Perry, but I'm late for a meeting with my set designer, so I really must go."

"Of course," Perry agreed, his eyes not missing the fleeting shadow that crossed her face. He rose.

"And think about that role, Perry. Algernon. You'd be amazing." She offered a brisk nod and then swept out of the cafe.

Perry watched her go. She knew more; he could feel it in his bones. Was it something to do with Marco and Vic? *There's only one way to find out…*

19

MEANWHILE, TUESDAY 22 JUNE

"So we'll get on with the toilets and hope we can get access to the dining room in the next few days," Charles said cheerfully to Bea and Ryan as they sat around the table in Ryan's flat in Clary House. "But be aware." He sounded serious all of a sudden. "If we can't get access by the end of the week, then we'll have eaten into all of our contingency time. Then a tough decision will need to be made — pay a premium so we can work weekends to get it completed on time or delay the opening."

Bea glanced at Ryan. His eyebrows had drawn together, and he rubbed one with his forefinger. She knew neither option was an attractive one for him and Simon.

"We can't delay the opening," he told Charles. "There's too much at stake."

"Fingers crossed then that the police will be done soon," Charles replied.

Can Simon talk to CID Steve and see if any pressure can be put on Finch to release the room quicker?

Charles pushed his chair back and rose, prompting Daisy,

who had been curled up under the table by Bea's feet, to get up and stretch.

"Oh, before you disappear, Charles. Did you know a builder by the name of Jack White? His company handled quite a bit of the work here, including the bar and the false wall where Vic...well, you know."

Charles lowered himself again. Daisy gave a huff and lay down. "Sure, I knew Jack White. He was a good craftsman. Him and his men did solid work. But there was a fire at a hotel during a job they did a few years ago —tragic business, really— the rumours spread like wildfire. Excuse the pun." He shook his head, his expression grim. "An old extension lead was found plugged into a socket in the hotel kitchen. Though the investigation ended inconclusively, many believed it'd sparked the disaster. Jack and his lads swore they'd never set foot in the kitchen during the remodel, but once suspicion takes root, it's hard to kill."

"That's unfair," Bea said, picking up the white mug Ryan had given her earlier with 'Chef [shef]. Someone who cooks stuff you can't' emblazoned in black on the side. "If nothing was proven..." She trailed off and took a sip of black coffee.

"I agree. But after that, work dwindled to a trickle, and poor Jack... He lost heart. He packed up and left for Spain, hoping for a fresh start." A brief silence fell before Charles' brows lifted. "On the plus side, well for me anyway, one of his former crew came to work for me—a fellow named Ed. He's downstairs if you want to talk to him about anything."

Bea and Ryan looked at each other. "Indeed. That would be really helpful," Bea said. "We'll be down shortly."

Charles rose and leaned down to pat Daisy on the head as she moved into a sitting position. "I'll see you later," he said as he headed out of the flat.

"Well, that's a stroke of luck," Ryan said. "This Ed chap

should be able to tell us what actually happened during the renovations here—"

Beep. Bea's phone vibrated on the table. She picked it up.

Simon: *Have arranged to meet Steve. I have news from Roisin — time of death fixed to between Friday evening and Sunday morning as we suspected. Vic didn't turn up for his flight to New Zealand and no financial activity over that weekend or after... x*

Bea showed the message to Ryan. "Well, that narrows it down a bit—"

Click. The flat door opened, and Daisy let out a low *woof* as she bounded towards the intruder. Bea looked at Ryan. *Who's that?*

A stout woman, her curly black hair arranged in a halo around her head, walked in through the door, carrying a large caddy chock-full of cleaning products. She halted and gasped, her free hand flying to her chest. "Oh, my apologies, Mr Hawley. I didn't mean to barge in on you." Her eyes flittered from Ryan to Bea. Her mouth dropped open. "Oh my goodness. Is that..." She looked back at Ryan and mouthed, "Lady Rossex?"

Bea stifled a laugh. Ryan nodded as he stood. "Dot, please come in. There's no need to apologise. I wasn't expecting to be here," he said with a large smile that showed off his perfect white teeth. He turned to Bea. "Bea, this is Dorothy Thoms, she runs Dot Dusts, the cleaning company that has the contract to clean Clary House, along with most of Windstanton from what I can gather."

He winked at Dot, who laughed, shaking her head. "Well,

now, not *everywhere*, Mr Hawley. But quite a lot of the businesses and large properties." She inched towards them in a bent position as she tried to pet Daisy at the same time.

Bea rose and held out her hand. "It's good to meet you, Dorothy. We'll leave and get out of your hair."

"Oh, please, my lady, don't leave on my account," she said as she placed the caddy on the floor and stretched out to take Bea's hand. "It's lovely to meet you. You wait till I tell my sister that I met you today. She won't believe me!"

Bea smiled, then pointed to her little dog, who was still dancing around Dot. "Oh, and this is Daisy."

Dot dropped Bea's hand as she rummaged around in the big front pocket of her overalls. With an, "Ah ha," she pulled out a dog treat. "Now, can you sit, Daisy?" she asked. Daisy immediately plonked her bottom on the floor and looked up adoringly at the cleaner. "Ah, what a good girl." Dot popped the treat into Daisy's mouth. "Aw, she's so cute," she said, her eyes shining.

That's another person under Daisy's spell!

Dot straightened and waved a hand at Bea and Ryan. "Please, you two carry on. Don't mind me. I'll just get some water, and I'll start in the bathroom." She picked up her container of cleaning supplies and walked over to the sink, Daisy trailing after her with an ever hopeful look in her eyes. As Dot unpacked various polishes and bottles of cleaning fluid, a faint smell of citrus and lavender wafted over to the table where Bea and Ryan had sat down again. When she'd finished, Dot slotted the empty caddy under the tap and turned it on. While she waited for the bucket to fill, she turned to Ryan. "Any more news on poor Mr Blackwell?"

Ryan shook his head. "It's early days. The police aren't even sure exactly when he died yet."

"Well, I can tell them that," Dot said with certainty, her

silver hooped earrings swaying as she moved her head. "It must've been Saturday night."

Did Dot see Vic over that weekend? That would be great news.

"Old Mrs Hall, who lives just over there," she continued, gesturing out of the window with one hand as she turned off the tap with the other. "She saw lights flickering about on Friday evening and again on Saturday night. Then nothing." She dipped her head, a look on her face that said, "See."

Okay. So if he was alive on Friday and Saturday, then he must have been killed between Saturday night and when he'd failed to turn up for his flight on Sunday morning. They should talk to this Mrs Hall to confirm what Dot was saying. Maybe she'd seen someone with him at his flat? *That can be a job for Perry. He has a way with the more mature ladies…*

Bea hesitated. Shouldn't they let Finch know too? If the police had fixed on the weekend, and this narrowed it down more, then… She picked up her phone and sent a text to Simon. *He'll know what to do…*

Daisy, appearing to have given up on more treats, sloped off and settled down by the window with a deep sigh.

"So did you know Vic Blackmore then, Dot?" Ryan turned his chair to face the cleaner, who was still standing by the sink.

"It was mainly my sister-in-law who did this flat back then," Dot replied, smoothing her apron down. "But occasionally I filled in for her. Tidy man, he was. Quiet though." She squirted a thick white liquid from one of her bottles into the water in her bucket. "That was when him and Liv —you know, Olivia Belmont from the theatre…She was his girl-friend— weren't having one of their rows." She took a breath and carried on, "They split a short month or so before he… well, you know."

"Indeed," Bea mumbled.

Dot continued, "Liv played it all tragic-like when she found out he was staying in Australia, but I say she was relieved. Had her eye on some other chap." Dot's thick black eyebrows arched knowingly.

Now that's interesting.... "And who might that have been?" Bea asked casually, her gaze fixed on Dot's face.

"Who knows?" Dot shrugged, her lips pursing. "But my cousin, who cleans up at the theatre, overheard Liv on the blower just before she and Mr Blackwell split. She was telling someone to hang tight, and she'd be free as soon as she'd 'sorted Vic out'."

Oh my goodness! Did Liv kill Vic so she could be with someone else?

With a pointed look that spoke volumes, Dot pulled the bucket towards her and grabbed the handle. "I'd best skedaddle. The bathroom won't clean itself. Nice to meet you, my lady."

"You too, Dot," Bea said as she rose, smiling.

Dot gave a lopsided curtsey, then disappeared out of the door that led to the hallway.

"That was interesting," Ryan said as he stood. "Dot seems to know everyone and everything in this town. She may be useful in the future if we need any more information."

Bea gave a cautious nod. Was it reliable information or was it just gossip? *Not that gossip doesn't have its uses*, she admitted. But they would have to be careful and check everything before they accepted it as fact.

"Shall we go and talk to Ed now?" Ryan asked, heading towards the door.

"Indeed, we might be on a roll," Bea said. She looked over to call Daisy, but the little dog was curled up fast asleep.

She followed Ryan, leaving Daisy gently snoring by the window.

————

Walking into the wide corridor on the ground floor five minutes later, Bea caught Charles' eye. He poked his head around the door that led to the bathrooms and shouted, "Ed!"

A few seconds later, he opened the door wide to let a short muscular man pass through. Bea instantly recognised him as one of the workman who'd been in the dining room when they'd discovered Vic's remains.

"Have you got a minute?" Charles asked as the man turned to face him.

"Sure," Ed responded, wiping his hands on a rag he was holding.

Bea and Ryan approached as Charles said, "This is Mr Hawley, who owns this place, and you know Lady Rossex from Francis Court."

Ed turned and gave a short nod. "Your ladyship."

"Charles tells us you were employed by Jack White and were one of the crew who worked on the renovations at The Seaside Lounge just over three years ago when the bar and stud wall was built."

"Aye. I can tell you for nothing, there was no one in it when we put it up. I think we'd have noticed." Ed chuckled, running a hand through his thinning hair.

"Indeed," Bea said, smiling. "Can you remember exactly when that was?"

Ed stuffed the rag he'd been holding into his overalls pocket and scratched his chin. "Well, let me think now. It would've been the last full day we were working here, which was a week before they were due to reopen. We only came back to tidy up and collect our gear on the Monday morning." He dipped his chin. "Aye, it was that Friday. It was our last job that day. It was only a stud wall, so it didn't take long to build. We did that while they fitted the bar out behind it. We plastered it the same day."

Bea blinked. "So the wall wasn't left with just the plaster board up overnight at any time?"

Ed shook his head, a wry smile on his lined face. "No, my lady. So if you're thinking someone put the body in there when the place was empty, I can tell you, they couldn't have done. We were in there the whole day, and by the time we left on Friday night, it was all plastered and done." He scratched his head. "I've been thinking about it ever since we found them bones, and for the life of me, I can't think how he got in there."

"Indeed." Neither could she.

"And when you came back on the Monday, it was as you'd left it?" Ryan asked.

"Well, we only came in to pick up our stuff as we'd finished by then, but aye, it was almost dry, just a few damp patches as you'd expect."

So how is it possible Vic's body got into the wall? And when? It must have happened after the builders had completed the job. But that was at least two weeks after the police think he was killed. So where had the body been kept in the meantime?

"Did anything odd or unusual happen during the time you were working here?" Ryan asked.

"Odd? Nah." Ed shook his head, then paused. "You know, things go missing sometimes. They get moved. Normal stuff."

"Such as?" Bea prodded, tilting her head. Could it be relevant?

"Let's see…" Ed scratched his chin again, squinting in recollection. "An old extension lead vanished the first weekend. The plaster's hawk went walkabout—"

"Walkabout?" Ryan's brows rose.

"Yeah. It disappeared for a weekend, then turned up somewhere different to where the plasterer swore he left it. Probably someone borrowed it to do some stuff at home. It happens all the time."

"Anything else?"

"Yep, some drill bits disappeared, along with a screwdriver. But like I said, all quite normal on a site." He turned and looked at Charles, who'd been hovering by Ed's side.

"Ed's right," Charles agreed. "It happens all the time during a project. The lads borrow each other's tools. Sometimes they take them home and forget to bring them back. It normally all rights itself by the time the job is finished."

Ed sniffed, then pulled the rag out of his pocket. "Will that be all? I really need to get back to work."

"Yes, of course." Bea smiled at him. "Thank you for your time, Ed."

"That's left us with a mystery," Ryan said when Ed and Charles were out of earshot. "How on earth did Vic's body get in the wall?"

How indeed! Bea stifled a sigh. After talking to Dot, she'd thought they were making progress, but now it felt like they'd hit a brick wall. Well, a stud wall, in fact.

20

ALSO HAPPENING, TUESDAY 22 JUNE

Simon nursed his coffee in the sunlit atrium of The King's Hotel in King's Town, watching the steam curling up from his cup as he took a calming breath. *Did that really just happen?* He could feel his blood pressure rising as he recalled his telephone conversation with Finch that had ended five minutes ago.

Having given the inspector the information that Bea had found out about the neighbour having seen lights over that weekend, he'd not expected Finch to declare his undying gratitude for bringing it to his attention. After all, they'd hardly been best buddies when he'd left the force. But as an ex-colleague trying to help, Simon had expected a least a polite thank you. What he'd not been prepared for was to be vilified for his assistance.

"Why the hell are you sticking your nose in, Lattimore? Think you can do a better job than me, do you? Think I haven't already got my men making door-to-door enquiries? Think I'm some dinosaur who's forgotten how to run a murder enquiry?"

Any hope that Simon had had that what had happened

between them all those years ago was forgiven had been dispelled in an instance.

Simon had taken a deep breath before he'd replied, "No, of course not, Finch. I just thought it would be helpful to know that there's a witness who saw some—"

"A witness that we would have found without your help, thank you very much. I don't care how much you want this resolved quickly, Lattimore, so you can open your poncey restaurant—"

Poncey? Simon should have cut the call there and then. It'd been clear that Finch had still been furious with him. Simon stifled a huff. If anyone should be indignant about the outcome of the complaint he'd made against Finch, it should be him, not Finch. His complaint had been dismissed. Lack of evidence, they'd told him.

"But I won't be railroaded by anyone, especially you and your royal...amateur sleuth" —Finch had spat the word out on the other end of the line— "into cutting corners! So I'm telling you now, you'd better keep your pretty little nose out of this investigation, sweetheart, or I will relish arresting you both for perverting the course of justice." He'd taken a rasping breath. "And I don't care if she *is* the niece of the king. I'll still chuck her in jail!"

Sweetheart? Put Bea in jail? Simon had started in disbelief. "Look here, Finch. That's bang out of—"

"No! You look here. I'll say it one more time just so we're clear. I know what I'm doing, Lattimore. I've been doing it for years. So I don't need the help of a poof in a pinny!" Finch had cut the call, leaving Simon staring at his phone in a haze of incredulity.

He'd taken a gulp of his hot drink. *That's one way to ensure that I'll not be sharing any more information with you!* In fact, he'd a good mind to find out who'd killed Vic *before* Finch. Then he would relish the moment when Finch had to say thank you for his help, and—

"Mucker!" A familiar figure navigated through the maze of chairs towards him.

"Steve, mate!" Simon let out a short breath and grinned as his friend joined him. "I ordered a pot of coffee," he said, indicating the large silver pot in the middle of the coffee table in front of him.

"Great! I need one. I can't believe it's only eleven in the morning." Detective Inspector Steve Cox threw himself into the leather armchair opposite Simon. "It's good to get out of the office for a break. We're knee-deep in a bank scam investigation at the moment. My head is bursting with numbers."

Simon suppressed a smile. Despite the weariness in Steve's voice, Simon could still detect a spark of determination that hadn't faded since they'd joined the police force together in their late teens. Steve loved his job, and he loved to complain about it too.

Steve helped himself to coffee, then taking a sip, he gave a satisfied sigh and relaxed back into the chair. His gaze met Simon's, and he frowned. "What's wrong? You look like someone's got your goat good and proper."

Simon huffed. "You could say that." He told Steve about his call with Finch.

"He said what?" Steve barked, shaking his head. "He can't talk to you like that." He picked up his phone. "We need to tell someone, mate. You need to make a formal complaint against him."

Simon reached out and put his hand on his friend's arm. "Yeah, and we know how well that went last time. It will be my word against his. Again." He dropped his hand and ran it through his hair. "There's no point."

Steve let out a heavy sigh. "He was a bigot then, and he's

still a bigot now," he said in a weary voice. "He shouldn't be allowed to get away with it."

Simon gave him a wry smile. "I know. But maybe he won't. You know what they say about karma…"

Steve dipped his chin. "Well, if I have anything to do with it, they'll be right," he said through gritted teeth. He picked up his coffee and took a slug of it. Then he put the cup down and crossed his legs. "So how's that restaurant of yours coming along?"

"Slowly," Simon replied. "We've had to rejig the work schedule as we still haven't been able to get back into the dining room. Unfortunately, that's where most of the work needs doing. I'm worried we won't get it done in time for the opening." *I can't bear to think about the extra cost if we have to work weekends.* He'd already sunk a boatload of cash into the project. Fingers crossed his latest book, *The Betrayal*, which was due for release next week, would shoot straight to the bestsellers list and fill up the coffers again.

Steve's brow creased. "So Finch hasn't finished with the crime scene yet?"

Simon shrugged. "No one's been there since the weekend, but we're still being told we can't get back in."

Steve swore as he rubbed his hand along his stubbly jawline. "That man! Um, let me see what I can find out. They should've finished in there by now."

Since the investigation had started, Simon had wondered if Finch was being difficult on purpose. Now there seemed to be no doubt about it.

Hopefully, Steve can chivvy things along a bit for us. "Thanks, mucker. That would be great." He picked up his coffee and took a sip. "So how's that godson of mine? Now he's back, is he raring to embrace academia in Edinburgh?"

"Well, he's back, that's for sure. Along with about six

months' worth of washing, much to Julia's horror. He's as skinny as a beanpole and has done nothing since he stepped in the door but eat. I get the impression they worked him hard in both New Zealand and Australia," Steve replied, a distinct note of pride in his voice.

"And knowing Callum, I bet he played hard too."

"He's keeping very quiet about that at the moment. I think he's trying not to worry his mother." They both laughed.

"And how's the brainy one?"

"Jenny had her last exam yesterday, thank goodness. She's been knee-deep in revision for her GCSEs for weeks," Steve said, a pained look on his face. "She's been a nightmare to live with, so we're *all* relieved they're over now. She thinks she's had it tough, so, of course, I've pointed out to her that it's just the beginning." He gave a wry smile. "I just got an eye roll in response."

"Of course." Simon grinned. "Isn't that the universal sign of teenage wisdom?"

Steve laughed. "Of course you'd know all about that now. How *are* things going with Isla?" He leaned forward, studying Simon over the rim of his coffee cup.

Simon hesitated, putting his cup down on the table and adding some more steaming hot coffee. *How are things?* That was a good question. It was difficult to know. He was navigating uncharted territory.

Steve had been one of the first people Simon had rung when Isla had appeared out of the blue just over two months ago, announcing that she was his daughter. Being the father of two teenagers, one of them a girl, Steve's advice on handling the delicate relationship Simon was trying to grow with a daughter he'd just met for the first time had been invaluable.

"It's early days yet," he replied, lifting his cup. "She's…

remarkable, really. How she's coping with the loss of her mother and planning to go back to Barcelona to study. We're finding our way. I just wish we had more time together."

"Yeah, she seemed a pretty together kid," Steve said. He'd met her a couple of times before she'd had to go back to Scotland to sort out her mother's affairs. "And the spitting image of Bridget." Steve and Roisin had been with him on the holiday in Spain where Simon had had a weeklong holiday romance with Isla's mother.

"It's the eyes," Simon agreed, recalling the moment he'd met Isla. Even before he'd known she was his daughter, he'd seen something in her eyes that had seemed so familiar.

"And how's Perry taking it all?" Steve prodded gently.

Simon set his cup down. "On the surface, he's the embodiment of cool. And Isla adores him." He paused, searching for the right words. "But sometimes when I talk about her, he deflects the conversation or goes quiet on me. Which, as you know, is unlike Perry."

Steve nodded, smiling.

"I can't help worrying if he's had his nose put out of joint a bit with Isla's sudden appearance. He's never been one for playing second fiddle, and I've been giving Isla a lot of attention, I suppose. I just want to get to know her before she disappears back to Spain, you know?"

"Sounds like he just needs some reassurance that he's not been usurped in your affections," Steve offered with surprising insight. "Big changes — they take a bit of getting used to, don't they?"

"True enough," Simon replied, mulling over the notion as he took another sip of his coffee. "Thanks, mate. I'll have a chat with him about it."

The conversation drifted momentarily until Simon's eyes landed on his wedding ring, sparking a memory from a few days ago. "By the way, I noticed Finch wasn't wearing his wedding ring."

Steve pulled a face. "Ah, yes. He and his wife got divorced a few years ago."

"What happened?"

Steve shrugged. "You'll have to ask Julia if you want all the details, but I believe his wife instigated it. Not a big surprise really. Who'd want to live with him? They sold the house he'd painstakingly done up in Windstanton, he bought a flat, and she's now in Fawstead with the boy. Finch's been like a bear with a sore head ever since the divorce came through." He put his hand up. "Not that that's any excuse for his behaviour, mind. We're all just glad he keeps to himself over at the Cold Case Unit."

All of a sudden, Simon's heart felt light. All the tension that had been with him since his conversation with Finch seeped out of his body. Finch might have said things meant to wound, but they'd been just words. Simon was the luckiest man alive. A rewarding career as a writer, a second hobby doing something he loved — cooking. A husband who made him laugh and loved him just as he was. Friends who made him feel valued. And now a daughter who he was already proud of and knew would bring even more joy and love into his life. He almost felt sorry for Finch. Simon didn't need to prove anything to this bitter, lonely man clinging onto the past. He stifled a smile. That was karma in action. They would continue to investigate their own way, and if they discovered anything important, they would still tell the police. *Just not Finch.* "So do you know how's he getting on with the case?"

Steve raised an eyebrow. "Not much apart for the time of death window, which I believe you already know." Steve raised an eyebrow at Simon, who gave him a sheepish grin.

Steve continued, "I think he's onto something, but he's keeping his cards close to his chest."

So what does Finch know that we don't?

"Rumour has it he wants to crack this on his own, so he can go out with a bang," Steve continued.

Simon's mouth fell open. "He's leaving?"

"Early retirement, so I hear."

Simon raised an eyebrow. "But isn't he only in his early fifties?"

"Ah, but you know the drill—retire one day, come back as a CIO the next. I think he's setting himself up for a cushy civilian role."

Simon tilted his head to one side. *This might work in our favour.* If Finch was keen to prove himself so he could secure a new role as a civilian investigation officer, then he had an incentive to close the case quickly.

"It's been great to see you, mucker, but unfortunately I need to get back to work," Steve said, draining the last of his coffee as he rose.

Simon stood up. "Me too. I—" He stopped, distracted by two men striding through the lobby just to their left. Simon recognised the one with the confident air of a man used to being observed but not the taller man with the slightly hunched shoulders.

"Who's that with Julian Thornton?" Simon tilted his head discreetly towards them, his curiosity piqued.

Steve glanced over his shoulder, nonchalant as ever. "Oh, that's the mayor of King's Town," he replied before turning back, an eyebrow arched. "Word is Thornton's got his eye on the mayoral seat in Windstanton."

"Really? He's a serious businessman, isn't he? I thought nowadays being mayor is all ribbon-cutting and handshaking —mostly ceremonial."

"On the surface, possibly." Steve gave him a knowing smirk. "But behind the scenes, it's all about building connections. Nothing feeds power like knowing the right people to talk to."

Simon's gaze lingered on Thornton's retreating figure. "Did you know Thornton owned Clary House before we bought it off him? It was his place when Vic met his untimely end. Vic supposedly sent an email to Julian saying he was staying in Australia and not coming back. Have you guys seen the email?"

"An email?" Steve's tone sharpened, his detective instincts kicking in. "It's not been mentioned to me, but that might be something Finch's keeping to himself. Do you think Thornton's involved?"

"He can't be ruled out. After all, he had access to the building, *and* if Vic never left, then was there ever really an email?"

"Interesting," Steve said, his eyes holding the steely glint of someone ready to dig a little deeper. "I'll try and find out more about this email and see if Thornton's on Finch's radar."

Meanwhile, we need to talk to Thornton. A shiver ran down Simon's spine. They needed to be careful. *If he killed Vic, then he has a very strong reason to want to keep it buried in the past.* After all, no one would vote a killer in as mayor.

21

AFTERNOON, TUESDAY 22 JUNE

"Thanks for coming with me, Ryan," Perry said, pulling at the collar of his shirt and undoing another button. The sun, beating down on their heads as they walked along the cobblestone path to the Windstanton Theatre, had taken him by surprise when it had come out a short while ago, the morning having been dull and overcast with no hint it would burn away to reveal such a hot afternoon. *I should've ditched my jacket before we set out.* He adjusted the cuff of his fitted blue suit, the fabric sticking to his skin. *Yuck!*

Ryan's large mouth broke into one of his trademark grins. "No worries, Perry," he replied with a casual shrug. "It's a great opportunity for me to introduce myself to a food critic. It's important to get them on side, you know?"

Perry screwed up his eyes against the sun's glare, mentally kicking himself. *I should've brought my sunglasses.*

"But are you sure he'll be here?"

Perry raised his eyebrows and smirked. "Don't worry. I have it on good authority he frequents the cafe at the theatre every afternoon." When he'd met with Liv this morning, he'd recognised the cafe manager. She'd been one of the part-time tour guides at Francis Court when she'd been a student. At the time, he'd headed up the team, and they'd got on very well. After Liv had left him, the manager and Perry had chatted, catching up on all the gossip. When Perry had casually mentioned that he'd needed to find Marco Rossi, his ex-colleague had told him to look no further as Mr Rossi came to the cafe every afternoon. He had the same table every day, she'd told him, where he sat working on his laptop while the staff kept him topped up with tea.

Sure enough, as Perry and Ryan walked into the cafe on the first floor of the theatre a short while later, they spied Marco at a large table over in the far corner, hunched over his laptop. The food critic's hands danced over his keyboard, stopping only long enough for him to refer to a small note-book lying open beside him.

Perry followed Ryan, who was making his way across the room towards a table for two next to Marco. As they sat down, the man looked across at them. Ryan smiled. "Mr Rossi?"

Marco stared as he gave a slow nod.

"This is serendipitous indeed," Ryan said. "I'm Ryan Hawley, and I was hoping to track you down. I have an invitation to the opening of my new venture, SaltAir, in Clary House. I very much hope you'll be able to come."

"Ah, the culinary maestro from London, no?" Marco's voice was rich, tinged with an Italian accent. "Would you care to join me?" He waved them into seats opposite him, moving his notepad and closing his laptop.

Clearly Ryan's charm had worked on Marco, and Perry mentally patted himself on the back for having asked the chef to accompany him to this interview.

Tea orders dispatched, Perry and Ryan settled into the velvet-lined chairs opposite Marco. The scent from the pot of

Earl Grey already on the table mingled with the aroma of freshly baked pastries being served for afternoon tea to the other patrons scattered around the room.

"Tell me, Ryan." Marco leaned forward, his eyes alight with professional curiosity. "What gastronomic delights do you plan to bestow upon us at SaltAir?"

The two of them delved into the depths of menus and wine pairings. When their tea arrived, Ryan was waxing poetically about sustainable produce and innovative flavour profiles. Perry poured his Darjeeling, hoping they would soon run out of steam, so he could get down to business. *I want to know about him and Vic, not about whether a pinot grigio or a Soave goes best with lemon sole.*

Perry seized his moment when Ryan paused talking to pour himself a cup of camomile tea. "So how will it feel to be back at Clary House?" he asked Marco, who was taking a sip of his Earl Grey.

Marco hesitated for a moment, the twinkle in his eye dimming slightly. "Well, er…it'll be interesting to see the transformation, I suppose."

"And do you have any thoughts on what might have happened to Vic?" Perry continued, watching Marco's fingers trace the handle of the tea pot.

"Well…er, I heard he was found stuffed in a wall somewhere. Quite extraordinary. I thought he'd hopped off to Australia and decided to stay there," he said, a shrug lifting his shoulders.

"Was there anyone who might have wished him harm, do you think?" Perry's tone was conversational, but his gaze was sharp.

Marco's laugh was dismissive, almost scoffing. "Vic wasn't always... shall we say, amicable. But deserving of harm? Who can say?"

Interesting. He clearly thinks it's possible. Was he of the same mind as Liv? It was worth testing the waters… "What do you make of Rob Rivers' success since those days at The Seaside Lounge?"

"Ah, Rivers," Marco sighed. "A talent long overshadowed, it would appear. One might wonder if he yearned for the spotlight Vic bathed in."

He wasn't being quite as emphatic as Liv had been, but was he hinting that he, too, thought Rob had had a motive for murder? Or was it a diversionary tactic to shift the attention from himself? He studied the man sitting opposite him. His hands, full of life when he'd been talking to Ryan, now sat motionless and rigid on the surface of the table. The easy smile had slipped off his tanned face, and now the corners of his mouth turned downwards ever so slightly. His eyes were guarded and evasive.

"And how was your relationship with Vic?" Next to Perry, Ryan shifted in his seat and cleared his throat.

A flicker of unease crossed Marco's face. "We had a good working relationship," he replied curtly, his eyes darting away from Perry's steady gaze.

Really? Perry recalled Maisey's pointed remarks about the cooling of the friendship between Marco and Vic in the months leading up to Vic's disappearance.

Ryan coughed and made to rise.

Perry ignored him. "Did you see him the weekend before he supposedly jetted off on his holiday?"

Marco's laugh was short, more a huff of indignation than amusement. "Why would I? We didn't mix socially."

So where were you then? Perry opened his mouth, the question teetering on the tip of his tongue, but Ryan jumped up, his chair scraping as it was pushed backwards. "It's been delightful, Marco. I'm really looking forward to welcoming you at SaltAir." Ryan held out his hand, and Marco took it, looking slightly bemused at the sudden change of direction.

Perry's chest tightened. *What's Ryan up to? I haven't finished yet...*

Ryan's hand dug into Perry's elbow as he tried to subtly get Perry to stand. "Come on, Perry," he said, a forced smile on his face. "We need to let Marco get on with his work."

Perry stifled a sigh as he rose. "Nice to meet you, Marco." Marco bobbed his head, then looking away, he flipped open his laptop. Perry could have sworn he spotted a look of relief wash over the man's face as he looked down at this screen.

You're hiding something. I know you are!

22

A SHORT WHILE LATER, TUESDAY 22 JUNE

Outside the theatre, Perry squinted as he and Ryan stepped out of the door and onto the street. Ryan stretched, rolling his shoulders. "I'm sorry, Perry. But Marco was done talking. You saw that, didn't you?" Ryan's tone was light, but there was a firmness there too.

Perry suppressed a sigh. Ryan was right of course. "But something's wrong. He's hiding behind those smarmy smiles and oh-so-casual shrugs," Perry muttered, frustration lacing his words.

Ryan nodded, the gesture slow, thoughtful. "I agree. But pushing him further wouldn't have got us anywhere. In fact, it could've backfired. I don't want to sour relations with the local food critic before SaltAir even opens."

Perry pursed his lips, conceding with a reluctant nod. "Fine, but I tell you there's more to his story."

Ryan patted him on the back. "All in good time, Perry. You'll figure it out; I have no doubt."

Not with you on my shoulder, Perry thought. Then he felt bad. He wasn't being fair. Ryan was in an awkward position. Most of their suspects so far were people Ryan and Simon had to impress if they wanted to make a success of SaltAir. *I shouldn't have put him in that position by bringing him along. I should do this on my own...* "Ryan, why don't you head back and check on Charles' progress?" Perry suggested casually. "Perhaps you can also give the police a ring too? See if they've loosened up about letting us back in the dining room. The sooner we can get in there, the less pressure we'll all be under."

Ryan's eyes narrowed for a moment as he stared at Perry.

Go on. You know you want to...

Ryan gave a slow smile. "Okay, Perry. But keep me posted, yeah?"

With a sharp nod, Perry watched Ryan's retreating figure before turning on his heels and heading in the opposite direction, towards Rivers By the Sea.

———

When Perry stepped inside the bistro a short while later, the place was humming with the low buzz of conversation. He scanned the room. A sprinkling of tables were occupied by guests finishing off what was left on their three-tiered china cake stands. He licked his lips. *A scone or a nice slice of cake would go down well right now.*

"Can I help you?" The front of house manager, poised elegantly in a smart fitted dress, approached Perry with a practiced smile.

"Rob Rivers, please," Perry said, his tone direct but friendly. "Please tell him Perry Juke from SaltAir has an invitation for him."

She inclined her head, then disappeared behind a set of swinging doors. Moments later, Rob Rivers emerged, his hair impeccably gelled, the very picture of a cool local celebrity chef. He extended a hand, and Perry took it, smiling. "Thanks for seeing me. I've heard great things about this place."

Rob smiled as he dropped Perry's hand. "Sonia said something about an invitation?"

"Oh, yes. You may have heard that my husband, Simon Lattimore, and Ryan Hawley, the judge on *Bake-off Wars*, are opening a new restaurant, SaltAir, on the sea front?"

Rob's face lit up. "Of course. It's the talk of the town."

"Well, I come bearing an invite to the grand opening." Perry handed over the invitation with a flourish. "We'd love to have you there, of course."

"Thanks, Perry," Rob replied, flipping the invite over in his hands. "I'd love to come."

Now what? Perry needed to get him on his own so he could question him. Time to pull out his trump card. "I told my business partner, Lady Rossex, I was coming to see you this afternoon. She was keen to know about this place." He looked around the room.

"Lady Beatrice?" Rob's face lit up in recognition, his charm dial turning up a notch. "She'd be more than welcome to dine here anytime she'd like. Would you like a glass of champagne while I show you around?"

Bingo!

"Thank you, that would be lovely."

Rob gestured to Sonia, who'd been lurking just behind them, and she tottered off in her sky-high heels before returning a few seconds later with a bottle in one hand and two champagne flutes in the other. *Pop!* She expertly poured a glass and handed it to Perry.

———

Twenty minutes later, seated at the bar, Perry said, "Your place here is charming." In fact, much against his expectations, he rather liked the elegant decor and furniture that was cleverly arranged to give a feeling of casual sophistication. It could do with a few tweaks here and there —the lighting was awful, and the wooden serving hatch would have to go— but generally, it was a pleasant environment. "I'm eager to see what you think of Clary House when you come to the opening."

"Ah, The Seaside Lounge," Rob said, swirling the fizz in his glass. "I've got fond memories of that place. I was so shocked to hear they'd found Vic's remains. I mean, we all thought he'd started a new life Down Under." He shook his head. "And all along, he was in a wall."

Perry stifled a snort and cleared his throat. "Do you think there was anyone who wanted him dead?"

Rob's smile faltered. "Vic? Nah, he was all right. You know, supportive and stuff. I wouldn't be where I am now if it hadn't been for him."

Because you killed him?

"So the two of you got on then, did you?"

A shadow of something whizzed across his face. *Unease?* "Yeah." His smile faltered, and his lips twitched in uncertainty before settling back into a confident grin. "He was my mentor, like."

"And there was no professional rivalry?"

"I was ambitious, I won't deny it. Maybe Vic felt that sometimes. We disagreed about ingredients too. He had expensive tastes when it came to produce. I wanted to keep it local, you know, less food miles and stuff. Also local produce from around here is great quality. But Vic thought more money meant it was automatically better. So he'd order crabs from the other end of the country, in Cornwall, even though we have amazing crabs just down the coast here in Tromer. And it's not like we were that busy some days. I honestly don't know how the place survived." He took a swig of champagne. "But generally, we mucked along just fine together. As I said, he was supportive, you know?" There was a slight stiffness in his shoulders.

He's hiding something too. Perry's stomach hardened. *Join the club!* No one he'd spoken to about Vic seemed to be telling the truth. "Did you see Vic the weekend he was due to go on holiday?"

"Me? No." Rob's answer was quick. *Too quick?* "After the deep clean at Clary House on the Friday. l left and was tied up recording a pilot for Fenshire radio for the rest of the weekend." He smiled. This time it was sincere and relaxed. "That was my first big break, you know." He raised his glass. "And, as they say, the rest is history."

Well, good for you! Perry wasn't sure if he liked this man or not. Was it all hot air, or was he really grateful to Vic for his support? Perry stood. "Thanks for the champagne. I'll see you at the opening."

Rob hopped off his bar stool. "Yes. I look forward to it. And please do let Lady Beatrice know she's welcome here anytime."

23

MEANWHILE, TUESDAY 22 JUNE

Bea stepped out of the back of the Bentley, then quickly turned to stop Daisy from following her. "I'm sorry, Daisy, but you can't come with us this time." The little dog looked up into Bea's face, her huge brown eyes wide with confusion. Bea's heart hurt. She turned to Simon, who'd got out of the other side of the car. "Will it be okay if I take her?"

Simon gave Bea an understanding smile but shook his head. "No, Bea, it's a business meeting." He turned to Fraser, who was in the driver's seat. "Fraser, would you mind looking after Daisy for us? We won't be long."

Fraser gave a short bow. "Of course not, Mr Lattimore." He then redirected his gaze to Bea. "There's a small lake with a path around it over there, my lady." He pointed to an area to their right. "I'll take her for an explore."

Bea smiled gratefully at her old family retainer as he retrieved Daisy's lead from the pocket of the car door and clipped it to the little dog's harness. "Thank you, Fraser. Be good, Daisy," Bea said as she turned around and surveyed Julian Thornton's office.

"It's a bit flashy for my taste," Simon said from beside her.

She had to agree. Although the modern glass facade with steel trimmings looked in keeping with the other buildings in the showy business park on the outskirts of Windstanton, she much preferred the elegance and history of the older buildings in the town centre. "I wonder why he bases himself all the way out here."

"I imagine it's because he owns the park, so he needs to set an example."

They entered the building, their steps echoing in the sleek, marble-clad lobby. A receptionist with a large headset mouthpiece blocking half of her lower face took their details before escorting them through to Julian's office.

"Ah, Lady Rossex, what an honour!" Julian boomed as they entered, rising from behind his mahogany desk with his hand outstretched.

"It's nice to see you again, Mr Thornton," Bea said, shaking his hand. "And you know Simon Lattimore, of course."

He bowed slightly. "Of course, of course." He chuckled, his salt-and-pepper hair catching the light streaming in through the floor-to-ceiling windows overlooking the lake. Bea could see Fraser over the other side, patiently waiting for Daisy, who had her head buried in a bush.

The men shook hands.

"Please take a seat." Julian gestured to an area in the corner of the office where four leather tub chairs were arranged around an oval glass table. They each took a seat. As Bea settled into the chair, she was disappointed she no longer had a view of the lake. *Who puts a seating area so far away from the best view?*

"Now to what do I owe this pleasure?" Julian lounged

back in the chair opposite her. A twitch in his left eye suggested he wasn't quite as relaxed as he was trying to make out.

"An invitation and a request," Simon replied. "Firstly, we'd like to invite you to the opening of SaltAir." He leaned over the table and handed Julian an invitation. "I do hope you can come."

Julian's face lit up. "That's great. I'd love to." He read the embossed card, then placed it on the table and leaned back, crossing his legs. "I hear you're doing exciting things at Clary House, Simon. Did I read somewhere there's going to be a monthly supper club along with the restaurant?"

The receptionist entered with their hot drinks, and Julian listened intently as Simon filled him in on the setup they had planned at Clary House. "I must say I'm impressed," he said when Simon had finished. "I always thought Clary House had potential, but since...well, things changed, and I just couldn't make it work."

"When Vic left?" Bea prompted.

"Vic? Oh... Well... Yes, I suppose so." Julian tripped over his words, his composure slipping. "I mean, yes, after he was no longer there, it all just became difficult."

Bea suppressed a smile. *Maybe Vic's spirit was hanging around in the building, bringing Julian bad luck...*

"Actually, Julian," Simon chimed in, seemingly oblivious to the sudden tension. "Do you have copies of the plans Jack White's company worked on? Our solicitor's away, and it would be a great help when we start work in the dining room."

"Plans? Oh, yes, those plans," Julian murmured, his surprise evident as he glanced between them. He uncrossed his legs and shifted in his seat. "I might have something lying around, but you know how it is—paperwork tends to get misplaced. I'll see what I can do." Julian's face twitched again, and he seemed unsure of where to rest his hands.

I think we've struck a nerve! "So how did you feel when Vic's remains were discovered?" Bea asked.

"Shocked, of course," Julian Thornton uttered, his voice betraying a tremor as he clasped and unclasped his hands. "When the police came and said he'd been found — I just can't fathom it."

"Indeed." Bea watched him closely as his gaze flitted about the room.

"He sent me an email, you know," Julian continued, his face looking a little flushed now.

Bea glanced at Simon.

"I hadn't seen him since we'd closed the restaurant on the Wednesday evening," Julian continued. "He'd seemed fine then. We said have a nice holiday to each other — I was off to Spain on the Friday, family holiday, you know, and he was going to New Zealand on the Sunday. So you can imagine my shock when I came back a few weeks later and got an email from him. It said he'd been offered a job in Australia, and so he wasn't coming back." His eyes darted to Simon, then back to Bea. "I mean…" He shrugged, then tucked his errant hands behind his knees.

"And did you give a copy of the email to the police?" Simon asked, catching Bea's eye.

"Ah…" Julian winced, his Adam's apple bobbing. "I'm afraid I deleted it. I never thought it would be important." He managed a weak smile.

How convenient! Bea was beginning to think Maisey was right, and there was no email. "But you're sure it came from Vic?"

"It was from a personal email address that was in his name. I had no reason to doubt it was real." He sighed. "But now the police — Well, they say an email address could have been set up in his name by anyone."

So the police believed there *had* been an email. *Did they find out something we don't know?* "What exactly was your partnership with Vic? Business-wise, I mean?" she asked.

"Partnership?" Julian echoed, the word seeming to catch him off guard. "Vic handled the culinary side. The restaurant was his domain. I owned the building and oversaw the business end of things. My accountant, Bryan Sinclair, managed the finances."

"How was the restaurant doing?" Bea leaned in slightly, her expression one of polite interest. She knew from what Rich had told them already that it had been profitable. *Can I get Julian to expand on that?*

For a moment, Julian appeared lost, the question hanging in the air like a bad smell. "Why do you ask?" His tone remained civil, but there was a steeliness behind it now.

It would appear not! Rats! Now what excuse could she give for having asked such a direct question?

"Pure curiosity." Simon jumped in to rescue her. "Ryan and I want to emulate your success. So any tips you might have about what worked and what didn't would be gratefully received." He smiled warmly at Julian, and the man relaxed back in his chair. He proceeded to tell Simon about showcasing suppliers, advertising in the region, and early bird specials.

Well played, Simon! Tension released from Bea's shoulders, and she let what Julian was saying wash over her. Had Julian's earlier discomfort been a sign of guilt? Was it possible he'd killed Vic? But why? Surely he would've needed the chef to continue bringing in the business and earning him profits? Another thought struck her. If Julian was the killer, then why would he have hidden the body at Clary

House? Wouldn't it have smelled those first few months, even through the plastered-up wall? Julian wouldn't have wanted that, would he? Talk about bad for business!

Oh! Wait. What if he'd used Vic leaving as an excuse to close the building and prevent anyone from discovering the body?

She started to gasp in surprise when she had a sudden thought.

Wait, no... He'd applied for permission to turn it into flats, hadn't he? Again, any work required would have led to the grisly exposure. And, she reminded herself, when he'd eventually given up and decided to sell, he must have been aware Ryan and Simon were going to have work done. If Julian was the killer, then why would he have pushed for development, knowing the risk? Had it been a ruse, or merely ignorance? Or did selling the building suggest he was innocent? *But then why is he so spooked by our questions?* It was time to poke the bear a little more...

She waited for Julian to finish lecturing Simon on how to run a successful business and then, much to Simon's obvious relief, she changed the subject. "Did you and Vic get on, Mr Thornton?"

Julian shifted his weight forward. "I respected him a great deal. He was a highly skilled and innovative chef. We made a good team." Surprisingly, his statement was made with a conviction that suggested he was telling the truth.

"So off the record, Julian," Simon said. "As you knew him well, was there anyone who you think would have wanted him dead?"

Julian immediately stiffened and he lowered his gaze. "No. I don't think so."

Bea recalled what Maisey had said about Rob Rivers.

"Not even Rob Rivers?" she asked.

Julian looked up. Was that relief she fleetingly saw across his face? He appeared to consider the question for a minute. "I suppose it's possible," he conceded. "Vic and Rob were a bit like oil and water, always at odds. Vic didn't think Rob had the creativity to develop the place. I trusted Vic's assessment."

"Yet Rob's place seems quite successful now," Simon said, his eyebrow arching with a silent challenge.

"Have you been there?" Julian scoffed, his laugh rich with derision. "It's like stepping back into The Seaside Lounge but with a posh hostess to greet you. He's merely rehashed Vic's old recipes, with only the occasional variation. There's nothing innovative about Rivers by The Sea."

He's not a fan then! "So is that why you didn't reopen after Vic left? You didn't have a chef who was good enough to replace him?"

The question made Julian's jitters practically palpable. His eyes darted quickly to Bea, then away. He swallowed. "Bryan, and er, well...yes... Bryan advised me that converting the building into flats would yield a better return. Sadly, planning permission for change of use proved...elusive." He glanced at his watch.

She caught Simon's eye. *Are we done?*

"Well, thank you for your time, Julian." Simon rose and held out his hand. "If you do find those plans, would you be kind enough to get someone to drop them off at Clary House, please?"

As Bea stood, Julian sprang up, his eyes dancing. "Of course," he said, shaking Simon's hand. "And it was a pleasure to see you again, my lady." His handshake was brief and his fingers clammy. *I doubt you mean that!*

24

EVENING, TUESDAY 22 JUNE

B ea leaned on the cool marble countertop and inhaled the comforting aroma of garlic and fresh herbs that wafted through Rose Cottage's open-plan kitchen. Her tummy rumbled.

Simon, stirring a pot on the stove with one hand, dipped a spoon into the deep-red sauce with the other. He took a taste, smiled, then turned the heat down and dropped the used spoon into a small jug of water by the side of the cooking range. He opened the oven door and peered inside before nodding and closing it again.

"What are we having?" Bea asked, licking her lips.

"A classic from my childhood," Simon replied as he diced up some cooked chicken, carrots, green beans, and sweet potato before pushing them off the chopping board and into a round bowl.

Is that some sort of side dish?

Perry appeared by her side and handed her a glass of red wine. "Where's that lovely man of yours? I'm hungry."

My man? She grinned. "He'll be here any minute. He texted me to say Fraser was bringing him straight here from the station." Her stomach fluttered. *Come on, Bea, get a grip. He's only been to London for the day!*

Woof! Daisy, who'd been snoozing in her favourite chair by the French doors, jumped down, did a long stretch, then came trotting past Bea and Perry. Ignoring them both, she stood by the door leading into the hall, her tail wagging furiously. *That will be him then,* Bea thought, and a few seconds later, a car pulled up outside the cottage.

Perry opened the kitchen door, and Daisy hurtled out. Perry gave a low laugh, then followed her.

Bea's pulse quickened as she heard Rich's deep voice greet Daisy, then Perry. Her heart lifted as he walked into the room and gave her a lazy smile. She moved over to meet him. "Hey, you. Good day?"

She raised her head, and he lightly dropped his lips onto hers.

"Meetings, meetings, meetings," he said with a sigh, then grinned. "But all the better now I've seen you."

"Cheesy!" Perry whispered loudly to Bea as he moved past them and joined his husband by the stove.

Rich laughed, and Bea gave him a playful punch on the arm. "Hey," he said, rubbing his arm. "What makes you think I was talking about you!" He leaned down and ruffled the terrier's ears. "I meant you, of course, little girl," he pretended to whisper to Daisy.

"Food's almost ready," Simon called from the kitchen as he opened the oven and took out a tray with a loaf of bread on it.

"We've been busy information gathering," Bea told Rich as she grabbed her glass of wine. "There's lots to tell you."

They made their way to the table, where Perry handed Rich a bottle of beer. "She means I've been proper sleuthing, and as always, she's just been in the right place at the right time, and people have told her stuff!"

They laughed as Simon arrived at the table, Daisy at his heels, with a huge dish of pasta and a wooden platter with large slices of bread on it. He placed them in the middle of the table, then, Daisy still trailing him, headed back to the kitchen.

Bea sat down and placed her wineglass on the table. "Oh my goodness, it smells delightful."

"Well, dig in then!" Simon called from the other side of the room as he picked up the bowl of chicken and vegetables and headed towards the French doors with it. "Here you go, Daisy," he said as he placed it on the wooden floor near her favourite chair.

Oh...so not a side dish then. Bea watched her little dog attack the food with gusto.

Simon joined them at the table. "So we have ravioli with rocket, artichokes, and almonds, along with a rosemary sourdough."

"Simon, you've outdone yourself," Rich said, spooning a large scoop of pasta into his bowl with visible delight.

The conversation flowed easily as they ate. Perry recounted his encounters with Liv, Marco, and Rob, ending with his observation that they were all hiding something.

Bea told them what Dot had confided to her and Ryan about Vic, along with the neighbour's report of the lights in Vic's flat, leading to her assumption that he'd still been alive on Saturday evening at least. She also gave them the details Ed had revealed about the timing of the stud wall going up three years ago.

As they devoured the delicious food, Simon described his and Bea's visit to Julian Thornton's office. "That man was definitely spooked by our questions," he concluded, then he dabbed his mouth with a napkin and leaned back in his chair with a satisfied sigh. "Oh, and the police now have the preliminary report on Vic's autopsy," he said. "It seems he was struck on the side of his head with an object that left quite the impression—literally. They found a large dent in his skull. At the moment, they don't know what made it, but they believe it's what killed him. They also found traces of his chef's jacket amongst the debris in the wall, and interestingly there were the remains of silica gel packs inside and outside of the plastic sheeting. They apparently absorb moisture and odours. You can get them anywhere. The plastic sheeting didn't tell them much either."

"Did you get that from CID Steve?" Bea asked.

Simon shook his head. "No. Roisin rang me an hour or so ago. But I saw Steve."

A look of something…*pain?*…flashed across his face, then it was gone. *What was that?*

Simon continued, "He said Finch is keeping the investigation close to his chest." He shared with them Steve's speculation that Finch was setting himself up for a civilian's role for when he took early retirement.

"So you say he needs a quick win?" Rich asked, wiping his mouth with a napkin.

"Exactly. He may even get to the bottom of this before we do," Simon replied, glancing at Perry.

"But we're not going to give up, are we?" Perry pouted, then looked at Bea for support.

Simon has a good point. We could just—

"You could just leave it to the police," Rich pointed out. "If this Finch guy is keen to get a result, he might easily get it wrapped up before the opening."

Perry's eyes pleaded with her. She crinkled her nose. "But

what if he doesn't? We'll have lost all that time. I think we need to carry on."

Perry gave her a grateful smile. "I agree!" He turned to his husband. "Do you want to leave it in someone else's hands and take the risk?"

Silence hung in the air. If Simon didn't want to continue, then Bea knew they would stop now. In or out, they were a team.

Rich's hand nudged hers under the table. She reached out for his fingers. "Okay," Simon said after what felt like an age. His jaw was set as he rose. "I'll keep in touch with Steve, and we'll pass anything we find on to him, okay?"

Not Finch? Despite what he'd said, perhaps Simon wasn't over his dispute with Finch, after all...

Simon was still talking. "When we've cleared the table, let's review our list of suspects and look at motive, means, and opportunity for each of them."

Rich's fingers quickly squeezed hers before he stood. Grabbing their bowls, he followed Simon into the kitchen. She caught Perry's eye as she let out a slow breath. He gave her a smile, and she returned it. She wasn't ready to give up yet either.

———

"So Vic's time of death was likely Saturday evening based on what the neighbour saw," Simon said, writing on the top of a piece of blank paper.

"You need to get that verified." Rich picked up his coffee cup. "It's a secondhand report about something that happened over three years ago."

Simon, his pen poised above a blank page in his notebook, said, "So we have Liv Belmont, Vic's recent ex-girlfriend; Rob Rivers, his ambitious senior sous chef; Marco Rossi, the front of house manager of The Seaside Lounge at the time; and Julian Thornton, the previous owner of Clary House. Have I missed anyone?"

Bea dredged her memory for what else Maisey had told them. "Oh, there's Bella DeMarco. We haven't spoken to her yet, but she worked with Vic in the kitchens too. She was the other sous chef."

Simon wrote her name down.

"We should deliver her invitation tomorrow and have a chat with her," Perry suggested.

"Great. That can be a job for you two," Simon said, writing a note on the paper.

"We can do that," Bea reassured him. "Until Charles gets going in the dining room, Perry and I can't really do much."

"Any more suspects?"

Perry shook his head. Bea pursed her lips. In the back of her mind, she had a vague feeling they'd missed someone. *But who?* She wracked her brains but couldn't think. Maybe it was nothing…

"So what do we know about each person's access to Clary House?" Rich asked.

"Each one had access via a set of keys or knew Vic well enough to get inside without much fuss," Perry replied.

"So basically they all had means," Simon said, ticking a box next to each of the names in his list.

"So what about motive?" Perry asked.

"Well, everyone I've spoken to has been quick to point the finger at Rob," Perry said. "He was ambitious and nipping at Vic's heels apparently. They argued quite a bit too. He may have thought that with Vic out of the way, he would get a chance to head up The Seaside Lounge."

"Although Julian was quick to point out to us that Vic didn't rate Rob that highly," Simon added.

"But was he delusional enough to think he stood a chance?" Bea asked.

"I spoke to Rob. He told me Vic was like a mentor to him. He did admit they argued over food sourcing. Apparently, Vic liked to bring expensive ingredients in from all over the place, whereas Rob wanted to buy local," Perry told them.

"Do you think he could've killed Vic?" Rich asked.

Perry shrugged. "I don't think he was telling me the truth about his relationship with Vic. But on the other hand, I didn't get the feeling he disliked him."

Simon tapped the end of his pen on his chin. "I'll put him down as having a possible motive. What about Liv?"

"Dot said she and Vic argued," Bea said. She turned to Perry. "Do we know who ended the relationship?"

"She told me she did," Perry answered.

"Dot implied Liv had another man in the wings. Did she mention that?"

Perry shook his head, then his eyes twinkled. "Oh, have we got ourselves a love triangle, do you think?" he asked hopefully.

"Could be. And they often lead to murder," Rich replied, dipping his head at Perry.

Perry rubbed his hands together, mumbling, "I love a good love triangle."

Bea stifled a giggle.

Simon put a big tick by Liv's name.

"I'm not sure Marco has a motive though. He said he and Vic got on okay, and Liv confirmed that," Perry said.

"Ah, but don't forget Maisey told us Marco and Vic had a falling out," Bea reminded him.

"I think we need to dig a bit deeper on that one then," Rich said.

Simon wrote TBC by the side of Marco's name. "We don't know much about Vic and Bella's relationship yet, so let's leave that for the moment." He put a question mark on his sheet by her name. "So what about Julian?" He raised an eyebrow at Bea.

"I can't see that he'd want to lose Vic as the restaurant was doing okay financially. And also there's the whole thing about Vic's body." She explained to them her thoughts about why it was unlikely that Julian would have left Vic's body in Clary House if he'd killed him.

"Good point," Rich said, smiling at her.

"But Maisey's convinced it's him. She thinks the whole email thing is made up," Perry pointed out.

Oh, yes! Bea had forgotten about the missing email.

"And he says he deleted it, so there's no evidence to back up that it ever existed," Simon added.

"I wonder if he showed it to anyone," Bea said. "We should have asked him."

"I agree with you, Bea," Simon said. "I don't think he has a strong motive at this stage, but we should try and find out if anyone else saw the email." He made a note next to Julian's name. "Right, so lastly let's look at opportunity. We know the time of death the police are working to is between Friday evening and Sunday morning. If we believe the neighbour's account of lights being on and off in his flat on Friday night and Saturday evening, then it seems most likely that he was killed between Saturday night after the lights went off and Sunday morning when he failed to turn up for his flight. So who has an alibi for that time that we know of?"

Perry took a sip of his coffee. "Rob told me he was

recording something for Fenshire radio that weekend, so that should be easy to check."

"And Julian said he was on holiday, didn't he?" Bea asked Simon.

Simon nodded. "What about Liv?" he asked Perry.

"She said she was knee-deep in writing her latest production. Assuming she was alone, then she doesn't appear to have one." He put his cup down. "And as for Marco, I didn't get a chance to ask him before Ryan shut me down," he said with a huff.

Bea suppressed a smile. Perry had told them how Ryan had scuppered his questioning of Marco.

"Um," Simon said, looking at the list. "I think we still have quite a bit of work to do."

"And then we need to think about how whoever did it got the body into the wall," Rich said, scratching his chin. "If it was constructed *and* plastered on the Friday, and the construction crew is adamant there wasn't a body in there when they built it, then when did the killer do it?"

"Could it have been placed there later?" Simon suggested. "Maybe after the news broke that the Seaside Lounge wouldn't reopen?"

"If so, where was Vic's body kept during that time?" Bea's gaze flicked to Rich.

"How about the flat?" Simon asked.

"It seems the most likely option," Rich agreed.

"Leave that one with me," Bea said. "Dot might know when it was cleaned before and after Vic was supposed to have left."

"Good idea." Simon put his pencil down and picked up his coffee cup. "I like it when we have a plan."

25

MORNING, WEDNESDAY 23 JUNE

The Bentley's engine purred to a halt outside The Fawstead Inn. "Are you sure Bella DeMarco will be here?" Bea asked Perry, who was sitting next to her on the back seat.

Perry peered over the rim of his sunglasses. "Yes. I asked Claire. She knows everything, of course. She's friends with the hotel manager. Even though Bella doesn't work here anymore, she lives in a flat around the corner, and she still comes in every morning to have a coffee and record some videos for her social media. The hotel doesn't mind. It's good publicity for them."

"My lady." Fraser had opened the back passenger door and was waiting on the pavement, his hand resting on the handle.

"Thank you, Fraser." Bea stepped out onto the pavement. Linking her arm through Perry's, she let him lead her up the steps to the covered entrance.

They walked into the sprawling lobby, all oak panels and weathered claret-coloured carpets that muffled their footsteps.

In front of them, the grand staircase wound its way up like a giant creeping vine.

"It's strange coming back here, isn't it?" Perry said in a hushed tone. Bea nodded slowly. The last time they'd been here had been to confront a killer. And indeed, it had been this exact lobby where she and Rich had agreed to stop keeping things from each other and move forward together as a team. It had been a turning point in their investigative partnership, but it had also been more. It had been the beginning of their opening up to each other. And that had led to...

A smile tugged at the corner of her lips as she recalled this morning's departure from The Dower House. Rich, Daisy by his side, had pressed a gentle kiss to her lips. His eyes had crinkled at the edges —she loved that— as he'd told her to have a good day, and he'd see her later. A picture of domestic normality that, for most, would seem mundane. But for Bea, who had grown up living a life that was far from 'normal', it was heaven.

Perry tapped Bea's shoulder. "There she is," he whispered. Bea followed his gaze through the cozy clusters of armchairs and coffee tables laden with coffee pots and folded newspapers to a green velvet sofa in a corner by the entrance to the dining room. A tall, willowy woman with perfectly curled long hair was nestled in the corner of the couch, huddled over a laptop.

Bea was suddenly conscious that a hush had descended on the lobby. She looked around to see what had caused the change in atmosphere, then realised all eyes were on her and Perry. She swallowed. *Oh no. It was a mistake to come here unannounced...* This wasn't Windstanton, where people were used to seeing her around the small town. And even if they were surprised to see the king's niece having a coffee in a local establishment, they were far too polite to stare. But this was Fawstead — much bigger, with many more tourists, and they were in the most popular hotel in town. *What was I thinking?*

She started as a man cleared his throat just behind her. Wide-eyed, she spun round.

The lanky man gave a short bow. "Lady Rossex, what a pleasure to see you here. Can I help you at all?"

Er. I don't know... Help! She looked at Perry.

"We'd like to have a chat with Isabella DeMarco," Perry told the hotel manager in a low voice. "She's over there by the dining room door."

Bea, now having regained her composure, added, "I'm so sorry, Mr" —she looked down at the gold name badge pinned on the lapel of his black suit jacket— "Cartwright. We seem to have caused a bit of a stir." She gave him a beaming smile.

"No, not at all, my lady," he blustered. "Would you like me to find you somewhere private you can conduct your business?"

"That would be lovely, if it's not too much trouble?"

"It's no trouble, I can assure you, Lady Rossex. Please come this way." He held out his arm and guided them towards a door marked 'Private' on the other side of the lobby. As they approached, he withdrew a bunch of keys and slotted one into the lock. "This is The Old Library, my lady. We use it for private functions. Please make yourself at home. I'll fetch Miss DeMarco. In the meantime, can I get you some tea or coffee?"

"Coffee would be great," Perry answered for them.

With a swift nod of his head, Mr Cartwright disappeared.

"Well, this is nice," Perry said as he walked over to a seating area containing two floral-patterned Chesterfield sofas, divided by an oval glass-topped table, its elaborate legs resting on a Persian rug. He plonked himself down and crossed his legs.

Bea made her way alongside the floor-to-ceiling book-shelves, spotting a number of first edition classics behind the perspex. "It just didn't occur to me we'd cause so much inter-est," she said, mooching over to join him.

"I don't think it's me they're interested in, my dear," Perry said, raising an eyebrow.

"But last time we came, it was no issue."

"Ah, but that was April. Now it's approaching peak holiday time, so—"

The door opened, and Bella DeMarco swooped in, followed by Mr Cartwright with a tray laden with coffee things.

Bea and Perry rose. "Miss DeMarco. Thank you so much for joining us. My name's Perry Juke, and this is Lady Rossex."

"Hi," Bella said breezily as she stopped in front of them, a faint smell of mint clinging to her person. Bea looked up into the striking face of the reality TV star as she shook her hand. Bella's piercing green eyes held a steely determination that suggested she was a woman who got what she wanted.

They sat as the manager finished emptying his tray. Bella had taken the sofa opposite Bea and Perry. She leaned forward when Mr Cartwright left and deposited her mobile phone and the electronic cigarette she'd been carrying on the table in front of her. Then she crossed her long legs and leaned back into the corner of the couch. "Please call me Bella," she said, stretching one lean arm along the back of the sofa. "Aren't you Simon Lattimore's husband?" Perry smiled in agreement. "And you're both working on the refurbish-ment of the new restaurant at Clary House? It's called Salt-Air, I believe."

She knows a lot... "Indeed."

She smiled slyly. "I read *The Society Page*, you see. It keeps me informed about what's going on in the area."

Ma will be pleased!

"Funny you should mention SaltAir," Perry said as he poured Bea a coffee and gave it to her. "We've come primarily to give you this." He handed the invitation across the table to Bella. "We'd be delighted if you came to the opening event."

She studied the card. "Oh, absolutely. My followers will love it."

Bea took a sip of her hot black coffee, then said, "Will you be okay going back to Clary House after what happened to Vic?"

Bella raised a slightly shaking hand to her chest. "Oh my goodness, what a shock that was! I still didn't believe it until that dour old policeman turned up asking questions."

"So you believed he'd gone to Australia and decided to stay, did you?" Perry asked, adding milk to his coffee.

"I mean, it was all out of the blue. One day Vic is saying, 'See you when we come back to work', and then we get told he's taken a new job, and he's not coming back. No goodbye. Nothing." She glanced down at her phone, then shrugged. "But we had no reason to disbelieve Julian when he told us, so yes, I thought that's what had happened."

Bea leaned forward. "Just out of curiosity, did you ever see the email that Julian mentioned? The one supposedly from Vic?"

Bella's brow creased before smoothing out again. "No. Julian told us about it, but..." Her voice trailed off, and something flickered in her eyes — a moment of realisation maybe. "Did Julian lie about it then, do you think?" Bella's laugh was short, tinged with disbelief. "But surely Julian didn't hurt him?" She answered her own question before Bea or Perry could respond. "No. Julian wouldn't hurt anyone."

"So did Vic have any enemies that you know of?" Perry asked.

Bella pursed her lips and twirled a lock of her wavy brown hair around her finger, seeming to ponder the question. "Enemies? No…I don't think so. He argued with a couple of the others — Marco Rossi and Rob Rivers. But I don't think it was anything serious." She pulled a face. "Rob was always eager to take the lead. But that doesn't mean he wanted to hurt him, does it? I mean, I was ambitious too, but I wasn't as vocal about it as Rob."

"So did you want to step into Vic's shoes too?" Bea asked.

Bella gave her a wry smile. "No, not at that place. The Seaside Lounge was sinking. Vic overspent on expensive ingredients, and we had too many days where we were less than half full. It felt like only a matter of time before it went under."

Really? But the financials had been solid according to Rich.

Bella smoothed down the skirt of her flowing maxi dress. "Anyway I'd already been headhunted by this place when Vic disappeared. Ironically, I was going to hand my notice in on the day we went back after our break. But when Julian said he was closing the place down, I didn't need to."

Bea glanced over at Perry. That explained what Maisey had said about Bella not seeming bothered when they'd found out about the closure of The Seaside Lounge. Bea hesitated, studying the woman. She was now staring down at the floor in a posture that gave the impression she was slightly bored with the conversation, but Bea couldn't help noticing how her breathing was shallow and rapid. *I think you're hiding some-*

thing behind that glamorous and cool exterior… "Why did you want to leave?"

Bella cleared her throat, then looked across at Bea. "As I said, they wanted me here. It was a promotion, and I was ready for a change." She tapped her elegant nails along the top of the sofa.

"So you came here as head chef?" Bea asked.

She crossed her arms. "Not initially, no. I was senior sous chef." She raised her chin. "But I was promoted to head chef within eighteen months."

"And how did you get on with Vic?"

Bella's eyes narrowed for a split second, then she shrugged. "We got on just fine."

I'm not so sure I believe you.

"So no arguments or creative differences?" Bea pushed.

She tossed her head of wavy brown curls. "No." She swallowed and looked away. Bea stifled a sigh. It was clear Bella was hiding something, but it looked unlikely she would give them anything more about her relationship with Vic right now. Bea glanced over at Perry and gave him a subtle nod.

"Er, so you said Vic argued with Marco. Do you know what about?" Perry asked, then took a sip of his coffee.

Bella quickly brushed her hand across her face, then raised her head and shook it. "No. But I got the feeling it wasn't about work, you know? They were a really good team and continued to work well together, but that last month or so, it was all business between them. None of the banter there used to be."

We need to talk to Marco again and try to find out what changed between them.

"Rob, on the other hand, he was always questioning Vic about his food choices. Vic would order from these expensive suppliers, but when the food came, honestly, it was no better than we could have got locally for half the price. I was with Rob on that one." She gave a wry smile. "In fact, that's the only difference between what Vic did then and what Rob does now at his new place. Because let's be honest, Rivers By The Sea is just a more showy version of The Seaside Lounge with a few subtle changes." A hint of smugness flittered across her face.

She wasn't the first person to have said Rob's style was very similar to Vic's.

"And it's no surprise really because Rob was a good sous chef; he just lacked new ideas. I swear some of the stuff he's serving now are things Vic was experimenting with before he left...I mean, died."

"Are you sure about that?" Bea probed.

"Absolutely," Bella replied confidently, uncrossing her long legs and leaning forward. "Vic had this black book, you see. It held all his signature recipes, along with the ones he was perfecting and his ideas for food combinations to try in the future. He'd refer to it all the time, and during our frequent quiet periods, he'd try out some of them, and I'd help."

So where's the book now?

"Do you know what happened to it?" Perry asked, his eyes bright.

"He never normally let it out of his sight," Bella replied, her green eyes clouding with memory. "But if he was due to go away, he may have put it somewhere safe?"

Perry glanced at Bea while tapping his foot on the patterned carpet. Nothing had been found during the refurbishment.

He's thinking the same as me... Did someone take it?

A crease formed between Bella's brows, and she gasped. Stretching over to absentmindedly pick up her orange vape pen, she turned it in her hand. A screen of curls bounced around her shoulders as she shook her head, then she mumbled, as if talking to herself, "I wonder…that would explain why his food is so like Vic's…"

Is she saying what I think she's saying? Does she think Rob took Vic's book? And more importantly, did he kill him for it?

26

LATE MORNING, WEDNESDAY
23 JUNE

"So what do you think of Bella?" Bea asked Perry over the low hum of the Bentley's engine.

Perry drummed his fingers on the leather seat. "Well, I can see why Maisey said she was a bit of a diva. You can tell she normally gets her way. She was clearly upset when you questioned her about her relationship with Vic. And she lied to us about being headhunted by the hotel."

They'd spoken to Mr Cartwright on their way out, and although he'd confirmed what Bella had told them about coming to work at the hotel as a sous chef just a few weeks after The Seaside Lounge had closed, his recollection of how she'd come to be employed differed to Bella's. According to him, she'd approached the then head chef about five weeks prior to ask for a job. She'd even worked for free while The Seaside Lounge had been closed just to prove herself. She'd been offered the sous chef role only a day before she'd been due to go back to work at Clary House.

"But then she could have said that just to big herself up to us. I can't think of a reason why she'd want to kill Vic, *and* she was leaving The Seaside Lounge anyway, so what would be the point of getting rid of him?"

"Um." Bea wasn't so sure. There was something about the smooth social media star that set her nerves on edge. "Her motive could be nothing to do with the restaurant. And don't you think it was rather calculated, the way she threw Rob under the bus?" *Was it just a distraction to stop me asking any more questions about her relationship with Vic?*

Perry raised an eyebrow. "I thought she was just trying to be helpful."

"And she doesn't have an alibi," Bea continued. Just before they'd left, Perry had asked Bella when she'd last seen Vic. She'd told them it had been when they'd finished with the deep clean on the Friday. Then she'd told them she'd been at home alone, enjoying her first weekend off for months.

"Could be. But the whole thing about the black book of recipes does give us a nice lead. It's possible the murderer took it."

And is that Rob? Bella hadn't been the only person who'd told them Rob's cooking was very similar to Vic's. Was that because he was using Vic's black book for inspiration?

"And you think that could be Rob?"

Perry shrugged. "He seems the most likely candidate."

"To have taken the book, perhaps. But don't forget he has an alibi for that weekend, so that rules him out as our killer."

"Allegedly," Perry corrected with a wry twist of his lips. He picked up his mobile. "I'm going to contact the radio station and see if I can get it confirmed right now."

While Perry waited for his call to connect, Bea sat back. The leather seat was cool against her skin as she watched the countryside pass in a blur. Her thoughts were disjointed as she allowed her concerns to bubble up to the top of her mind. She grabbed onto the first one. Why did everyone who'd worked at The Seaside Lounge have the impression that it'd been floundering when Rich's investigation into its finances had suggested it had been a healthy business? She chewed on the inside of her cheek. *Had he missed something?*

She fished her phone out from the pocket of her black jeans. It was worth double-checking.

Bea: *More than one person has indicated they thought The Seaside Lounge was in trouble with Vic overspending on ingredients and with a lot of periods when the place was very quiet. Is it worth double-checking the financials? xx*

"Ha!" Perry exclaimed, dropping his phone down on the seat beside him with a flourish. "Rob was definitely recording a pilot on the Friday night. But get this." He waggled his eyebrows. "They have no record of him being scheduled to record anything on the Saturday night!"

Bea's pulse quickened. "So he lied to us?" *Why would he do that unless he had something to hide?*

"We need to pay Mr Rivers another visit." Perry's eyes sparkled. "Let's go straight there now."

"Oka—"

Beep! Bea stopped and looked down at her phone.

Rich: *Sure. I'll ask Fred to have a look. How are you getting on? xx*

She hesitated. She'd been about to agree with Perry that they should go see Rob right now. But Rich's text was a timely reminder of the promise she'd made to him months ago at The Fenshire Inn. No more lone wolf forays. They were a team. "Actually, Perry, I think we should run it past Rich and Simon before we talk to Rob."

He cocked his head at her. "Really?"

"Look, if he's the killer, then we can't just barge in and accuse him of murder. We have to be much more subtle. Simon and Rich know how to do these things properly."

Perry leaned back and crossed his arms. "We've managed before with just the two of us," he pouted.

"Yes, and we've almost got killed a couple of times too, remember?"

He gave a long sigh. "Okay," he said, a touch of petulance still in his tone.

She reached out and squeezed his arm. "Thank you."

"But let's get them right now then," he huffed. "If we're quick, we can turn up at Rivers By the Sea in time to get a table for lunch."

————

"Remember, we're aiming for subtlety," Rich reminded them from the passenger seat as Fraser navigated the sleek car into a parking spot outside Rivers By the Sea.

"Subtlety is my middle name," Perry said straight-faced as he reached for the door handle.

Simon grunted noncommittally while Bea stifled a giggle as they got out of the car.

The hum of conversation and the clink of cutlery greeted them as they walked up to the desk. The place was a hive of activity, buzzing with the lunchtime rush. Bea pressed her lips tight and sneaked a glance at Rich. *It doesn't look like they can fit us in.*

"A table for four please, Sonia," Perry said confidently to the immaculately dressed front of house manager.

Rich winked at Bea. His face said, "Just wait."

"Ah, Mr Juke. How nice of you to come back so soon," the slim woman said with a smile. "Unfortunately" —she glanced around at the rest of the group— "we're fully—" Her eyes rested on Bea. Her smile faded and was replaced with what looked like sheer panic.

Perry reached back and grabbed Bea's hand, pulling her to the forefront. "And as I promised Rob, I've brought Lady Rossex with me. It will be her first time dining here."

"Of course, my lady." Sonia bobbed awkwardly. "Please give me a moment." She scurried away as fast as her four-inch heels would allow, then returned moments later with a nod towards the kitchen and an enormous smile. "Chef Rivers would be honoured if you joined him at the chef's table."

"We'd be delighted," Perry replied as he gave Bea a smug smile, then followed the manager, who led their little procession through the dining room and to a table set into a booth in the bustling kitchen. The air was heavy with the scent of sizzling meat, fragrant herbs, and rich sauces. Bea's stomach growled with anticipation.

After they were seated, Rob Rivers approached them with a charming smile and introduced himself. "It's a real pleasure to have you all here," he said warmly, wiping his hands on a cloth attached to his chef's jacket. "My staff will look after you. Enjoy your meal, and I'll join you later," he told them before returning to his cooking brigade.

The food was excellent, each dish a well-balanced combination of flavour and presentation. *If Vic's food was this good, then I can see why Rob wants to mimic it*, Bea thought.

"That was delicious," Perry told Rob when he took a seat

with them after they'd finished eating. "Vic must have been quite a mentor for you."

Rob's smile faltered for a fraction of a second before he recovered, his posture stiffening. "Of course, I've developed my own style since then," he said, a touch defensively.

He must get fed up with constantly being compared to Vic.

"We were talking to Bella today," Perry continued. "She told us about Vic's black book, the one that contained his signature recipes and ideas for new dishes."

Simon cleared his throat. "Er, Perry—"

Perry wasn't listening. "She said your food is exactly like his."

The colour drained from Rob's face.

He must have actually taken it!

He wiped the sweat off his forehead with the back of his hand.

"Did you take the book?" Bea asked in a soft voice.

Before he had a chance to answer, Perry leaned in towards him. "And did you kill Vic?" he hissed.

Perry!

Next to her, Rich choked on his water, coughing into his napkin while Simon's brow creased in dismay.

Rob, meanwhile, was shifting in his seat as his eyes searched theirs. "No, no, of course not," he stammered, his hands gripping the edge of the table. Then he bent his head down, his eyes fixed on the table. "But, yes. I...I took the book," he mumbled.

Bingo!

Rob quickly looked around the kitchen, then leaned in towards them. "Look, Vic had left, and after Julian sacked us, I thought—why not? It was the least he owed me," he told them, his voice barely above a whisper.

"What do you mean 'owed you'?"

Rob let out a sigh. "Vic owed me money."

"And that's why you killed him?" Perry jumped in before anyone could stop him. "We know you weren't recording for the radio the entire weekend."

Rob frowned. "Wasn't I?" He shook his head. "I can't exactly remember. It was three years ago. But I didn't kill him. I swear. Why would I? The man owed me twenty thousand pounds!"

"That's a lot of money. What did he want it for?" Rich asked.

"This place."

Bea's brows creased. *Here?*

Rob took a sip of water. "It was his idea. Vic wanted to get out of The Seaside Lounge and have his own place."

Really? So Julian was going to lose his chef anyway?

"He said he liked my idea of focussing on local produce, but Julian had given him a list of approved suppliers to use, so he'd never have the option to do that while he stayed at The Seaside Lounge."

Why would Julian get involved with telling Vic where to get his produce? Maybe he set all that up to get the best value he could?

"To my surprise, he asked me if I would go with him. He'd be the executive chef, and I'd be the head chef. I was excited. I'd always wanted to run my own kitchen, so I agreed. But all his capital was tied up in his flat in Bristol. He was going to sell it eventually, but he had a tenant via an agency on a rolling agreement who required six months notice to leave, so he asked if I could raise the money to cover the first year's lease. As it happened, I'd had a small inheritance from my grandmother, so I agreed to front the payment. He said he'd pay me back after the sale."

"And then he disappeared?" Bea prompted.

"I was furious. I thought he'd left me high and dry. I tried ringing but with no luck. We'd signed the lease by that stage, but I knew there was a cooling-off period of fourteen days, so I could still get out of it. Then Julian told us he was closing the restaurant, and I didn't have a job anymore. I knew Vic kept the black book in his office when he was away. So I took it. I thought if I had it, I could open the restaurant on my own. Vic was always the creative one, you see. I just love to cook. But with his book, I had enough material to give it a real go." He shrugged. "It seemed like fate, you know?"

Bea could see how Rob could have convinced himself he deserved the book to make up for Vic having left him in the lurch. "Did you actually see the email Vic sent, Rob?" she asked.

He shook his head. "No. Julian just told us about it." His eyes widened. "Was he lying?"

"Not necessarily," Rich replied. "It could have been sent by someone pretending to be Vic."

"Poor Vic. When I think how I cursed him when I thought he'd abandoned me and our plans, and all that time he was dead." Rob shook his head.

He looks sincere. Bea glanced at Rich, who was watching Rob. *Does he believe him?*

"Look. Please don't tell anyone about the book. My reputation…" He trailed off, his eyes shifting around the table.

If he's telling the truth, then he doesn't deserve to be exposed. And the food *had* been excellent. She looked at the others; it seemed they agreed. "Your secret is safe with us," she told him while adding in her mind the caveat, *Unless you're the killer.*

———

They ambled out of Rivers By The Sea, and the gentle salty breeze was a welcome relief from the hot and humid kitchen of the restaurant.

"Well, you were as subtle as a sledgehammer, Perry," Simon said, a sliver of amusement in his voice as they stood outside waiting for Fraser to bring the car around.

Perry blinked, looking baffled. "But he talked, didn't he?" He glanced at Bea for backup, and she nodded, trying to stifle a grin.

"It was an interesting technique," Rich added with a smile. "I think you may have shocked him into telling the truth."

So he believes Rob when he says he didn't kill Vic? It now seemed like their number one suspect had a stronger motive to have wanted to keep Vic alive than to have wanted him dead. They would have to go back to the drawing board...

The car purred around the corner, and the four of them got in. As she sat down next to Rich and Perry, Simon having taken the front seat this time, Bea recovered her phone from the middle console in the back seat and switched it on. *Beep!* She looked down at the screen. Her heart sank.

Ma: *Darling, do you have a man living at your house? If not, there's a handsome burglar using your library as an office!*

27

MID-AFTERNOON, WEDNESDAY
23 JUNE

"So how did she know?" Perry asked from the large squishy sofa in the middle of the morning room at The Dower House. Beside him, Daisy was curled up fast asleep, the occasional twitch suggesting she was dreaming.

Bea had just told him about the text from her mother and the subsequent call she'd had to make. "She came around to drop off some post for me. That's what she said anyway, but then in the same breath, she complained she never sees me these days, so I imagine it was really an excuse. I think she hoped I'd be here, and we could have a coffee together," Bea told him as she perched on the edge of the window seat.

Have I been neglecting her recently? Princess Helen wasn't the sort to be clingy, but Bea had to admit that until recently, when she'd lived in her apartment at Francis Court, she'd seen her parents at least two or three nights a week when she'd joined them for dinner. *I should visit more.* "Anyway, she gave Fraser the letters, then went back the other way. She saw Rich as she went by the library window."

"Ah…"

"He didn't see her. He was busy on a call. But, of course,

she recognised him and put two and two together." Her mother had informed her with great satisfaction that she'd guessed Bea had a secret man because of the weekends she'd spent away when Sam hadn't been at home, and, as she'd put it, "The fact that these days, you look like the cat that's got the cream."

"So you're well and truly busted," Perry said.

"Indeed. And now I have to take Rich to have dinner with my parents on Thursday night."

"Ohhh…meet the parents."

"In fairness, they have both met him before, when he was here doing his job."

"But this is different. This time they'll be vetting him to see if he's future son-in-law material," Perry pointed out gleefully.

What? Bea's stomach tumbled over. "Don't be ridiculous. No one is talking about marriage."

"Yet…" Perry said with a cheeky grin. "But be honest; that's what they'll be looking at."

Her heart sank. *Oh my goodness, is he right?* "And it gets worse." Bea huffed. "Grandmama will be there too."

Perry raised his hand to his chest. "Yikes! They're bringing out the big guns early."

Bea's maternal grandmother, Queen Mary The Queen Mother, was a force to be reckoned with. A formidable woman in her mid-eighties who split her time between Francis Court and her own home in Scotland, she was ambitious for her grandchildren when it came to partners and had her own suitability criteria, with few ticking even half of the boxes, let alone all of them. Bea licked her dry lips. *How will Rich measure up?*

"Don't worry, Bea. If anyone can handle it, Rich can," he

said reassuringly as he picked up a *Country Life* magazine and flipped through it.

Bea lifted her legs up onto the window seat and wrapped her arms around her knees. *I hope he's right!* When she'd told Rich they'd been found out and that her family had summoned them to dinner, he'd been very nonchalant about it, even going as far as having said it was about time. A shiver ran down her spine. *I need to persuade Sarah and Fred to come too.* There was safety in numbers. She stared out the window and into the back garden, which was bathed in the afternoon sun. *Breathe, Bea. Think about the rose garden you want to establish...*

Five minutes later, Perry glanced up from the magazine resting on his lap. "Still worrying about Rich and this dinner, are you?"

"Actually, no, I wasn't," Bea said proudly. She had other things in life to think about apart from her love life! "I was going over the plans for the rose garden in my head. Pete is coming to see me later this week so we can properly map it out." Pete Cowley was the head gardener at Francis Court, and Bea's parents had agreed to let her borrow him while she was developing the garden at The Dower House.

"That reminds me," Perry said, folding the magazine closed and popping it on the side table. "He's taking Ellie away for the weekend to Paris." He dipped his chin and gave Bea a knowing look.

Bea smiled. "Ah, that's nice." Pete and Ellie had been dating for almost a year now, and Pete had recently moved into Ellie's cottage in the village, which she rented from Perry.

"Bea!" Perry shrugged his shoulders and raised his hands. "He's...taking...her...to...*Paris*," he repeated slowly as if she were a child.

She frowned. *So?*

"Oh my goodness!" He threw his hands up in the air. "*Paris!* The most romantic city in the world…"

Ohhhhh… "You think he's going to propose?"

"Finally! Yes. Of course he is. It's Paris."

"Perry, I think sometimes people go to Paris just to see the sights." She caught his eye, but he looked away.

"But—" he mumbled in protest.

"Does *Ellie* think Pete is going to propose?" she asked quickly.

"Er, well, um," he spluttered.

She had a bad feeling about this. "Perry, what did you do?"

"Nothing," he pouted.

"You told her you thought he was going to propose, didn't you?"

He rubbed his nose as red spots appeared on his perfectly high cheeks. "But it's *Paris*, Bea."

She let out a deep sigh. "Let's just hope Pete sees it that way. If not, we're going to have a very disappointed catering manager on our hands when they get back." She gave him a pointed look just as the door creaked open.

Mrs Fraser bustled in, a silver tray balanced expertly in her hands. "Tea's ready, my lady," she announced cheerfully as she set it down on the table in front of Perry. "I'll let Mister Richard and the others know."

Bea hopped off the window seat. "Thank you, Mrs Fraser."

As Mrs Fraser departed, Bea glanced at Perry as she sat on the sofa opposite him, an impish twinkle in her eye. "You've been saved by the bell!"

"Do you think I should talk to Ellie and try to reset her expectations?" he asked rather sheepishly.

Bea shook her head, the corners of her mouth twitching. "Ellie's not an incurable ⌡romantic like you. She'll know better than anyone if Pete's likely to propose and will set her expectations accordingly, regardless of what you've said." *And I might just have a word with Pete later this week and see what his plans are...*

The door opened, and Rich and Simon breezed in. Daisy opened an eye, then stretched as they joined her and Perry. When Rich sat opposite Bea, Daisy immediately shifted, placing her paw on Rich's leg, her tail wagging furiously. Rich fussed over the small dog while he reached for the cup Bea held out to him. "Thanks," he said, smiling. "I need this." He gently returned Daisy to the space in-between him and Perry, then took a sip of his tea. "Oh, before I forget, I passed the financials for The Seaside Lounge to Fred to have a look at. Let's see what he has to say."

"I've just got off the phone with Steve," Simon told them, picking up a biscuit. "He's pushing for Finch to release the dining room back to us, so fingers crossed."

That would be great.

"And he told me something interesting." He turned to face Bea. "Do you remember Julian mentioning his accountant to us, a chap called Bryan Sinclair?"

That's it! That was the other person Bea knew had been mentioned in connection with Clary House, but she hadn't been able to pull his name. She nodded.

"He's on Finch's radar as a suspect, according to Steve."

"Why?" Perry asked.

"Finch wasn't very forthcoming, unfortunately."

"We should have a chat with this Bryan person ourselves," Perry suggested, setting down his teacup with a delicate chink against the saucer. "Is he local?"

"Er, I'm not sure." Simon grimaced, the corners of his

well trimmed beard dipping in a frown. "It depends where he's buried."

Rats! That's not much help...

"Dead?" Perry echoed, his eyebrows shooting upwards. "So how does Finch plan to accuse a dead man?"

"It will be a challenge, that's for sure. But from what he said to Steve, Bryan's wife is flying in from Spain in the next couple of days to visit her daughter. He thinks she can help."

"Then we'll need to talk to her too," Perry said.

Bea took a sip of her tea. "We also really need to talk to the neighbour, Mrs Hall. But how? It's not like we can just knock on her door and interrogate her about what she saw that weekend."

Before Simon could respond, the door swung open, and Ryan strolled into the room. "Sorry I'm late, everyone. I was on the phone with the police."

"Good news, I hope?" Simon asked.

Ryan flashed his trademark grin. "Better than good—we've got the green light to reclaim the restaurant on Monday."

Bea's shoulders relaxed. *Phew!*

"Brilliant!" Perry cried, clapping his hands together. "That means we'll only be just over a week behind. It could be worse."

"Don't worry. I've spoken to Charles, and although it will be tight, he thinks he can claw back the time with little to no extra cost," Ryan reassured them, pouring himself a cup of tea.

"That's great news, Ryan." Bea beamed at the chef. "I was just saying I need an excuse to approach the neighbour across the road from Clary House and try to clarify what she saw the weekend Vic was killed."

"How about I invite her over for a sneak peek at the

supper club's dining room? With any luck, she'll be too flattered to refuse."

"Oh, and I could just happen to be there?" Bea asked, arching an eyebrow.

"Exactly," Ryan confirmed with a conspiratorial smile.

"Ryan, that's a stroke of genius," Bea said, raising her teacup to him.

"Let's circle back to our suspects, shall we?" Rich said, shifting to the edge of the sofa and placing his empty cup on the table. "The only person who seems to have an alibi is Julian Thornton, who was on holiday. We need to find out exactly when he left, just to be sure."

"He told us he went on the Friday," Simon told him.

"I can get that checked," Rich said. "We know Rob has an alibi for Friday night but not Saturday. Liv, Marco, and Bella have nothing for the entire weekend. I think we should concentrate on those three for now."

They all agreed.

"I'll talk to Liv again," Perry said. "I'll pretend I'm interested in playing Algernon in her play and see if I can find out who this man is that Dot thinks she was having an affair with."

His air was casual, but Bea couldn't help wondering if he really *was* interested in playing the lead in Liv's next production. She glanced at Simon from the corner of her eye. He was trying unsuccessfully to suppress a grin.

Ryan cleared his throat. "I'm not comfortable about pushing Marco any further just yet." He explained he was worried about turning the food critic off and the damage it could do to SaltAir. They all agreed to leave Marco for the moment.

"What about Bella?" Bea asked. She was still convinced the woman was hiding something.

"I was thinking we could do the same with her as we're doing with the neighbour," Simon said to Ryan. "We could show her around…"

"Good idea. She might put something out on social media. Get a bit of advance interest," Ryan said.

"Great." Rich rubbed his hands together. "So we all have jobs to do then. Let round two begin."

28

LATE MORNING, THURSDAY 24 JUNE

"I'm knee-deep in wallpaper swatches here," Perry moaned to Bea. She moved the mobile phone to her other ear and leaned back against the wall of the supper room on the first floor of Clary House. She stared out of the window. *Where is he?* Ryan had gone to collect Mrs Hall from her flat across the road. It seemed like ages since he'd left. Bea looked over to her early warning system, but Daisy was curled up under a chair in the corner of the room, snoozing.

"Is chartreuse too bold for the walls?"

What? Bea was instantly back in the room. "Chartreuse is always too bold, Perry," she said in a hurry. "Can't we go with the teal? It's soothing."

He sighed. "Yes. There's teal in the first mural option I sent you. Shall we go for that one then?"

Bea switched the call to speaker and flipped to her photos. *Yes, that will work.* "Indeed. I think it's the closest to contemporary vintage we can find," she said of the ink-sketch style of the Victorian conservatory scene she was looking at. "I love it."

· "Okay. Fab. I'll get it ordered now. I'm seeing Liv this afternoon."

"Great. We have Bella visiting here this afternoon. In the meantime I'm still waiting for Ryan to arrive with the neighbour. I've no idea what's keeping them." There was silence at the other end of the line. "Perry? Are you all right?"

"Isla has confirmed to Simon that she'll be coming to the opening."

"That's lovely, isn't it?" Bea said, a smile tugging at her lips despite the tension she could hear in Perry's tone. It would be great to see Simon's daughter again. The more time she spent with the young woman, the more she liked her.

"Simon certainly thinks so."

Bea could imagine Perry pouting right now. "Of course he does. She's his daughter, and he's keen to get to know her better. We all are."

Perry huffed at the other end.

"Listen, Perry," Bea said, her tone softening. "You and Isla got on great before you knew she was Simon's daughter, remember? She could bring so much into *both* of your lives if you just give her the chance."

"I suppose so," Perry admitted reluctantly.

"Tell you what, when she arrives, why don't we take her off for a spa afternoon at Oakwood Manor? Just the three of us. A bit of pampering and some time where you can talk to her without Simon around."

"Maybe," he mumbled.

Woof! Daisy wiggled out from under the chair and headed towards the door.

"Right, that's them arriving now. Just think about it, okay?"

"Okay. I'll talk to you later."

She cut the call, then scampered after Daisy, who was already halfway down the stairs.

"Ah, Lady Rossex, what a surprise," Ryan called up from the bottom of the grand staircase, a smile spreading across his face. Beside him stood a white-haired woman with an eager look in her eyes. Ryan turned to her. "Well, this is a treat, Mrs Hall. Lady Rossex is overseeing the design of this place for us." Daisy had reached the bottom of the stairs and was now sniffing the newcomer. "Oh, and this is Daisy," Ryan explained.

Mrs Hall briefly looked down and mumbled, "She's sweet," before gazing back up at Bea as the wrinkles on her face moulded around a huge grin.

"Hello," Bea said, smiling as she reached them. "How nice to meet you, Mrs Hall." She held out her hand.

The older woman executed a low curtsey, then shook Bea's hand, barely putting any pressure on her fingers before dropping it like a hot potato. "Oh, please call me Carol, your ladyship. It's so lovely to meet you." Her hands fluttered in front of her like a pair of excited birds. "And how's that lovely mother of yours?" she asked, then carried on before Bea had time to respond. "I met her once at a dinner we were giving for the hospice, you know. So elegant and very kind, she was. She told me the flower display I'd done in the reception was beautiful. I'll never forget that." She gave a wistful sigh.

"Mother is fine, thank you, Carol. So what brings you here?"

"This handsome young man offered to show me what you've done with that lovely room upstairs. How could I resist?"

The sideways smile she gave Ryan left Bea wondering if

it was Ryan rather than a chance to see the room that she couldn't resist.

Ryan offered Carol his arm. "Let me escort you upstairs then. I think you'll love what we've done with the place."

"Lead on, young man," Carol beamed, taking his arm as they ascended the staircase together. Daisy shot up ahead, leaving Bea to fall in beside them.

"So…your brother's found himself a nice girl," Carol said to Bea. "She seems bubbly and friendly."

"Indeed. Summer is great. We all like her very much."

"Good. So when are you going to snag yourself a good man, dear? Someone tall, dark, and handsome to sweep you off your feet?"

Bea stumbled slightly. She caught Ryan's eye as he grinned at her over the woman's head. "Er…I'm more focussed on raising my son, Sam, at the moment, Carol."

"Fair enough. A boy needs his mother. But you can't hide yourself away forever, you know. What happened to your husband was awful, but you're too young to never have love in your life again."

Bea smiled into the bright eyes of the lady beside her. She hoped everyone would be as understanding as Carol if she ever went public with her relationship with Rich. "I'll bear it in mind, Carol."

They reached the top of the stairs, and Ryan led the elder lady through the huge open doors of the supper room.

"Isn't this just splendid?" Carol exclaimed as she entered the room. She dropped Ryan's arm, her gaze immediately drawn to the ornate ceiling. "I'm so relieved you're not turning it into flats. Such a lovely building deserves to be cherished."

"We want to bring it back to life," Ryan explained. "Now can I get you a drink of some sort?"

Carol looked over at the glass bar running along the far wall. "A small sherry would be nice." She turned and winked at Bea. "It's five o'clock somewhere, isn't it, my dear?"

Bea stifled a giggle. "Indeed."

Ryan returned with Carol's drink.

"That Julian Thornton was after my house ten years ago, can you believe it?" she said, accepting the glass with a delicate hand. "But I told him where to stick his offer."

Good for you! Now down to business. "Did you hear about Victor Blackwell?"

Carol nodded, her expression sombre. "Yes, my cleaner told me they'd found his body. Such a shame." She shook her head. "I thought he went to Australia, and all that time, he was propping up a wall."

Ryan snorted, then coughed.

"Do you remember that weekend, Carol?" Bea asked. "It was the weekend after the restaurant closed for the refurbishment in January three years ago."

"Oh, yes, dear. I remember it. Lots of to-ing and fro-ing for a couple of weeks after, there was." She took a sip of her sherry. "Then after Vic didn't come back, they closed it down permanently. Sad if you ask me." She turned to Ryan and patted his arm. "I'm so glad it will be open soon. It will have a purpose again."

"We're looking forward to it," Ryan agreed.

Come on; back on track. "So the police believe Victor died sometime over that first weekend after the restaurant closed and before the building work began on Monday." Bea said, trying to sound casual.

"That's terrible." Carol swirled the liquid in her glass. "I saw the lights on that weekend..."

Bea observed a slight falter in Carol's gaze, a flicker of uncertainty. "But...?" she prodded gently.

Carol set her glass down on the sideboard. "It was odd, you know. On Friday, after the main lights had gone off, there was still a glow behind the curtains. A small light—perhaps from a lamp? It lingered throughout the night." She gave a short laugh. "I don't sleep well these days. My son says it's because I nap too much in the afternoons."

Bea quirked an eyebrow at Ryan, his puzzled look mirroring hers. "Er, can you elaborate on that, Carol?" he asked.

"Of course, dear." She leaned forward, lowering her voice as if sharing a secret. "Vic was a creature of habit. He always had the big light on. But not this time. No, this time was different. There was no light on in his bedroom, just this small one on in the living room." She gave her bony shoulders a shrug. "I thought he'd just dozed off, you know, watching the television."

"And did you see lights on Saturday evening, Carol?"

Carol shook her head. "I was out Saturday night. I went over to my sister's for dinner. I got back around ten. By that time the lights in Vic's flat were all out and all the curtains were open.

So Vic wasn't there at ten. Had he already been dead by then?

"Did you see Vic at all over the weekend?" Bea pressed gently.

"No, dear. Sorry."

"Did you see anything or anyone else that weekend?" Bea asked. "Did anyone visit Clary House, do you know?"

"There was a car skulking away from the back car park at around ten when I got back on Saturday. I saw it leave as I got out of my brother-in-law's car. He kindly dropped me off home after dinner that night."

Bea's fingers tingled. *Could that have been our killer leaving?* "Can you describe this car?"

"Describe?" A frown added to the wrinkles on her forehead. "It was long and a dark colour. That's all I saw. I'd seen it, the same car that is, before, on the Friday around half-six, when I went off to bingo."

"It could've been anyone from those flats down the road," Ryan said, stroking his goatee. "I've been warned they might try to use our parking spots at night."

Rats! That's more likely it.

Carol picked up her drink again, taking a sip. "You could be right," she agreed. "I've been complaining for years about the number of cars using that car park. I even told the police. It's dangerous the way they come hurtling out of there. But they said it was a private car park, and I needed to tell the owner. I told Julian Thornton. He said he'd put a sign up. It hasn't made a lot of difference."

"Was the car one you'd seen before that Friday?" Bea asked, her eyes shining.

Carol frowned. "I don't think so."

She didn't sound sure. *Perhaps it's nothing…*

"Anything else?" Ryan coaxed.

"Nothing," Carol confirmed with a shrug. "I spent most of my Saturday sitting by the window enjoying the sea views and doing crossword puzzles." She paused, her face folding into frown. "The only odd bit I remember Saturday was Vic's bedroom curtains."

What about them?

"They were drawn tight." She knocked back the last of her sherry. "All day."

29

SHORTLY AFTER, THURSDAY 24 JUNE

Having said goodbye to Carol Hall, Bea and Ryan followed Daisy up the wide staircase to his flat on the second floor. As Bea climbed the stairs, her mind was a whirlpool of questions. *Why did Vic leave a small light on all night? Why didn't he open his bedroom curtains all day Saturday? Who was in the car seen on Friday and Saturday, coming out of the empty car park?*

As she entered the flat, the warmth hit her, wrapping around her like a welcome hug. Immediately, Ryan went to the coffee machine and switched it on. By the time Bea sat down at the dining table, a rich aroma of coffee was wafting through the air. She inhaled deeply. *Is there anything better than the smell of coffee?*

With two mugs in hand, Ryan joined her at the table. "Was Carol's info any good, do you think?" he asked, handing her a mug.

Bea took a sip, letting the rich flavour settle on her tongue as she pondered the question. "It's got my mind spinning," she said, tapping her finger idly against the ceramic inscribed with 'Don't make me use my chef voice' on the side. "You know how after what Dot told us about the lights, we thought Vic had been killed on Saturday night?" Ryan nodded. "Well, now I'm not so sure."

"Really?" He raised an eyebrow, leaning in with interest. "What's got you second-guessing?"

"Bits and pieces," she said, her gaze drifting off to the rooftops visible through the window. "Things aren't adding up. Why would Vic have left the curtains drawn all day in his bedroom on that Saturday?"

Ryan shrugged. "He could have been having a duvet day?"

It was possible. "But you'd think the day before he was leaving to go on holiday for nearly three weeks, he'd have too much to do."

"That's true. So he could've just not bothered to draw the curtains if he was busy packing."

Perhaps…

"Well, then there's the car. I get your point that it could have been someone just taking advantage of the restaurant being closed and using the car park. But then again—"

There was a knock at the door. Daisy jumped up and hurtled towards it. Ryan put his mug down and strolled to the door. As he opened it, Bea heard Dot's apologetic voice. "Sorry to disturb you like this, Mr Hawley. But you said today would be a good time for us to deep clean the bathroom."

"Dot, you know you don't need to apologise," Ryan assured her, stepping aside to open the door wide.

She swept into the room, her cleaning caddy swinging from her arm, followed by another woman with a slightly flustered expression on her face, also carrying a case full of cleaning products. Dot immediately leaned down to fuss over an excited Daisy. "This is the cute little dog I was telling you about, Ange," she told her companion as she straightened up.

Both women clocked Bea. Dot's face broke into a smile, but before she could say anything, the taller, thinner woman gasped, her hand fluttering to her chest. "Oh Lordy, you're Lady Beatrice!" she exclaimed, her voice tinged with disbelief.

"Guilty as charged," Bea replied with a chuckle, extending her hand. "And you are?"

"Angelia," Dot answered for her, gesturing towards the woman who was standing stock-still with her mouth open. "My sister-in-law. She works with me."

Angelia suddenly came to life, aiming a curtsey at Bea before taking her hand and shaking it eagerly. "Please call me Ange; everyone does."

"We've just seen old Mrs Hall outside," Dot informed them. "She said she had a lovely time seeing what you've done to the place, Mr Hawley."

"I clean for her, you know," Ange added to Bea.

A thought sparked in Bea's head. "Ange, you're not by any chance the one who cleaned this flat when Victor Black-well was living here, are you?"

Ange smiled smugly. "Yes, I cleaned this flat and the offices downstairs. My sister and her hubby cleaned the restaurant." Her face clouded over. "I was so sad to hear he'd died."

"When was the last time you cleaned Vic's flat, Ange?" Bea asked.

"Let me see now. I cleaned first thing on the Monday morning after he'd gone on holiday. Monday was my regular day to clean here." She walked a little further into the room, then placed her bucket down.

"Did you notice anything odd?" Bea pressed, still smiling reassuringly at the cleaner.

"Odd?" Ange paused, tilting her head. "Not really. Although there wasn't much to do. It was very tidy for a change." She pursed her lips. "Even the bins were empty." Then she paused. "Oh, hold on." She leaned in, her voice dropping conspiratorially. "The red toothbrush I used for scrubbing in the bathroom—it had gone. I remember thinking, *Now why would he pack that for Australia?*"

"Anything else?"

Ange's brow furrowed. "Oh, yes. There was another thing. His father's travel alarm clock — he loved that clock. It was one of those old-fashioned ones that fold up, you know. Red leather. He kept it on his nightstand. He always took it with him when he went away."

So whoever cleared up the flat to make it look like Vic had left, didn't know him well enough to know he wasn't very tidy, the red toothbrush wasn't his, and that the travel clock had sentimental value and would never be left behind. Although her head was still crammed with thoughts, a picture was emerging.

"And was that the last time you came here?"

She dipped her head. "Yes. I was due to clean the Monday after Mr Blackwell should've come back from his trip, but when I found out he wasn't coming back, I checked with Mr Thornton, and he told me not to bother."

"I think we'll get on, Mr Hawley, if that's okay with you?" Dot said, picking up her caddy.

Something was niggling at the back of Bea's brain. Something Ange had said… *Oh, I remember!*

"Sorry, Dot. Just one more question for Ange if I may?"

"Yes, of course, my lady."

"Ange, you said you found out Mr Blackwell wasn't coming back. Can I ask how you found out?"

Dot and Ange exchanged a look that bore the weight of a secret.

Bea's tummy fluttered. There was something they knew. *Am I going to get lucky here?*

Dot's hand fluttered to her chest "Lady Rossex," she said, her voice quivering slightly. "You've got my word. We meant no harm."

Bingo! "Of course, not. I understand."

Dot gave a short nod at Ange, who, with a sheepish tilt of her head, said, "I clean the offices at The Parade, including the one Mr Thornton uses. I was there on the Wednesday evening, the day before Mr Blackwell was due to come back. I saw a printed-out email, just there on the desk. I had to move it to wipe the surface."

So there was an email! Julian had been telling the truth after all. "Did you read it?" Bea asked, then held her breath. *Please say yes.*

Ange looked a bit sheepish adding, "I did more than that, my lady. I took a picture on my phone. I wanted Dot to see it."

"Do you still have this picture?" Again she held her breath.

"No. Sorry. I lost my phone a few years back and all my photos with it."

Bea exhaled slowly. *It was too much to hope for.*

"Hang on though. You sent me a copy, Ange." Dot was scrambling for her mobile phone in the front pocket of her apron. "I still have all my photos."

There was a lightness in Bea's chest. She caught Ryan's eye, and he gave her a discreet thumbs up.

"Here you go," Dot said as she tapped the screen of her phone and handed it to Bea.

It was a photo of an email that had been printed out. In the margin was a handwritten note 'Talk to B'. *Bryan maybe?* The email itself was short, only two paragraphs, simply signed off 'Vic'. It said he'd been offered an amazing opportunity in Australia, so he was staying. He apologised for the short notice but stated that he knew Julian would understand. The final sentence particularly caught Bea's eye, 'So as you can imagine, I had no choice but to act on this.' *No choice? What an odd way to phrase it...*

30

LUNCHTIME, THURSDAY 24 JUNE

B ea's fingers tingled as she hurried into the Breakfast Room at Francis Court, her mind racing with the new information she'd gathered from her trip to Clary House. Ahead of her, Daisy strained against her harness, keen to get to Rich and Perry, who were at a table over in the far corner. At that moment, Rich raised his head and, seeing her, grinned. She waved. *I can't wait to tell him my theory…*

When Bea got clear of the other tables, she bent down and unclipped Daisy's lead. The little terrier immediately hurtled towards Rich and with one jump landed on his lap. Perry looked up. Giving a mock sigh, he said to Bea. "I think we both know who Daisy's favourite is these days."

"Well, her eyes aren't painted on," Rich said, grinning.

"And he's so smug about it," Bea said to Perry, lightly tapping Rich on the arm as she sat down next to him.

"If you think I'm sharing my lunch with you now, young lady, you can think again," Perry said, leaning over to Daisy, who was perched on Rich's lap. She tried to lick his nose.

"I ordered you a tuna toastie," Rich told Bea as he pushed a coffee pot towards her.

Aw, that was thoughtful. "Thanks," she said, smiling. "Where's Simon, by the way?"

"He was still on the phone with his publishers when I left. They're trying to organise a book tour to start in October. I left him to it."

She jiggled her legs. "Okay, so, er, shall I tell you how I got on?"

"Don't you want to wait until we've eaten?" Perry asked, looking hopefully towards the door that led to the kitchen.

Rich grinned as he carefully placed Daisy on the floor under the table. "I don't think she'll be able to wait that long."

Perry raised an eyebrow. "Okay, then all right. Fire away."

"I think it's a game changer," she began. She told them about her conversations, first with Carol Hall and then with Dot and her sister-in-law, Ange. And, of course, the email, which she showed them a copy of.

Their food arrived just as she finished. "So you now know everything I do. But I've had more time to think about it, and I have a theory." She cut her toasted sandwich in half and took a bite.

"Let's hear it," Rich said through a mouthful of food.

"First, we need to go back to Friday night," Bea said, her words tumbling out in a rush. "I think Vic was killed then, and the killer tampered with the lights and closed the bedroom curtains in his flat to throw anyone off the scent. They then returned on Saturday to do the same thing, when they switched them all off and opened the curtains. I think they then cleared up the flat and took some of Vic's things to make it look like he'd left to go on holiday. That would explain what Carol saw and why the flat looked as if Vic had left when Ange cleaned it on Monday." She took another bite of her food.

"Interesting," Perry said, spearing a pasta shell on his fork. "That means the person Carol saw in the car both nights could be our killer."

"Indeed." A surge of satisfaction went through her at their shared understanding.

"Do we have a description of the car?" Rich asked.

Bea wrinkled her nose. "Not a very good one, I'm afraid. Just that it was long and dark."

"I wonder if any of our suspects have a car that fits that description?" Perry asked.

"It's something we can try and find out," Rich said. "Although it was three years ago…"

Bea continued, "There's more. Our killer messed up on a few things. They tidied the flat too much. Ange gave me the impression Vic wasn't normally very neat. They also took a red toothbrush, not knowing it was one that was used by the cleaners. They presumably thought it was Vic's. But they left a travel alarm clock, you know one of those fold-up ones, which Vic would have taken according to Ange as it had sentimental value."

"Suggesting the person who did this didn't know Vic or his habits very well," Rich said, putting down his fork.

"Indeed."

"Okay, but what about the body?" Perry asked, his brow furrowed. "Where was it all this time if Vic was killed on Friday? It couldn't have been in the wall as it didn't exist at the time. It only went up two weeks later."

"Good question," Bea replied, her excitement momentarily waning as she considered the possibilities. "We have the same issue as before, but now at least we known it wasn't in the flat during that time."

"And I think we can safely say it wasn't in the restaurant, or they would have discovered it when they started the renovations," Rich added.

Indeed. "So where was it?" Bea asked.

"Perhaps the killer had a hidden storage space somewhere?" Perry suggested, his blue eyes gleaming. "Or could they have transported it away somehow and then returned it to the scene later?"

"Transporting a body isn't exactly easy," Rich pointed out. "Particularly for one person on their own. I think there would be too big a risk of being seen."

"Especially with eye-eagled Carol Hall across the way," Bea added.

Perry looked disappointed.

"I'm not saying it's impossible, Perry. Just unlikely." Rich pushed his plate to one side. "Anyway, let's not get too sidetracked." He took a sip of his coffee. "If Bea's right and the murder took place on the Friday, then our next step is to review who has an alibi for Friday night."

So he thinks I could be right about the murder having taken place on Friday...

"Rob definitely does," Perry said, picking up a piece of chicken from his plate and dropping it under the table to Daisy. "I checked it myself. So that leaves Liv, Marco, Julian, and Bella to consider." He looked up at the ceiling. "Oh, and the dead accountant chap Finch thinks it was," he added.

"Oh, yes, I forgot about him. Bryan Sinclair," Bea said.

"I'm still trying to confirm Julian's flight details, but if he left on Friday, then that rules him out full stop for Friday *and* Saturday," Rich said.

Perry wiped his mouth with a napkin. "But if he left Friday night, couldn't he have committed the murder before he left?"

Bea cocked her head to one side. "But then who went in and opened the curtains and switched the lights off on Saturday?"

"An accomplice?" Perry suggested.

Rich raised an eyebrow. "We can't rule it out. But it would mean two people wanted Vic dead, and at the moment, we're struggling to find a reason anyone would." He continued, "So, in other news, I can confirm Rob and Vic signed the lease for the restaurant premises together, just as Rob said. He made the payment too." He dipped his head at Perry. "I agree we can fairly much rule Rob out now. He would've wanted Vic alive, not dead."

Bea suppressed a huff. *So we're really no further forward.* Even if they assumed the murder took place on the Friday, it really only ruled Rob out, and they'd already established he probably hadn't killed Vic. She pressed her lips together. *So much for my big news being a game changer!*

"Right," Perry said, shooting up from his chair. Daisy emerged from under the table, her tail wagging. "I should get going. I'm meeting Liv soon." His eyes sparkled with anticipation.

"Be careful, Perry. Just remember, she could be the killer," Rich said.

Really? "But hold on. We've just said the person who killed Vic didn't know him well enough to have known about the toothbrush or the alarm clock. Surely Liv would have? She was his girlfriend, and no doubt stayed over at his flat when they were together."

"That's a consideration," Rich said.

"But then she would also have had a key," Perry pointed out, leaning forward and resting his hands on the back of his chair. "And the toothbrush thing could have been new. They split up a good month before Vic disappeared. Also, she could have been in a bit of a rush, so not thinking about the details. I'm sure she's hiding something."

"About another man?" Bea asked.

"Exactly. Maybe the two of them were in it together?" Perry suggested. "One way or another, I intend to find out."

"Just remember, proceed with caution. Tact is the key," Rich said firmly.

"Why does everyone keep reminding me about being tactful? Subtlety is my—"

"Middle name!" Bea and Rich completed for him. She grinned, adding, "Yes, we know."

"Exactly," Perry said as he reached down and patted Daisy on the head. He straightened. "I'll see you later."

Bea watched him weave around the tables and disappear through the large glass door leading to the terrace. *I hope he finds out something new.*

Under the table, Rich took her hand in his. "I know it's frustrating, but we'll get there. We just need more information to put the pieces of the puzzle together."

She knew from other investigations they'd been involved in that you inevitably felt like you'd hit a brick wall. *But this feels different.* "I think it's the lack of motive I'm struggling with. Normally, more of our suspects have a reason to want our victim dead. But here — well, Liv had broken up with Vic. So what would she have gained from his death? Bella already had another job lined up and was moving on with her life. Rob, we know, needed Vic to make their new restaurant work. Marco and Vic seemed to get on according to the others. Bryan, we know nothing about, but why would an accountant want to kill Vic? Vic had nothing to do with the business side of things according to Julian."

"Let me see what I can dig up on this Bryan Sinclair," Rich said.

"And finally, talking of Julian, he needed Vic to make him money." She shrugged. "Why would *any* of them want to kill him?"

Rich squeezed her hand, then dropped it and frowned. "Here's a thought," he said, rubbing his chin. "What if Julian found out Vic was setting up his own restaurant with Rob? He'd be losing his head chef *and* his senior sous chef all at once..."

"And that could be a strong enough motive to kill Vic?"

Rich swayed his head from side to side. "No, probably not. He'd lose Vic either way, so it would defeat the purpose." He shrugged. "It was just a thought." He smiled at her. "So what are your plans now?"

"Now we've decided on the colour palette for SaltAir, I have furniture shopping to do. Then we've invited Bella to have a look around Clary House. You?"

"More meetings that really should be an email," he said, rising with a sigh. "Do you want me to take Daisy back with me?" At the mention of her name, Daisy sat and looked up at Rich, her tail sweeping the floor.

Bea rose too. "Yes, please. That would be very helpful." She looked down at her little dog, who was gazing up at Rich like a love-struck teenager, and added, "I think she'd rather be with you than me anyway!"

31

AFTERNOON, THURSDAY 24 JUNE

Perry sipped his cappuccino, then licked his lips to remove the foam clinging to his upper lip as he listened to Liv Belmont's animated pitch in the busy theatre cafe in Windstanton.

"Algernon is charming, brilliant, and witty," Liv said, her blue eyes lighting up with excitement.

Perry lifted his chin. *I can do that...*

"But he's also vain, shallow, and has no moral compass." She leaned in closer, lowering her voice conspiratorially. "You'd be perfect for the part."

Rude! I know right from wrong...

"Wilde based the character very much on himself, including the pithy one-liners. He's both complex and fun. What do you think?"

Complex and fun... He had depth. "He sounds like quite the character," Perry said nonchalantly, leaning back in his chair. "And you certainly have a way of selling a part, Liv."

Liv's eyes glinted with pride. "I do my best, Perry. And honestly, I think you'd bring something special to the role. And then, of course, there's the costumes!"

Perry imagined himself dressed to the nines in Victorian finery. A dark-blue fitted coat, a paisley patterned cravat, a shirt with a high white collar, pale leather spats on his brown shoes. *Dapper.* That was how they would describe him in the reviews.

Wait! You're here for a reason, Perry. He needed to find out why Liv had *really* split up with Vic. *And who the other man is…*

Perry took another sip of his coffee, savouring the rich taste. He'd been waiting for the right moment to ask her, and it seemed now was as good a time as any.

"Before we get too carried away and I just say yes without proper consideration," Perry began, shifting in his seat. *Be subtle.* "Can I ask you why you really ended things with Vic?"

"Vic?" Liv's eyes widened, and her smile faded ever so slightly. "Perry, I've already told you," she said, her voice wavering just a bit. "I was fed up with his obsession with food. I felt like it was more important to him than I was."

"But was it just that?" Perry pressed gently, studying Liv's face for any signs of deception. "Or were you looking for an excuse to move on and be with someone else?"

Her cheeks flushed crimson, and she fidgeted with her napkin. It was clear he'd struck a nerve. "I don't know what you're implying, Perry," she stammered, avoiding his gaze. "And whatever it is has nothing to do with you playing Algernon."

Have I pushed too hard? Perhaps she'd throw him out now, and he still wouldn't have the answers they needed. *Forget subtle.* He had to go straight to the heart of it. "Come on, Liv." He tried to keep his tone gentle yet firm. "You can be honest with me. Did you leave Vic for someone else?"

Liv's eyes flashed with indignation as she glared at Perry,

her hands trembling. "I don't know why you would think that," she snapped.

Well, you asked... Perry leaned in closer, his voice low and steady. "Liv, you were overheard on the phone telling someone to hang tight, and that you'd soon be free once you sorted Vic out." He shook his head gravely. "Can't you see how that sounds? If the police find out, they might think you meant you were going to kill him."

Tears welled up in her eyes. Perry looked down at the floor. *Was I too brutal?* He glanced up in time to see Liv's lips quiver.

"Perry, I swear, I would never have hurt Vic. We had history — we were happy once, believe it or not. But things changed, and out of the blue, I fell in love with…er, someone else." She grabbed her glass of water and took a large gulp. She sat up straighter. "And anyway, why would I need to kill him when I could just end the relationship, which is exactly what I did?" She wiped away a tear that had strayed down her cheek with the back of her hand and lifted her chin to stare at him.

She seemed to be sincere. *So who's this someone else?* "Who was it?"

"I can't say," she replied, her voice barely audible.

"But, Liv, you have no alibi for the weekend Vic died, do you?" he asked gently.

Did she understand the precarious situation she was in? Her eyes darted from his, going around the room. Leaning closer, she whispered, "Actually, I have an alibi, Perry. I was with someone that weekend. We went away together."

His eyebrows shot up. "Why didn't you say?"

"Because we were trying to keep it quiet," she murmured, her face flushed. "It's…complicated."

Ah... "You mean he's married?"

She shot back and raised a hand to her chest. "No! I don't mean that at all. Who do you take me for?" Her jawline was set in a sharp line.

Perry shook his head. "I'm sorry, Liv."

She took a deep breath. "It's just that he and Vic… Well, they knew each other. "

Julian? No, he's married. Bryan? Also married. Rob? Oh, now that would be interesting… "Come on, Liv. This person is your alibi. Who is it?"

"Look, you're not the police," she snapped, a hint of anger in her eyes. "I don't have to tell you."

Perry opened his mouth to argue but was at a loss for words. *She's right.* He wasn't the police, and he had no right to know. *Blast!*

Just then a table scraped back. Perry looked over his shoulder to see Marco Rossi making a beeline for their table. And he didn't look happy. "Liv! Are you all right? What's happened?" he cried as he reached them. He leaned in and stared at Perry, his eyes dark and menacing. "What did you do to upset her?"

"Marco, it's okay," Liv reassured him, resting her hand on his arm. "We were just talking."

The way Marco looked at her—protective, gentle, and utterly devoted. *Marco? Of course, Marco!* Single and friends with Vic. And suddenly not big buddies like they'd used to be. It all made sense. *Marco is the other man!* But would he admit it? *Only one way to find out…* "Marco, Liv's in a bit of a bind," Perry said, his eyes studying the man's face. "She has no alibi for the weekend Vic died, and there's some incriminating evidence against her. She says she was away with someone, but she won't say who. Maybe you can persuade her to—"

Marco's eyes flicked from Perry to Liv, lingering on her

tear-streaked face. "Everything will be okay, Liv," Marco murmured, squeezing her hand reassuringly. Turning to Perry, he raised his chin. "I was with Liv that weekend. We went to a hotel together."

Yesss!

"And now, if you don't mind, we'd like you to leave."

32

LUNCHTIME, THURSDAY 24 JUNE

Bea drummed her fingers on the mahogany sideboard, the sound echoing softly in the empty supper room at Clary House. *I should have brought Daisy. She always makes people feel at ease.* But the little dog had looked so settled in her bed in the library at home with Rich, that she'd not wanted to disturb her.

Where are Ryan and Bella? Bea had a feeling that beneath Bella's composed exterior lurked answers about Vic, and she was set on coaxing them out of her.

As if summoned by her thoughts, Bella finally sauntered into the room, escorted by Ryan, a wide grin splitting his face. Bea suppressed a smirk. Ryan was clearly pulling out all the stops to charm the social media influencer.

"And this," Ryan announced with a flourish, "is the supper room where—"

Please don't say the magic happens…

"—we'll be entertaining our guests who join SaltAir Fine."

Thank goodness!

Bella moved around the room, taking snaps. "You and Perry really did an amazing job with the renovations, Lady Beatrice. It looks so different," Bella gushed, her gaze flitting around the room. "It's very tasteful and totally in keeping."

"Thank you," Bea replied. "We wanted to pay homage to the history of the building in this room. Downstairs, we'll have a bit more fun with the decor."

"Well, I look forward to seeing that in a couple of weeks," Bella replied, popping her phone into her jacket pocket.

At that moment, Ryan's mobile rang. He glanced at the screen. "Sorry, I need to take this. One of my key suppliers wants to talk prices." He left the room, his phone to his ear.

"Tell me, Bella," Bea said, leaning in slightly. "How does it feel to be back in Clary House after all these years?"

"Fine," Bella replied, her nonchalance betrayed by a faint quiver in her voice. "Like I said, it all looks so different now."

Bella's discomfort was clear. But why? *Should I do a Perry and just ask her outright?* Bea took a deep breath. "I get the feeling there was more to your relationship with Vic than you've admitted to us. Were you two having an affair?" *Oh my goodness, where did that come from?* Until this moment, Bea had been unaware that she'd suspected they'd been having an affair. *Is this what it feels like to be Perry?*

Bella's jaw dropped, her green eyes widening in shock. "What? No, of course not!" she stammered, her cheeks flushing crimson. Her voice was steely as she said, "In fact, you couldn't be any further from the truth." Then with a loud huff, she turned on her heels and bolted from the room.

Rats! What was that all about? Bea shook her head, then hurried after Bella.

Bursting through the back door into the car park, Bea

spotted the tall woman over the other side, vaping furiously. A minty haze enveloped Bea as she approached, causing her to cough lightly.

"I wish I never gave up smoking," Bella grumbled, taking another drag on her electronic cigarette.

"Look, Bella, I'm sorry," Bea said softly, stepping closer. "I shouldn't have brought it up. It's none of my business."

Bella took a shuddering inhale, then she shrugged. "No, it's not your fault. But for the record, there was no affair with Vic. The truth is…just after he and Liv split up, he invited me to go on his trip to New Zealand and Australia with him." Bitterness laced her tone. "I thought it would be fun, you know, a culinary tour, so I said yes."

"So what happened?" Bea prompted gently.

"I went up to his flat after work. We were discussing a possible itinerary and looking at flight options. It was all going fine, but when I went to leave, well suddenly he…he tried to kiss me," she spat out. Red spots appeared on her cheeks. "I mean, what was he thinking? That I was *that* desperate? He was ten years older than me and hardly a looker. He could never get someone like me as a girlfriend," she sneered.

Someone thinks a lot of herself…

Bella's green eyes blazed as she continued her story, "I told him exactly where he could stuff his holiday and stormed out. How dare he think that I would ever be interested in him!" She took a dramatic puff from her electronic cigarette, then a mischievous grin spread across her face. "And wouldn't you know it, I ran into Julian Thornton in the hallway. He was just coming out of his office downstairs."

Julian? Bea's eyes narrowed as Bella's expression shifted into one of smug satisfaction. It was as if she'd just won a coveted prize, her lips curling into a triumphant smirk that sent shivers down Bea's spine.

Bella continued, "I told him what had happened and how I was going to sue Vic for assault. The look on his face was priceless." She gave a sharp laugh.

Bea's shoulders tensed. *What a vindictive little—*

"He got so flustered that he gave me the money for a cab home." She smiled coyly. "Then the next day, when I went into work, Julian called me into his office. Vic was there."

That must have been an uncomfortable encounter.

Bella looked down at Bea, her eyes flashing. "He apologised. It was pathetic. He said he'd misread my signals." She huffed. "As if I would give signals to someone like him. What a fool!"

Bea wrinkled her nose. She almost felt sorry for Vic. "So what did you do?"

Bella lowered her eyes. "I accepted his apology."

Just like that? Bea frowned. It had happened over three years ago, and yet Bella was still clearly very annoyed about the whole thing. *I think you're lying! I wonder what really happened?* she thought. "If it was all sorted so easily, then why did you leave?"

She shrugged dismissively. "Things were awkward after that. I just couldn't get over the fact that he thought *I'd* been interested in *him*. So I started looking for another job. A friend told me a sous chef at the Fawstead Inn was leaving, so I approached them, and that's how I got the job."

"Indeed." That sounded more like the story the hotel manager had given them.

Bella took a deep draw on her vape pen, the minty smoke dissipating around her. "Okay. I must go," she said, taking a car key out of her pocket. "I'm heading up to London for a few days to do some filming with one of my sponsors. I'll see you at the opening." She pointed the key at a sleek black sports car in the far corner of the car park and headed towards the flashing orange lights.

Bea watched Bella hurry towards her car. Just how enraged had Bella been at Vic? Angry enough to kill him? After all — she had no alibi for the night of Vic's death, and now she had what looked like a big fat motive.

33

BREAKFAST, SUNDAY 20 JUNE

B ea's heart fluttered in her chest like a trapped bird as she sat in the drawing room at The Dower House, waiting for the evening to begin. She glanced over at Rich, who, in stark contrast, seemed calm and relaxed. He was dressed impeccably in a dinner suit; the light hanging overhead picked up the silver in his temples as he leaned back in his chair and crossed his legs.

Bea reached out and stroked the wiry hair on the top of Daisy's head. *I wish you could come with us, Daisy-do. But unless I can get you reclassified as a support dog, Grand-mama will not allow you at the dining table. Perhaps we could do a swap?*

"Are you trying to negotiate with Daisy for her to take your place so you can stay here instead?" Rich raised an eyebrow in mock horror.

How does he know? Heat rose up her neck. She smoothed down her dress with shaky hands, the delicate chiffon sleeves rippling down her arms as she did so. She tucked her red hair behind her ears. "I don't know what you're talking about," she said, feigning innocence.

"Relax, Bea," Rich said, taking a sip of red wine. "You look beautiful, and everything will be fine."

She attempted to smile, although she suspected it looked more like a grimace. "I just want it to go well."

"And it will."

How can he be so sure? It was true he'd met most of her family already because of his job, even her fierce grand-mother. But that had been in a work capacity. This was differ-ent. Tonight they were meeting him as her…what? *Boyfriend?* That seemed such a juvenile word to use to describe something that felt so much more grown-up. She remembered Perry's comment. *Future husband?* She bit her lip. *Oh my goodness.* She glanced at Rich, who was flipping pages over in a magazine, and her heart wanted to burst out of her chest. She loved this man. He was funny, smart, support-ive, tolerant of her situation, and most of all, he got her. The real her. *I can't lose him now.*

And yet, despite what Perry had said about Rich having given up his job for her, and even though she could see in his eyes that he cared a great deal for her, she wasn't sure if his show of confidence wasn't hiding an insecurity that came from their very different backgrounds. There was no hiding it; in normal circumstances, they would never have met socially.

It didn't matter to her. She was an adult and could have a relationship with whomever she wanted. But she had to accept that being a royal came with expectations both from within the family and from the press. And their scrutiny, she knew from bitter experience, could be relentless and unforgiving.

I just don't want anyone to make Rich feel like he's not good enough. And that was why she needed her family's support. If *they* loved him, then they would be a united front against any criticism from the press.

Beep! Her phone vibrated on the table in front of her. *Probably a message from Ma warning me not to be late.* She picked up the phone and smiled when she saw Perry's name pop up.

Perry: *We wanted to say good luck for tonight. Don't worry. You and Rich are great together. They will see that xx*

Bea smiled. *I have the best friends!*

Perry: *PS while you're sipping champers, we've invited Julian Thornton to Clary House to have a look around *winking face*

"Anything interesting?" Rich asked, putting down his magazine.

"Just Perry and Simon wishing us good luck for tonight," she replied. "Oh, and they're seeing Julian Thornton again."

Rich nodded thoughtfully. "So where does that leave us with our suspects?"

"We can clear Rob. And Liv provided Perry with the hotel name before he left the theatre. They confirmed Marco and Liv were there that weekend. So they're both cleared too."

Rich raised an eyebrow. "I'm surprised she told Perry anything after he upset her with his questions."

Earlier, Bea had relayed to Rich Perry's commentary of his encounter with Liv and Marco. *Oh, I missed something out!* She laughed. "Sorry, I forgot to tell you. Perry agreed to play Algernon in Liv's next production, *The Importance Of Being Ernest*. I think that went a long way to placate her."

Rich snorted with laughter. "Perfect casting!"

When they'd got themselves under control, Bea continued, "Anyway, that only leaves Julian, Bella, and Bryan. Bella has no alibi, and there's no doubt she was furious about what had happened between her and Vic, so maybe that's a strong enough motive for her to have killed him." She shook her head slowly. "But I'm not too sure. I've asked Perry to get Julian's side of the story. Let's see if that matches hers."

"Sounds good. And Bryan?"

"His wife hasn't appeared yet, so that's still an unknown," Bea replied.

"And then there's Julian." Rich furrowed his brow. "Do you think Perry and Simon will get anything new out of him?"

"Who knows?" Bea shrugged. "But it's worth a shot."

"What about the police? Do we know how Finch is getting on?"

Bea sighed. "Simon has spoken to Steve to bring him up to date with what we've found out, but Steve told him that Finch isn't sharing."

Rich humphed as Fraser appeared in the doorway. "Would you like me to drive you up to the house, my lady?"

Rich arched an eyebrow at her. It was a beautiful evening, and the walk would be romantic, just the two of them. Then she looked down at her black sandals with their towering heels. "I don't think I can walk that far in these shoes," she said apologetically to Rich.

He grinned. "Can we have the car in ten minutes, please, Fraser?"

"Yes, Mister Richard," Fraser replied before leaving them alone once again.

Bea rested back in her chair. She was glad her brother — Fred, her sister — Lady Sarah, and Sarah's husband — John had agreed to join them for dinner. She was fairly confident they would help smooth her and Rich's path with her grandmother. Especially Fred, who was The Queen Mother's favourite.

"Bea." Rich's voice cut through her thoughts. "Hey." He reached over to touch her hand. "Don't worry. I'll be on my best behaviour, I promise. Now, just remind me, which fork do I use first, the big one or the small one?" he said, looking confused.

Bea's eyes widened as her heart sank, then she caught the twinkle in his eye. He winked at her. She grinned and playfully swatted his arm. "You're terrible, and you're doing nothing to settle my nerves."

And anyway, it's not you I'm worried about, Rich. It's them.

A sudden buzzing broke through their laughter.

Rich pulled out his phone to check an incoming text message. As he read the contents, his relaxed expression shifted into a clouded frown.

Oh no. What's happened? "Is everything okay?" she asked, concern tingeing her voice.

Rich ran his hand through his hair. "It's from Elise. My mother's cancelled her trip to visit this weekend."

Bea's heart sank. She'd been looking forward to meeting Rich's mother for the first time at his sister's. "Why did she cancel?"

"Why do you think? Desperate Dougie, of course," he muttered darkly. Rich and Elise always referred to their mother's long-term partner as Desperate Dougie or Double D for short. Neither of them seemed to like him much, claiming he was taking advantage of their mother's kind nature, expecting her to wait on him hand and foot.

"He's ill, apparently," Rich continued, shaking his head. "And it's just typical of her, putting Dougie before her own children. Why can't one of his lay-about offspring look after him for a change?" He clenched his jaw as he ran his hand along it.

Bea reached across the distance between them, offering a comforting touch. "I'm so sorry, Rich. I really wanted to meet her, but Elise once told me your mother is only happy when she has someone to look after."

His fingers intertwined with hers, and he offered a weak smile. "It's not your fault. I just wish she could see there's more to life than catering to that man's every whim."

"It's only Thursday. It's possible he'll make a speedy recovery, and she'll decide to come, after all."

"I suppose so. In the meantime, please don't let my mother and Double D spoil our evening," he said, his voice soft yet firm. "If she hasn't made it down here by the time the restaurant is open, I'll take you to Leeds to meet her. All right?"

"I'd like that," she replied just as a car beeped outside. Her stomach churned with a fresh wave of nerves.

"Ready?" Rich asked, rising and extending his hand to her.

"As I'll ever be," she muttered, accepting his hand and rising to her feet. Her fingers trembled slightly, but he held on firmly as he steered her out the door.

Bea couldn't help but marvel at his unflappable self-assurance as they stepped out into the warm night air. As they slid into the backseat of the Bentley, she closed her eyes and inhaled deeply. *It will be fine.* She could do this. With Rich by her side, she could face anything—even the judgment of her own family.

34

MEANWHILE, THURSDAY 24 JUNE

Perry glanced at his watch, then huffed. *He's been on the phone for thirty minutes now, and Julian will be here in ten.* He watched his husband pace the wooden floor of the supper room at Clary House, talking on his mobile phone. His free hand waved in the air as he chatted and laughed. *Thirty minutes!* From the time they'd left the house (Perry had had to drive, of course), Simon had had his phone glued to his ear. Perry drummed his fingers on the bar. *What can they be talking about that takes this long?*

He refilled his glass with tonic water and took a sip, then looked over at Simon again. The evening sun filtering through the high windows of the room was casting a bright light on his husband's face. The excitement in Simon's eyes was palpable as he let out a roar of laughter. Perry sucked in his lips. *He doesn't laugh like that with me.*

"Okay. That's great. We're looking forward to seeing you." Simon grinned as he listened to the person at the other end. "Yes, me too." He was still smiling as he cut the call. "Isla's going to drive down from Scotland next week now. She'll be here a few days before the party and hopes to stay on afterwards," Simon told him as he strode to the bar.

"Oh great!" Perry mumbled, pushing a glass of wine across the counter.

Simon stopped and stood still. His mouth fell slightly open as his brown eyes widened.

Rats! Perry kicked himself. *Did I say that out loud?* "I'm sorry, love. That came out wrong." *Am I being selfish? This isn't about me, and now I've hurt the man I love.* He remembered Bea's advice about embracing Isla in their lives. "I—"

Simon reached across the bar and grabbed Perry's hands. "No, *I'm* sorry. I forget this is different for you. I get carried away. It can't be easy having another person shoved in your face all the time. Just know my feelings for Isla don't diminish my love for you in any way, Perry."

Perry swallowed, feeling a tad lightheaded. He squeezed Simon's hands gently. "I know," he whispered, almost choking. *I'm an idiot!* Of course he knew that. He'd just lost sight of it. *Time to get over myself...* "Actually, do you think it would be okay if Bea and I took Isla for a spa day when she's here? We could spend some quality time together..." He trailed off when he saw Simon's brown eyes filling up. For a moment, they stared deep into each other's eyes. *It will be okay. We'll make it work.*

Simon dropped Perry's hands to swipe at his face. "I think she'll love that," he said, his voice a little hoarse. "You know you're going to make a great stepdad." He grinned. "You can be the fun one."

Stepdad!? Perry's breath caught in his throat. *Me?*

The doorbell rang, its shrillness cutting through their intimate moment. With a shared glance, they both took a deep breath, then moved towards the door.

Downstairs, Simon opened the heavy main door and

greeted Julian Thornton. "Julian. Welcome, and thanks for coming," he said warmly. "This is my husband, Perry. He and Lady Rossex have been doing the refurbishment, as you know."

"Ah, yes," the stocky man replied, shaking Perry's hand. "I've heard about your excellent work." He turned back to Simon. "Thank you for inviting me to see the progress you've made here. I'm looking forward to joining the supper club."

———

"Can I get you something to drink?" Simon asked, gesturing towards the well-stocked glass bar in the supper room.

"Ah, yes, a glass of wine would be most welcome, thank you," Julian replied, his gaze drifting around the room. "This is amazing."

"We wanted to create a comfortable space where people could relax and focus on eating good food and drinking excellent wine," Perry explained.

"And you've done just that. I can already tell it's going to be a tremendous success."

"Well, that's good to hear," Simon said, handing Julian his drink.

Right, niceties over. Let's cut to the chase and see what he has to say about Bella. "I understand Bella had a run-in with Vic a few weeks or so before his death?"

Julian's eyebrow's shot up. "Er, how did you—"

"She told us Vic made an inappropriate advance towards her."

Julian's complexion changed to a deep red as his nostrils flared. "That's her version," he snapped.

Perry leaned back slightly. *Whoa!* That wasn't the response he'd expected.

Julian continued, "I hope you didn't fall for her little victim routine. I did at first. When she came tearing down the stairs from Vic's flat that evening and practically knocked me flying, I believed her when she said Vic had made a pass at her. I calmed her down and told her to go home. I said I would deal with Vic and see her in the morning." He took a sip of his drink. "But when I talked to Vic, he was in shock. He told me he'd asked her to go on his trip with him earlier that day, and she'd been very keen. After she arrived at his flat that evening, they had a few drinks, and he said they'd been flirting. She was talking about their time away together as if they were going as a couple. So when she got up to say goodbye, he tried to kiss her. According to him, she freaked out and then fled."

"Do you think she led him on?" Simon asked.

Perry raised an eyebrow. *Is Simon taking Vic's side?*

Julian cocked his head. "Let me tell you what happened the next day." He took another sip of his drink. "She turned up in my office and said she'd decided to go to the press. She started spouting all this stuff about setting an example and how male predators shouldn't be allowed to get away with it. Well, I told her I thought she should listen to what Vic had to say as it seemed to me it had all been a bit of a misunder-standing."

Perry's body tensed. Why was it always the woman who had misunderstood the man's intentions? He took a deep breath. *Hold on though...* Hadn't Bea said that Bella had seemed more affronted that Vic had thought she would ever have considered being his girlfriend than upset that he'd tried to kiss her? So if she hadn't felt truly threatened by his actions, then why had she made so much fuss about it the next day? A tingle shuffled down Perry's spine. *Unless she decided to capitalise on the situation...*

Julian carried on, "Anyway, I got Vic in. He was mortified about the whole thing. Before she'd even opened her mouth, he apologised profusely. He said he'd totally misread the signals, and he was very sorry he'd upset her. Honestly, the man was sincere, I tell you." He flattened his lips. "But she wasn't having any of it. She refused to accept his apology, but then hinted that she could be persuaded not to take it any further if there was compensation on the table 'to help her deal with the mental scars', I think that's how she put it. I couldn't believe she was blatantly trying to blackmail him in front of me!"

Perry's eyes widened. *I was right!* And what was more, Bella certainly hadn't told Bea that was what she'd done. Perry huffed. *What a bi—*

"Really, the cheek of the woman!" Julian scoffed. "So I told her in no uncertain terms that no one was giving her any money, and as Vic said it was a genuine mistake, and he'd apologised, there was nothing more to say as far as I was concerned."

Perry leaned in. *So what did she do?*

"She wasn't happy, as you can imagine. She stormed out of my office but not before telling Vic he hadn't heard the last of it."

Is that when she decided to kill him? Perry shot a glance at Simon. His forehead was creased as he stared at Julian, his mouth slightly open. "So what happened then?" Perry asked.

Julian cleared his throat, then shrugged. "Er, nothing."

Perry's shoulders dropped. *Oh...*

Simon was still frowning. "Nothing?"

Julian blinked, then gave a strained laugh. "Nothing. She came back in to work the next day as if none of it had happened, and that was that. As far as I know, no more was said about it." Julian rubbed his nose as he gazed at the floor.

So she just dropped it? Perry suppressed a sigh. Perhaps she'd realised she wasn't going to get anything out of them? But talk about awkward — he could understand why she'd started looking for another job. Oh well, he'd tell Bea tomorrow and see what she thought of it all. In the meantime, they needed to know if Julian had an alibi for the night Vic had died. "So how does it feel being back at Clary House, knowing Vic died here?"

Julian's eyes darted around the room, and he shifted uncomfortably in his polished shoes. "Er, it's certainly a bit... um, strange, but I'm glad to see the building being restored. And I must say, I'm looking forward to the opening of the restaurant."

That was a politician's answer if ever I've heard one. But I'm not giving up that easily. "I heard you were away the weekend Vic died?"

Simon shifted on his feet and took a gulp of his wine.

"Y-yes," Julian stammered, avoiding eye contact. "I was on a family holiday in Spain."

Perry studied Julian's face for any signs of deception. "And when did you leave for your trip?"

Simon cleared his throat.

"Er, on the Friday evening." Julian's voice cracked ever so slightly, as his fingers tapped an erratic rhythm on the stem of his glass.

Just then, Julian's phone rang, its shrill tone slicing through the tense atmosphere. He glanced down at the screen, a flicker of panic crossing his face before he quickly gave them an apologetic smile. "Excuse me, I really need to take this," he said, depositing his glass on a nearby sideboard as he hurried out of the room, then closed the door behind him.

"Perry!" Simon ran his fingers through his short hair. "Subtle, remember?"

"Oh, come on, love," Perry said, shaking his head. "Did you see how he changed the minute I mentioned Vic? He's like a cat on a hot tin roof. Something's off," he whispered, his blue eyes narrowing. "And I'm going to find out what's going on." He crept towards the door.

"Are you sure this is the—"

"Trust me, love. I know what I'm doing," Perry interrupted as he put his fingers to his mouth, hissed, "Shush," then cracked open the door.

Listening intently as Julian's voice echoed up from the hallway below, he crept out of the room and noiselessly closed the door behind him. He paused on the landing where he could still hear Julian's conversation while remaining hidden from view. Perry's heart raced. He took a deep breath, concentrating all his focus on Julian's voice.

"Look, I'm just worried it'll all come out." He sounded flustered, his voice strained with anxiety.

So there is *a secret he's hiding. I knew it!*

"That's all very good, but how can you be sure it will go away?"

Who's he talking to? An accomplice, maybe?

There was a pause. Perry leaned closer to the bannister.

"Fine," Julian snapped. "I'll meet you tomorrow evening at the back of the old bingo hall. Ten o'clock sharp. And you'd better come with a plan."

Crikey! Perry jumped up. He lurched towards the supper room, his heart pounding in his chest, as he grabbed the handle and yanked the door open.

"Is everything okay?" Simon whispered as Perry dived through the doorway and hurried towards the bar.

"Tell you later," Perry replied breathlessly, darting behind the bar to catch his breath. *Phew!* As he stood with his back to the room, Julian walked back in.

"Sorry about that," he apologised to Simon. "Just a minor work issue to sort out."

Perry took another deep breath as he poured himself a tonic water. *Something's going on, and I bet it's linked to Vic's death.* Licking his dry lips, he took a sip of his drink. *And I have every intention of finding out what — even if it means skulking around old bingo halls in the dead of night.*

35

LATER, THURSDAY 24 JUNE

B ea's heels clicked a steady rhythm on the wooden floor as, walking on the arm of her elder brother, they followed the procession of diners from the dining room to the drawing room of Francis Court. Bea's phone buzzed discreetly in her hand.

"Who's that?" Fred asked, peering over her shoulder as she looked at the screen.

Perry: *The suspense is killing me. How did it go? xx*

She couldn't suppress the smirk that teased a corner of her mouth.

"You better put him out of his misery," Fred said. "Tell him I'm no longer the golden boy around here." He tipped his head at the couple a few paces ahead of them, where Queen Mary The Queen Mother, was hanging off Rich's arm. As he leaned down to tell her something, she let out a bark of laughter. Fred huffed.

Bea grinned as she unlinked her arm from her brother's and swiftly typed a reply.

Bea: *Put it this way, QM has invited Rich to Scotland to go fishing and to stay at Foxhall with her! xx*

Perry: *How does he do that?* 😂😂 *xx*

Bea shook her head. *I've no idea!* She returned the phone to her bag and took Fred's arm again. "I hope you're not too upset to have had your favourite person status revoked," she said in a teasing tone.

"And by someone who isn't even officially part of the family," he replied, nudging her. "Yet…"

"Indeed." Bea didn't want to discuss that right now. She was still taking in the revelation that Rich had charmed her family so quickly and so smoothly. "I wish Summer was here," she told him, changing the subject.

"You and me both. Don't get me wrong, I'm so proud of the success she's been having since she was such a hit as a presenter on *Bake Off Wars,* but I wish it didn't take her away filming so much. I miss her…"

They reached the dimly lit drawing room at the other end of the corridor and walked in, the flickering candlelight creating a warm ambiance. While Fred fetched them both a coffee from the sideboard, Bea glanced around the room adorned with antique furniture and impressive oil paintings until her gaze rested on Rich. He was helping her grandmother settle into an armchair by the window. He looked up, and their eyes met. Winking, he flashed her a cheeky grin before bending down to say something to the older lady. Bea stood up a little straighter. *Why did I doubt he could pull this off?* She should've known by now that his confidence wasn't misplaced. He was simply comfortable in his own skin.

"So when are you two going public?" Fred handed her a delicate china cup filled with steaming black coffee.

Her stomach churned. "Public?" The word left a sour taste in her mouth. "I can't even think about it at the moment. I want more time here, in our little bubble. Away from prying lenses and wagging tongues."

"It's going to happen eventually, Bea."

"I know. I just worry for Rich and especially his family." It would be the last thing his mother needed while she nursed her sick partner. "They didn't sign up for this circus."

"Rich knew what he was getting into, Bea. He saw it firsthand over the years working for PaIRS. And he'll know what to do to protect his family. He's tougher than you give him credit for, you know."

"Perhaps," Bea conceded. "But am I?"

"Hey, now." Fred reached his arm out and put it around her shoulders. He pulled her close and kissed her forehead, his voice dropping to a conspiratorial whisper. "Don't you worry, Bea. I've got something up my sleeve that might just ease the transition."

"Really?" She eyed him suspiciously. What was he up to? Then it hit her. *Oh my goodness! Is he going to propose to Summer?* "Are you—"

He shook his head. "I can't say anything more. Just watch this space, little sis. Watch this space."

Bea returned her coffee cup to the sideboard and spotted her grandmother moving towards her.

"Grandmama," Bea called softly, gliding across the room to intercept the matriarch's course. "Are you leaving?"

"Beatrice, my dear." Queen Mary smiled warmly, her silver hair catching the light from the crystal chandelier above her.

Bea leaned in, offering a cheek for a goodnight kiss. But the Queen Mother held her there, clasping Bea's hands in her surprisingly strong fingers. "He's charming," she said, her voice low. "And he fishes! A man after my own heart." Her green eyes sparkled with pleasure.

"Thank you, Grandmama," Bea replied, her cheeks heating at the unexpected praise.

"You deserve happiness, Beatrice. Don't forget that." With a last pat on Bea's cheek, she accepted her granddaughter's kiss and withdrew.

Well, that's a turn up for the books.

As she looked around for Rich, she clocked him deep in conversation with her brother-in-law, John. However, as she moved to join them, she saw her parents preparing to leave too. She changed direction and, smiling, she walked towards them.

Her father, a man of few words, simply enveloped her in a bear hug.

"Goodnight, Pa," Bea murmured, absorbing the comfort of his embrace.

"He's a good sort. I like him," he mumbled before releasing her and ambling off.

Her mother, elegant in a gown that whispered grace with every fold, stepped forward. "Your handsome man has done very well tonight, darling," Princess Helen said, her lips curving into a knowing smile. "Grandmama is utterly smitten."

"Is she?" Bea feigned surprise, though she felt a flutter in her chest. *My handsome man is a success!*

"Absolutely," her mother said, brushing an imaginary speck from the sleeve of Bea's dark-green dress. "And Beatrice, please don't be a stranger. We miss you and Sam."

Bea swallowed. "Yes, Ma," she said in a shaky voice.

"Goodnight, darling. And when you're ready, we'll orchestrate Richard's debut into the public eye."

———

Lady Sarah's stiletto heels clicked on the hardwood floor as she approached Bea. She wrapped her arms around her sister in a tight embrace that smelled faintly of her expensive perfume. "Anyone who can knock my twin brother off his favourite person perch is fine by me," she whispered, grinning. Then she pulled back just enough to peer into Bea's eyes. "It couldn't have gone any better, Bea."

"I was so worried," Bea admitted, squeezing Sarah's hands.

Sarah's voice softened. "Trust yourself more. Give this— give Rich everything you've got. You both deserve that." She kissed Bea's cheek before taking her husband's arm and slipping away with a final wave.

Bea took a deep breath, then pivoted on her heels away from the door. She headed over to join Rich and Fred, who were sitting by the fireplace. Rich stood as she neared and held out a Tia Maria to her. "I thought you might need this," he said, smiling.

She sat down, exhaling noisily. "I'm glad that's over." She lifted her glass to Rich. "You were amazing. Thank you."

"Yes, congrats, old chap," Fred said, clapping Rich on the back. "You've officially replaced me as my grandmother's favourite." He held his glass up. "And I can inform you now, I intend to fight back."

When the laughter died down, Fred announced, "I've got news."

Bea's heart skipped. *Is he going to tell us he's proposing to Summer?* It would certainly give the press something to keep them busy.

He continued, "Your hunch about the financials? Spot on. I had a forensic accountant take a look. There was definitely something fishy going on at The Seaside Lounge."

Bea's pulse quickened. *Really?* This could be the breakthrough they needed.

"The restaurant's books are a masterclass in creative accounting, apparently. Cash sales were high. Too many temporary staff and premium suppliers nobody's heard of. All classic signs of money laundering."

"Money laundering?" Bea frowned. She'd heard of it, of course, but how did it work in practice? "How?" she asked.

Rich jumped in to explain. "Essentially, you have a load of money from something illegal. Drugs, bribes, that sort of thing. You can't just take it to the bank and put it in an account."

"Too many questions would be asked," Fred added.

"So you put it through a legitimate business like The Seaside Lounge. You declare the money as sales, but you don't want to pay tax on it, so you make up expenses. In this case, temporary employees paid in cash or suppliers, neither of whom really exists. That way, you disguise it and pass it through the system." Rich shook his head. "Who would have been privy to the scheme, do you think, Fred?"

"Most definitely the accountant," Fred said, taking a sip of his cognac.

So now we know why Bryan Sinclair is under Finch's microscope, Bea thought. She caught Rich's eye, and he nodded.

What about Julian? Hadn't Rob said Vic had been fed up with being told what suppliers to use? *Well, that makes sense now.*

"Probably the owner," Fred continued. "And most definitely whoever was pumping in the dirty money if it wasn't one of those two."

"Was Vic in on it, do you think?" Fred asked. "Perhaps he got cold feet and needed silencing?"

"Or he stumbled upon the truth and paid the price," Rich replied, his eyes narrowing.

"I think that's more likely," Bea said. "Vic had complained to Rob about being forced to use certain suppliers as dictated by Julian. I don't think he'd have said that if he'd known that was part of the scam."

Rich tilted his head. "Good point."

"But at last," she said with a satisfied smile, "we've finally got ourselves a compelling motive."

36

BRUNCH, FRIDAY 25 JUNE

Bea, having caught everyone up with what Fred had told her and Rich last night about the money laundering that had gone on at The Seaside Lounge, leaned back in her chair around the dining room table in Ryan's flat in Clary House and took a sip of her coffee. Around her, the scent of fresh pastries wafted through the air, and Daisy, who had already found a sunny spot on the rug by her side, eyed the bakery spread with poorly disguised greed.

Bea looked over at Perry. When they'd all arrived at Ryan's earlier, he'd been unable to contain his excitement about Julian and his secret meeting. Before Ryan had even unpacked the breakfast treats and made their hot drinks, Perry had told them all about what he'd overheard. The evidence against Julian was mounting up. Perry caught her eye and bit into a chocolate twist, grinning.

Bea's stomach turned at the thought. *How can he eat chocolate this early in the day?* She looked away from him to Rich, who, fresh from his triumph last night, was munching his way through an almond croissant. As he bit into the flaky pastry, a shower of crumbs cascaded onto his lap, and Daisy was by his side in an instant.

Him too! What's wrong with these people? Bea shook her head and turned to Simon.

"That explains a lot," Simon said, juggling a plate containing a Danish *and* a cinnamon roll.

Has no one here eaten for days?

"I agree. Bryan and Julian were most likely involved, but I'm still on the fence about if Vic was mixed up in all this mess or not," he continued, brushing along his well trimmed beard with his hand. "However, we have a snag. I spoke to Steve this morning and, according to Bryan's wife, who's now in the country, they were at a rotary club dinner on that Friday night. They were at home together on the Saturday night getting ready for their trip to Spain, although she admitted he'd disappeared for an hour or so to get some last minute holiday supplies."

Bea's heart dropped. If she was right and Vic had been killed on Friday night, then Bryan couldn't be the killer.

Rich put his hand up as he swallowed his latest mouthful. "Hold on. I have something about Bryan." He tapped the screen on his phone. "Ah, yes…here it is. I'll just give you the essentials. So Bryan Sinclair. Qualified Accountant. Died two years ago, aged forty-eight. Cause of death was drowning in a boating accident in Portugal. Left a wife, Ann, and two daughters. Owned a house in Fawstead, sold after his death. Wife moved to Spain a few months later. She lives near Benidorm in a house they purchased ten years ago. In his will, he left everything to her. Total value of his estate was a cool four million."

He must have been paid well for his creative accounting skills!

"Seems like he was involved then," Ryan said, delightedly tearing into a pain au chocolat. "You wait until I tell Faye about this local bakery I've found," he added.

"We should make this a regular thing," Perry suggested, putting down a mug adorned with 'Did I roll my eyes out loud?' on the side and grabbing a blueberry muffin. "You know, like on a Saturday morning."

Ryan, Rich, and Simon all agreed through mouthfuls of food.

Bea rolled her eyes. "You just want an excuse to eat more pastries, Perry."

"Absolutely!" Perry laughed, his blue eyes twinkling.

We need to get back on track... "So what about Bella?" she asked. Perry had also filled them in on Julian's side of the story about the encounter between Vic and his sous chef.

Simon rubbed his chin. "Honestly, I don't know. If she really wanted to blackmail him, I can't see what she would gain from killing him."

But Bella had been livid... Was it a strong enough motive?

"Funny you should say that," Perry jumped in. "I was thinking earlier that Julian seemed outraged that Bella had threatened Vic with going to the press, then asking for money, but when we asked him what happened next, he was suddenly cagey. I'm not sure he was telling us the truth when he said nothing further happened. I think she might've tried again."

"We should try and talk to her again when she gets back from London," Simon said.

Bea took a sip of her coffee. *I'm not talking to her again!* Perry coughed. Bea looked at him and subtly shook her head.

"I can do it," Perry offered, winking at Bea. Her nose creased as she gave him a look.

"So do we have any more new information?" Simon asked.

"I have something else… Hold on." Rich wiped his hands on a disposable napkin and picked up his phone. "Okay, so Julian and family caught a flight at eleven on Friday evening from Fenswich Airport to Alicante," Rich informed them. "He returned on the Sunday evening just over two weeks later."

"Ah ha!" Perry cried, putting down his mug. "That means Julian could've killed Vic before he left."

"Perhaps," Bea said, her brow furrowing in thought. "But he definitely wasn't there on Saturday night to open the curtains."

"Perhaps he had an accomplice?" Perry paused, then his eyes lit up. "Like Bryan!" He gave them all a knowing look. "Think about it. Julian kills Vic on Friday night before he goes off to Spain when Bryan has an alibi, and then Bryan goes to the flat and takes Vic's stuff on the Saturday night in that hour his wife said he disappeared."

That would work.

"Exactly!" Perry cried, nodding vigorously. "If we're right, then we've cracked this case wide open."

"All right, Crockett and Tubbs, just calm down a minute," Simon said slowly. "There's still one critical thing we can't explain. How did Vic's body end up in the drywall?"

The room fell silent as everyone pondered this question, their gazes drifting towards the ceiling or the window as they searched their minds for answers. Daisy, seeming to sense the tension in the room, perked up her ears, her eyes darting between Bea and Rich.

"He had to have been hidden somewhere else first," Rich offered, shrugging. "But where? And how did he get moved with no one noticing?"

Ryan's phone rang, pulling everyone's attention away from the unanswered questions. He glanced at the screen, muttered an apology, and stepped out of the room to take the call.

Something was nagging in Bea's mind. *Hold on!* "If Julian and Bryan did it, then who's Julian meeting tonight?"

"That's a good question," Rich said. "There's a possibility it's nothing to do with Vic's death at all."

Bea tilted her head to one side. "You mean it's a coincidence? Come on, Rich. You don't believe in coincidences!"

He smiled. "You're right. Maybe there's a third person in all of this."

A thought struck Bea. "Could someone be blackmailing him? Someone else involved in the money laundering perhaps?"

"Exactly!" Perry took a gulp of coffee. "We should go to this rendezvous tonight and find out for ourselves," he said, excitement dancing in his eyes.

Simon and Rich exchanged a glance, shaking their heads in unison. "No, Perry," Rich said firmly. "It's time we talked to Finch direct and told him what we've found out. The police will want to be there. It needs to be done properly."

Bea's stomach clenched. *Really?* They'd done all the hard work, and now they were just going to hand it over to Finch?

"Bea." Rich put his hand on her arm. "There's a possibility Finch knows all of this already. After all, Bryan was his prime suspect days ago, don't forget."

Rats! He was right. Finch could have made all these connections himself…

Ryan re-entered the room, a serious expression on his face. "That was DI Finch on the phone," he told them. "He wants to see me and Simon this morning, here at Clary House. He's on his way now."

37

MEANWHILE, TUESDAY 22 JUNE

Wrapping her hands around a fresh cup of coffee, Bea breathed in the bitter aroma. Rich, standing next to her, shifted his weight from one foot to the other while looking around the table. "Should we all really be here, do you think?" he asked, raising an eyebrow. "Finch only asked for Ryan and Simon, after all."

Perry scoffed, crossing his arms over his chest. "I have no intention of leaving. I want to find out what Finch knows and if he agrees that Bryan and Julian killed Vic."

Sorry, Rich, but I'm with Perry. Bea gave him an apologetic smile. "I want to stay too, Rich. We're all involved in this now."

"I wouldn't worry," Perry added with a smirk. "Finch is hardly going to throw out a member of the royal family, is he?"

Simon mumbled, "I wouldn't be so sure."

Bea looked at him, frowning. He shrugged.

Rich tilted his head to one side. "Well, if everyone else is staying..."

Just then, Daisy's ears perked up, and she let out a low

woof. Bea looked at her just as they heard the main doorbell ring downstairs.

"That's him," Ryan said, straightening up. "I'll go."

Daisy jumped up and went running after him. Recalling Finch's disinterest in the little dog the last time they'd met, Bea called Daisy back and lifted her onto her lap. "You stay here with me, darling. Not everyone appreciates you like we do," she whispered in the terrier's furry ear.

A few minutes later, the door opened, and Ryan led Finch into the room. The accompanying faint smell of cherry made Bea's nose tickle. The inspector's grey eyes scanned the room, his thick moustache twitching. He looked at each of them in turn, his expression stern. "Lattimore," he grunted, then skipping Perry, his eyes landed on Bea.

I hope Perry's right, and he won't throw me out.

"I wasn't expecting to see you here, my lady," he said, his words clipped.

She lifted her chin. "We're working here, if you remember, inspector."

"Hmmm." He turned to Rich, his weathered face crinkling into a frown. "Who are you?"

Bea held her breath. *How would he react to having such a senior police officer here and clearly involved in the case?*

"Oh, just a friend of Simon's and Ryan's," Rich replied, offering no further explanation.

Will he accept that?

Finch stared at him for a few seconds, then took a deep breath. "Right. Well, I've come to tell you the case is now closed, and you can have your restaurant back with immediate effect."

That's it? Bea's shoulders dropped. She'd expected something a bit more dramatic… What information did he have that they didn't? Did he know about the money laundering? How had Vic's body ended up in the wall?

"We know what happened," Perry said with confidence. "But how did Vic's body get into the wall? That's the bit we're stuck on."

Finch's eyes narrowed on Perry. "Oh really?" he challenged. "Then I'd love to hear your version of events."

"Okay," Perry replied, seemly unfazed by Finch's attitude.

Go Perry!

"The Seaside Lounge was being used to launder money. Vic found out and was murdered to keep him quiet. He was killed on Friday night by Julian Thornton before he flew off on holiday. Then Bryan Sinclair came here to Vic's flat on Saturday to switch the lights on and off and open the curtains, making it appear as if Vic was still alive. At some stage over the next couple of weeks, Bryan disposed of Vic's body and he or Julian set up a fake email account in Vic's name that was then used to send the email saying he was staying on in Australia that Julian could pretend to find when he got back from holiday."

As Perry spoke, Bea watched Finch's reaction closely. Was he impressed by their sleuthing or merely humouring them before revealing his own findings? When Julian's name was mentioned, he shifted uneasily, but his face remained inscrutable throughout Perry's explanation. *Are we on the right track, or are we about to be proven wrong?*

Bea's fingers quivered nervously against Daisy's wiry coat as they waited for Finch to respond. She swallowed hard. *Come on; get on with it!*

When he finally spoke, it wasn't the question she'd been expecting.

"How did you find out about the money laundering?" he asked, rubbing his salt-and-pepper beard as he spoke.

Perry glanced at Rich, who stood rigidly against the wall, trying to blend into the background. *Rats!* Was their information network about to be exposed? Bea jumped in before Perry could say anything incriminating. "It was an educated guess," she said nonchalantly, hoping her voice sounded more confident than she felt. "Are we right?"

Finch shot a look of disdain at Simon before turning back to Perry. "Yes," he admitted with reluctance. "We believe the restaurant was being used to launder money, and like you, we think Mr Blackwell was killed because he discovered something suspicious was going on."

Bea suppressed a smile.

"However, you're not right about when the murder took place. Victor Blackwell was killed Saturday night, not Friday," he continued.

What? But she'd been so sure it had been Friday night… The police must have evidence to suggest otherwise. *And if it was Saturday then Julian—*

"And Julian Thornton wasn't involved," he concluded.

Bea's heart sank. *Did we really get it that wrong?*

"So who *did* kill Vic?" Perry asked wearily.

Finch hesitated, then gave a small satisfied smile. "It was Bryan Sinclair."

38

A FEW MINUTES LATER, FRIDAY 25 JUNE

B ea's heart pounded in her chest as she tried to come to terms with what Finch was telling them. "Are you saying Bryan was working alone?" she asked, her voice trembling slightly.

It seemed inconceivable that Julian could've been completely ignorant of what had been happening right under his nose.

Inspector Finch inclined his head slowly. "Yes, our investigation has led us to believe Sinclair was the mastermind behind it all. He used Julian's business to launder money gained through selling drugs locally."

So it was drug money. "I had no idea Windstanton was such a den of iniquity," she said.

Finch shrugged his heavy shoulders. "These days we have it under control. But back when the town wasn't so prosperous and before all the investment was made, there was much more deprivation, and it was a real problem."

Bea looked over at Simon, and he dipped his chin.

"Anyway, Thornton isn't exactly financially savvy," Finch continued, rubbing his thick beard. "He relies heavily on his advisors, and he trusted Sinclair implicitly. In turn, the accountant took advantage of that trust."

She glanced around the room, taking in the perplexed faces of her friends. Rich was staring at the floor, his brows furrowed, while Perry was giving Finch daggers, clearly not happy with what he was hearing. Simon was watching Perry. *Is he worried Perry will say too much?* Ryan, as ever, was calm and appeared unfazed by Finch's conclusion.

Daisy, sitting on Bea's lap, seemed to sense the tension and looked up at Bea with concerned eyes. Bea wrapped an arm around her and squeezed her gently. Bea couldn't shake the nagging feeling something wasn't adding up. She took a deep breath and let it out slowly. "If Bryan was running the entire operation, then how did he keep it hidden from everyone else?"

"Sinclair was a clever man," Finch replied, his voice tinged with grudging admiration. "He had a knack for staying under the radar. That is until, presumably, Vic found out. We'll never know how that happened, but we can be confident it's the reason Bryan Sinclair killed him."

Bea recalled the immense value of Bryan's estate. It made sense. Perhaps they'd been concentrating too much on Julian and had not given Bryan enough consideration.

"Just out of curiosity, inspector, do you know how Bryan disposed of Vic's body?" Rich asked.

"Of course, we can't be certain," Finch replied, shaking his head. "Sinclair is dead, and there's no forensic evidence left that can help us. However, our working theory is he killed Vic in the kitchen and stashed his body in the walk-in freezer. No one would be using it for three weeks, and it was off-limits to the workmen."

Bea's eyes widened. *Genius! Why didn't we think of that?*

As long as Bryan had moved Vic's body before everyone got back, then it would have been the perfect solution.

Finch continued, "After the workmen left on that last Friday they were here, we believe Bryan took Vic's body out, wrapped him in heavy-duty plastic, dismantled one side of the stud wall, placed him inside, stuffed the space with silica gel packs, and then re-boarded the wall and plastered it. Bryan was quite the DIY enthusiast, so he could've easily managed it by himself."

Perry's eyes narrowed as he stared at Finch, his lips pressed into a tight line. "Even if Bryan devised the whole scheme, how can you be so sure Julian wasn't involved too?"

"Mr Juke," Finch said, his tone unwavering. "We've done a full and thorough investigation. I'm satisfied with our conclusions."

"Really?" Perry shot back, clearly unconvinced. "Because I overheard Julian arranging to meet someone tonight. He told them he's, and I quote, 'Worried it will all get out'. Now that sounds like he's involved to me."

Finch visibly stiffened but quickly regained his composure. "That could be about anything, Mr Juke. Julian Thornton is planning on running for mayor, after all." He smirked, adding sarcastically, "Perhaps he has a lover he doesn't want the public to know about."

Bea glanced at Perry. There was still a determined glint in his eyes. She knew her friend wouldn't let this go easily. But she had to admit Finch had a point. They wanted answers, but were they seeing connections that weren't really there? She suppressed a sigh, rubbing Daisy's soft ears as she tried to get her thoughts together. She recalled her and Simon's meeting with Julian. He was definitely hiding something. *I think Perry's right.* "But I find it hard to believe Julian knows nothing, inspector. He seemed so...nervous when we talked to him and mentioned Vic."

Finch looked like he'd taken a spoonful of sugar and it had turned out to be salt. "You've been interviewing Mr Thornton about Vic's death?"

Rats!

"Er, no, Finch," Simon responded. "Myself and Lady Beatrice simply went to enquire about some plans for Clary House I wanted copies of. Naturally, Vic's name came up in conversation. And I have to agree, he seemed very uncomfortable talking about it."

"Sometimes people act strangely for reasons unrelated to a crime, Lattimore. You know that," Finch snapped out, crossing his arms. He turned away from Simon. "As I've already said, our investigation leads us to believe Bryan Sinclair was the one responsible. It's unfortunate he's no longer here to face justice or answer all our questions—"

Convenient more like!

"—but we've done what we can, and now we need to draw a line under this and close the case." He lifted his chin and held Simon's gaze. Simon hesitated for a few seconds, then looked away.

We need to leave this now before Finch loses patience, and we get in trouble for talking to suspects.

"Shouldn't the police at least check out this meeting tonight?" Perry insisted, a note of stubborn determination in his voice.

Bea's eyebrows shot up. *Perry!*

"Fine," Finch relented, his moustache bristling with irritation. "I'll pass the information along to CID, and they can decide how to proceed." He flashed a tight-lipped smile at Perry, who reluctantly nodded. He gave Finch the details of the rendezvous.

Ryan rose. "Thank you, inspector," he said, holding out his hand. "Congratulations on solving this case so quickly. Hopefully, we can all move on now."

Perry huffed. Bea exchanged a look with Rich. He winked, and she suppressed a grin.

Finch took his hand and shook it. "You've been very patient, Mr. Hawley." He cast a sideways glance at Perry, then returned his attention back to Ryan. "I hope your opening goes well." With a last nod to the rest of the group, he pulled his vape pen from his pocket, turned, and left.

39

SHORTLY AFTER, FRIDAY 25 JUNE

The room fell silent as the door clicked shut behind Finch. Bea shifted in her seat. The maze of clues had abruptly ended, leaving her stuck in the middle with more questions than answers. She glanced around the room at the others, all of whom were wearing similarly deflated expressions.

Perry finally broke the silence, his voice tinged with disbelief. "Is that really it?"

"It certainly feels less satisfying than our previous cases, doesn't it?" Bea agreed, absentmindedly stroking Daisy's fur. The little dog fidgeted. Bea opened her arms and let her jump down.

"Maybe we're just disappointed because we didn't crack this one ourselves," Rich suggested, running a hand through his hair.

"And in fairness, Finch's theory isn't terrible," Simon said with a shrug. "It makes as much sense as ours."

"So you believe Julian knew nothing about the money laundering, do you?" Perry asked his husband.

"I think the police have no evidence he did. In much the

same way as we don't." Simon put a hand on Perry's arm. "I know you're disappointed, Perry. But sometimes cases aren't wrapped up in a nice bow. Sometimes they're messy and unsatisfying."

Perry huffed.

"He's right, I'm afraid." Rich agreed. "It's frustrating, but Finch and his team will have done their best. It happened over three years ago. Cold cases are tough and often the only resolution is a plausible theory."

Ryan glanced at his watch, a frown creasing his brow. "Well, I, for one, am just glad it's over, and we can now focus on the restaurant. We've still got a lot to do." He stood. "I should probably head back to London now. We're moving Faye's last few things to the flat this weekend." He smiled. "Thanks for all your help on this, everyone."

"I'll talk to Charles and give him the good news," Bea told him as they all rose and headed for the door.

The door clicked shut behind them, leaving them on the quiet landing of the first floor of Clary House.

Simon rubbed his chin. "Sorry, but I need to head home; I've got a call to make."

"And I need to get back to work," Rich added, looking at Bea and smiling. *Perhaps we can discuss the case, just the two of us, when we get back to The Dower House.* She would like that.

"Bea." Perry's voice held a note of urgency. "Will you stay behind? I'd like to go over everything in the dining room now that we have access again. Make sure we have it all covered."

Really? Now?

"And we can ring Charles together," he added, tilting his head to one side.

Bea suppressed a huff. She wanted to spend some time

with Rich, but her best friend's pleading gaze was hard to resist. "All right," she agreed with a tight smile. "I'll stay here with Perry." She looked at Rich. *Sorry!*

Rich leaned over and gave her a peck on the cheek. "See you later, trouble," he whispered. Her heart gave a gentle flutter. He turned to Simon. "Can you give me a lift back?"

Simon nodded, and they all headed down the stairs. In the hallway, they parted, Daisy trotting off after Rich, who picked her up as they reached the door. With a last grin at Bea, he disappeared outside.

She turned to Perry. "This really could have waited, you know, Perry. We've got everything covered, and I can ring Charles when we get back to the office. He can't do anything today, and we're already set for Monday. I—"

"I know!" Perry hissed as he grabbed her arm and pulled her down the hall and into the dining room. He closed the door. His eyes narrowed. "I'm not buying Finch's theory. Are you?"

Bea hesitated. *Am I?* It *was* tempting to just accept it. They could move on and focus on the opening, which was in less than two weeks now. Sam would be home from school soon. Isla would be here too. And she wanted to spend some time with Rich talking about something other than Vic's death. But... She looked into Perry's blue eyes. She sighed. "No. Neither am I," she admitted reluctantly. "I don't agree Vic was killed on Saturday."

"Exactly!" Perry pulled his phone out of his pocket and fired off a text. "Julian was the one who told Vic to order from those fake suppliers, remember? That supports our suspicions, not Finch's conclusions."

"And Bryan couldn't have acted alone if Vic was killed on Friday, like his closed curtains all day on Saturday suggest." Bea twirled the rings on her right hand. "There are still too many loose ends for my liking."

Perry pocketed his phone, determination etched on his face. "We just have to keep digging until we find the truth."

"Indeed," she said, her mind kickstarting again. "I think we need to speak with Julian." Her heart quickened at the thought.

"Way ahead of you," Perry replied, tapping his pocket with a sly grin. "I've already sent out feelers to find out where he is."

"But remember, we're just going to talk to him," Bea stressed, brushing a strand of hair behind her ear. "He could still be the murderer, so let's make it somewhere public."

Perry grinned. "Don't worry. *I'm* not making that mistake." He winked.

"Oh, ha ha," Bea chided. She didn't need reminding that back in March, during Perry's bachelor weekend, she'd unwittingly followed a killer down into a hotel basement on her own.

"He should be relieved now Vic's case is supposedly closed," Perry said. "Let's see how he reacts."

Yes, indeed. Her stomach fluttered. They would get the answers they needed!

The ping of an incoming text made Bea jump slightly. Perry read the message and smirked. "Okay, so Julian's at the theatre cafe."

"Perfect," Bea said, a rush of adrenaline running through her limbs. "Let's pay him a visit."

40

AFTERNOON, FRIDAY 25 JUNE

The jangle of glassware and the soft murmur of conversation filled the air as Bea and Perry walked into the Windstanton theatre cafe.

"There he is!" Perry hissed, indicating the far corner of the cafe where the distinguished-looking Julian Thornton was reading a newspaper and drinking tea. "Let's go." Perry charged off in Julian's direction, slowing down only to have a quick word with the cafe manager as he weaved in and out of the tables.

Bea suppressed a smile as she followed. Perry really was determined to get to the bottom of Julian's involvement. *I just hope he'll be subtle.* She checked herself. *This is Perry. He's as subtle as a steam train!*

"Ah, Julian!" Perry called out as he got closer. "Fancy meeting you here. Do you mind if we join you?" Leaving the poor man no choice, Perry gestured towards Bea. "You know Lady Rossex, of course." Julian jumped up as he caught sight of Bea just behind Perry.

"Of course, Lady Rossex. How lovely to see you again. Yes, please join me." His smile didn't quite reach his eyes.

Perry pulled out a chair for Bea, then sat down himself.

"This is a delightful surprise," Julian said, his voice strained as he sat down again. "What brings you two here?"

"We've just had a visit from Inspector Finch, who's been investigating Vic's death," Perry said, leaning back in his chair and crossing his legs. "He says the case is closed, so we can carry on with our dining room restoration. We're here to have a celebratory pot of tea."

As if on cue, a server appeared with their hot drinks.

"Really?" Julian's eyebrows shot up, and for a moment, Bea could see genuine relief in his eyes. "That's great news. I'm glad everything's back on track for the SaltAir opening. I'm looking forward to it." He picked up his napkin. "Please apologise to your husband for me. I couldn't find a copy of those plans he asked for. I think the solicitors must have them."

Perry raised an eyebrow at Bea. She gave him a quick smile, then said to Julian, "Not to worry, Julian. We'll manage without them until the solicitor is back from holiday."

"Anyway," Perry said, clearly keen to get back on track. "Bryan—quite a shock to find out he was using the restaurant for money laundering, wasn't it?"

Julian squirmed in his seat, his face uneasy. "Er, yes... I couldn't believe it when the police told me."

"Finch came to tell you, did he?" Bea asked. *Does he also know Bryan is the killer?*

"Uh, no," Julian stammered, his eyes darting around the room. "Not the inspector. I hardly know him. It's the sergeant who's been my primary contact."

He's jumpy again. He must be involved in the money laundering. Her mind was racing. Had he been compensated by Bryan for the use of his books? Or was it Julian who'd needed dirty money laundered? "Did Bryan launder money through any of your other businesses?"

Julian's face flushed, and he struggled to find the right words. "I, um, well... That's still being looked into."

Bea shot Perry a look. He winked at her. She turned her attention back to Julian. Beads of sweat were forming on his brow. His eyes darted around the room as though searching for a way out.

"And not just a money launderer but a murderer too," Perry said, his voice deceptively light.

"What?" Julian's face drained of colour as his eyes pinged wide.

"Bryan killed Vic," Perry told him.

Bea's stomach dropped. Clearly, this was news to him. *Should we have said anything if he's not been told yet?* "Er... Finch told us, though it isn't public knowledge yet," she added, trying her best to sound nonchalant.

"Bryan killed...Vic?" Julian stammered. His dismay seemed genuine. "When?"

"On the Saturday night," Bea replied, her words punctuated by the tinkle of Perry's teacup against its saucer as he drank his tea. "The police think he put Vic's body in the freezer first, then came back later to hide it in the wall."

"Apparently, he was quite the DIY expert," Perry added, putting his cup and saucer down.

"Was he?" Julian's face contorted into an expression of disbelief, his hands visibly shaking. He took a deep breath and ran his fingers through his hair. "I can't believe when I saw him in Spain, he'd just killed someone," he mumbled, almost to himself.

Bea studied Julian's face, searching for any hint of deception. There was none.

"What about the email? Did Finch say anything about

that?" Julian asked, seemingly attempting to regain control of his nerves.

Bea raised an eyebrow. *Why has Julian brought up the email?* If Julian had been involved with Bryan, he would have known it had been a forgery. *Did Julian kill Vic or not?* "Finch didn't mention it," she said, watching Julian's every move.

"Bryan must have set up a false email account in Vic's name and sent it from there," Perry said with little conviction. *Does he still think Julian is our killer?*

Julian stared at him, then hesitated before replying, "Well, he fooled me." The words were heavy with resignation as they hung in the air.

Bea's head was spinning. Everything she thought she'd known was now being challenged. She needed time to think. *I need to talk to Rich.* She shot a quick glance at Perry.

"Right," Perry said, standing up. "We need to get back. The dining room won't redesign itself. It was nice to see you, Julian."

Bea rose. "Yes. Thank you for letting us gatecrash your afternoon."

"Er...no problem," Julian mumbled, forcing a smile.

Placing an arm through Bea's as they moved away, Perry gave her a quick squeeze, then stopped and turned around. "Oh, and have a good evening, Julian."

Perry!!

41

AFTERNOON, FRIDAY 25 JUNE

"Mrs Fraser certainly outdid herself tonight," Perry remarked, sipping his steaming coffee, his blue eyes twinkling with satisfaction.

Bea let out a sigh as she patted her tummy, now full of shepherd's pie and apple crumble. "Indeed."

"I'm thinking of adding a Mrs Fraser section to our menu at SaltAir — offering classic comfort food. What do you think?" Simon asked, relaxing back with his coffee in an oversized armchair in the drawing room at The Dower House.

"I think she would love that," Bea said, stroking Daisy, who was curled between her and Rich. He reached over and squeezed her hand, giving her a swoon-worthy smile. Her belly fluttered.

It's like he's always been here. She smiled back. She could get used to having this man next to her for the foreseeable future. Her heart sank slightly. *But does he feel the same?* His sparkling brown eyes when they met hers seemed to say yes. *At the moment.* But would that change when they were forced out of their protective bubble and had to face the attention and scrutiny of the outside world? Inevitably, that day was just around the corner. Would they survive? *I'm not ready to find out yet.*

Perry cleared his throat, his fingers drumming against the armrest of his chair. A nervous energy radiated out from him.

He's going to ask again, Bea thought, braving herself for another heated debate on whether they should or shouldn't go to Julian's rendezvous in just over an hour's time. Ever since she and Perry had told Simon and Rich over dinner about their chat with Julian, there had been a divide among them. Perry was insistent Finch's conclusion was flawed, arguing Bryan couldn't be Vic's killer because he had an alibi for Friday night. His money was still firmly on Julian. Simon was of the opinion they should leave it to the police now. Rich seemed to be of the same opinion as Simon, although when pushed, he agreed he wasn't satisfied with Finch's conclusion. Bea was torn. She agreed with Perry that the murder had most likely taken place on the Friday, but after their encounter with Julian this afternoon, she no longer believed he was the killer. In the end, unable to agree, they'd opted to postpone any further discussion until after they'd eaten.

Perry leaned forward, his blue eyes holding a determined look. "We need to go. The meeting is in an hour's time, but we should get there early so we're there when they turn up," he said, his voice low and urgent.

Simon shook his head. "Perry, CID will have it covered. If there's anything more to it than just a lover's tryst, Steve will fill us in tomorrow. Let the police handle it." His voice was calm but firm.

Rich, his hand absentmindedly stroking Daisy's fur, said, "Simon's right. We should leave this to the professionals. If you're right and Julian's involved, they will deal with it."

Bea bit her lip. Her gut was telling her they should go.

She glanced at the antique grandfather clock in the corner of the room, the ticking growing louder in her ears. Time was running out. "What if it's something more serious than a secret affair? What if it *is* connected to Vic's death? CID might not realise," she said hesitantly. "I think we should go just to make sure everything is okay. If we don't recognise the person who turns up, then we can leave without anyone knowing."

"See!" Perry said triumphantly, looking at his husband. "Bea agrees with me."

Simon puffed out his cheeks. "Only a bunch of idiots would go to the back of the old bingo hall in Windstanton at this time of night."

———

The moon cast an eerie glimmer over the decrepit old bingo hall as Fraser pulled the Bentley up along the pavement on the street next to the back entrance. The quiet streets of Windstanton were empty. The only sound was the purr of the car engine.

Simon, sitting in the back with Bea, Perry, and Daisy, mumbled, "I can't believe I agreed to this," as Fraser cut the engine.

"Er, what now, Mister Richard?" Fraser asked Rich, who was sitting next to him in the front of the car.

"We wait," Rich told him.

Bea looked at her watch. It was nine forty-five. She peered into the darkness, searching for any sign of activity. *No police yet.* "What time will the police be here?" she asked Simon.

"It's probably too early, but I'd better let them know we're here anyway," Simon muttered, pulling out his phone.

After a few rings, a man answered. "Steve? It's Simon. We're at the back of the old bingo hall in Windstanton. What time are you getting here, mucker?" Steve's voice at the other end was indistinguishable. "Home?" Simon repeated in a confused tone. "Are you sending someone else?"

Oh no, this doesn't sound good. Bea glanced at Rich, who was leaning up against the open perspex divider in the car. He pulled a face as he strained to hear what was being said.

"Julian Thornton's secret meeting," Simon said tersely into the phone. "CID were supposed to have it covered." There was more dim mumbling from the other end, then Simon said, "Okay, mate, see you soon." Simon cut the call with a deep sigh. "They never got the message," Simon grumbled. "Steve's trying to get a couple of uniformed officers here as soon as he can, but CID are a good thirty minutes away."

Finch hadn't taken their concerns about Julian seriously, so maybe he'd just been humouring Perry when he'd said he would pass the details on. Perhaps he'd had no intention of doing so? Bea scraped her bottom lip with her teeth. *So what now?*

"Well, we're here now," Perry said, determined. "We should go and find out what's going on. We don't want to miss them arriving." He looked around the car. "We can all go."

Really? Bea was torn between a desire to know who Julian was meeting and not wanting to venture out into the dark and face the unknown. What had Simon said earlier? *Only a bunch of idiots would go to—*

"No," Rich cried, then cleared his throat. "I mean, four is too many. We'll make too much noise. Simon and I will go. We've got more experience in this type of situation. You two stay in the car with Fraser and Daisy."

Bea's hackles rose. So she and Perry were to be 'kept safe' and were not allowed to get involved in the action? She glared at Rich, but his expression, a mixture of concern and something else she couldn't quite put her finger on, something soft and, at the same time, compelling, made her rethink. *Is it really such a bad thing if he wants to protect me?* Didn't she want to protect him too? A shiver went down her spine. Was it a good idea for him and Simon to go out there without backup? "Are you sure it's safe?"

"Positive," Rich replied, reaching through the open screen and giving her hand a reassuring squeeze. "We'll be careful. Besides, the police will be here soon. All we want to do is find out who he's meeting."

"Text us if you need anything," Perry said. For all his bluster a few minutes ago, he sounded a tad concerned now too.

"Will do," Simon replied as he patted his husband's arm. He leaned forward and glanced at Bea, a glint of resigned amusement in his eyes. "See? I told you only an idiot would do this."

42

AFTERNOON, FRIDAY 25 JUNE

Rich let go of Bea's hand. Her eyes were wide with concern. His chest tightened. He couldn't help but feel a pang of guilt for not letting her come, but he had to keep her safe. He gently patted Fraser on the shoulder, then pulled the handle and let himself out of the front passenger door. Closing the door softly, he tried to focus on the job ahead, but his mind raced with thoughts of Bea.

He loved how she threw herself into investigations. Her passion for solving mysteries lit a fire within him. He understood the thirst to prove someone you loved innocent and the need to get justice for someone whose life had been cut short in an untimely act of violence. *Our moral compasses are aligned.* That was so important to him. And she was funny. And smart. She got him. The real him. *But does she love me?* He suppressed a smile; the way her eyes sparkled when he smiled at her seemed to say it all.

And yet, there was always a hint of hesitation in her gaze. She loved him...but. What was the but forcing her to pull back from making their relationship public? Was she ashamed of him? His background was nothing like hers. There were no princes, princesses, dukes, or duchesses in his lineage. *More likely violent Norsemen pillaging and murdering!* But then she'd introduced him to her friends, her son, her family even. *No.* He didn't think it was that.

Was it because of James, her first husband… Did she still have feelings for him? She'd been upset when she'd discovered the secret he'd taken to the grave, but she'd also been happy she'd been right all along about his feelings for her. Content. Relieved. Sad even. But no, he'd not felt it was more than that.

It always seemed to come back to her fear of the relentless press and their unyielding scrutiny. He tried to understand the world she lived in, but he knew he could never truly comprehend the pressures of being a royal. He'd seen glimpses of it when he'd worked at PaIRS, of course, and he could remember the speculation when James had been killed in the car crash with a female passenger beside him. *It must have been awful for her.* But it had been fifteen years ago, and she'd faced it alone. Now she had him. *I'm sure we can handle the press together. But is she?*

"Ready?" Simon's low voice snapped him back to reality as the ex-police officer joined Rich by the side of the car.

Rich nodded. "Let's go." Beneath the silver moonlight, he motioned for Simon to move cautiously, his eyes darting about as they approached the back of the bingo hall. The darkness played tricks on his vision, but the rumble of raised voices was unmistakable. *They're here already?* Had Perry got the time wrong? "Wait," he mouthed to Simon, signalling with his hand for them to stop and watch.

Peering around the corner of the building, he could see two figures under the dim gleam of a flickering light.

Simon leaned in closer, whispering into his ear, "That's

Julian for sure. The one facing us. I can't see the other one clearly."

Rich strained his eyes, trying to discern any features of the second figure, but their back was towards them. They were taller than Julian but only by a few inches. Thinner definitely, even in the dark hoodie they were wearing. *Is it a man or woman? They're just under six foot*, he estimated. His gut told him it was a man. *But then it could be a tall woman...* Rich gave a heavy sigh, willing the second person to turn around.

Julian was standing upright, his chest pushed out slightly, his shoulders firm as he fronted up to the other figure. His voice was raised now, but Rich still couldn't make out what he was saying. The other person appeared more relaxed, their hands flapping in front of them in, Rich assumed, an attempt to get Julian to calm down.

And then, without warning, everything changed. The taller figure's hand shot into their pocket, producing a blunt object that connected with a sickening *thwack* to Julian's skull. Rich's stomach tensed.

Time seemed to slow as Julian crumpled to the ground.

43

A BIT BEFORE, FRIDAY 25 JUNE

B ea peered out the window, her eyes squinting under the dim light of the streetlamp. Rich and Simon were standing in the distance, seemingly rooted to their spot. *Aren't they meant to be out of sight waiting for Julian to arrive?* In the front seat, Fraser flipped the pages of his magazine, seemingly oblivious to the tension brewing in the back. Daisy lay curled up on the floor of the car at Bea's feet, snoring softly.

Perry leaned over her shoulder, his breath tickling her ear as he whispered, "Why are they just standing there and not hiding?"

"Perhaps it's the perfect spot for them to wait?" Bea replied, unsure. *And we should be there too, not relegated to the back seat of the Bentley like the reserve squad.* With a huff, she turned to Perry. "I can't believe they left us in the car."

Perry shrugged. "I'm actually quite grateful. I don't have suitable shoes to run in, and there will no doubt be some running soon."

Bea smirked. "Perry, you never have suitable shoes to run

in," she pointed out, glancing down at Perry's exquisite designer shoes.

"Exactly!" Perry exclaimed, grinning.

As the seconds ticked by, Bea couldn't shake the feeling something was about to happen. She glanced back out of the window, her gaze darting between Rich and Simon. Julian, and possibly Vic's killer, were out there, and all she could do was sit and wait. She sighed as she slumped back in her seat.

Who *was* there with Julian? Her mind raced, trying to put together the pieces of the puzzle. *Rob?* No. He'd had no reason to want Vic dead. *Marco or Liv?* No. They both had alibis. *Bella?* She'd still been away, according to Perry's contact at the Fawstead Inn. But had she come back early just to placate Julian? It was possible. After all, she could have killed Vic, and Julian had found out. But then, there was no indication she'd been involved in the money laundering, and that was what this was all about, wasn't it? She turned to Perry. "I just can't think of who Julian would be meeting at this time of night in such a dodgy place."

"Maybe it's someone we haven't considered yet," Perry suggested, fidgeting with the edge of his waistcoat.

She tipped her head to one side. *What, like a secret woman?* Was Finch right after all, and they'd wasted their time staking out a private liaison?

Her brow furrowed as a new thought struck her. There was one other person who kept coming up in their investigation: Bryan Sinclair. Finch was convinced he was the killer, so logically, ignoring the fact he was dead for the moment, he would be the most obvious person meeting Julian if he was indeed the murderer. *But he* is *dead... Isn't he?*

Bea's fingers flew across her phone screen, frantically searching through her emails. "I need to find the report Rich sent me," she muttered under her breath.

"Report? What report?" Perry asked, clearly startled by Bea's sudden urgency.

"The one about Bryan Sinclair." She glanced up at him. "I have an idea. It's out of the box, but it would explain everything." She resumed her search, then with a triumphant exclamation, she found the report. "Here it is!" she cried over the loud beating of her heart.

"Bea, what on earth are you talking about?" Perry demanded, his eyes wide as he tried to peer over her shoulder at the screen.

Her eyes skimmed the section she wanted. Her heart felt as if it would burst from her chest. *Bingo! Oh my goodness. I might be right...* "Okay, listen," Bea started, her voice trembling with excitement. "I think I know who the killer—"

Before she could finish her sentence, Fraser suddenly sat up straight in his seat. "Mister Richard and Mr Lattimore are on the move, my lady," he announced, his voice tense.

Have they spotted someone arriving early and recognised them?

Perry almost scrambled over her to get to the window. They gawked out just in time to see Rich and Simon disappear around the corner. *Where have they gone?* She cracked the door open a little to see if she could hear anything. The chilly night air whipped her hair around her face. Then there was a shout. *Have the police arrived?* But, no, it sounded like Simon.

"What's going on?" Perry hissed in her ear.

"I don't know." Bea squinted into the darkness. She couldn't hear anything. *Have they caught the murderer?* She opened the door a little wider. *Do they need help?* She turned to ask Perry if they should go and see just as Daisy took advantage of the situation and leapt out of the car, bounding out into the darkness.

"Wait! Daisy!" Bea hissed, but the dog was already a blur of fur and determination. She grabbed Perry. "Come on. We can't let her go alone!"

"I had a horrible feeling you would say that," he murmured as they tumbled out of the car.

"My lady!" Fraser cried in alarm from the front seat. "Don't you think you should—"

"It's fine, Fraser. We won't be long!" Bea called behind her as she and Perry began their pursuit of her little white terrier.

44

BACK OVER HERE, FRIDAY 25 JUNE

Rich's heart raced. Blood pounded in his ears. *What the?* Julian now lay motionless on the ground. *Please don't be dead!*

"Julian!" Simon shouted, the sound ripping through the air as he charged towards the man in a heap on the floor. Rich, feeling the adrenaline pouring into his veins, hared after him, taking out his mobile phone at the same time.

As he dialled the emergency services, his eyes scanned the scene, a sense of dread creeping up his spine. He caught a movement out of the corner of his right eye. The assailant was running. *Should I follow them?* But what about Bea? *Is she safe?*

"Hello. Which emergency service do you require?"

No! Julian had to be their priority. Bea was with Fraser, Perry, and Daisy. *She's fine.* Julian had to be their priority. Rich asked for an ambulance as he arrived by Simon's side. "And your location, sir?"

"Here," Rich said, thrusting the phone in Simon's direction so he could treat Julian with both hands. Simon grabbed the mobile without hesitation, barking out their location to the operator. His usual casual demeanour had vanished, replaced by a fierce yet calm efficiency. Rich looked down at where a pool of something dark was spreading on the floor. He immediately unbuttoned his shirt and removed it. The cool air made the tiny hairs on his arms stand up. *Just as well I have a T-shirt on too,* he thought as he wadded the shirt up, then dropping to the floor, he gently moved Julian's head. *A brick!* He'd landed on a brick. No wonder there was so much blood on the floor.

Rich quickly shoved it to one side and pressed the shirt firmly against the gash on the back of Julian's head. A further cut was bleeding on the side of his forehead where a large lump had appeared. Rich groped for a sleeve that had fallen out of the bundle he was holding under Julian's head. He held it onto the cut. With both hands putting pressure on the wounds, his mind turned back to Julian's attacker. There was no sign of them. *They'll be long gone by now...*

———

A few streets away, Bea's heart pounded in her chest as she sprinted after Daisy, who had darted around the car and across the street. Their footsteps were muffled by the grass as they ran across a verge. The only noise she could hear were the *ahs* and *ouches* coming from Perry right behind her.

"Ugh, my feet," he moaned between pants. "Why do you always make me run?"

"It's just pain, Perry!" Bea threw back at him, her focus locked on Daisy, who was now rounding the corner ahead of them.

"That's easy for you to say in those ugly trainers," he cried back.

She grinned.

"So who do you think the murderer is?" he wheezed.

"I'm pretty sure it's Bryan Sinclair," Bea called back over her shoulder, her breaths coming out ragged.

"But he's de—"

Suddenly, ahead of them, a hooded figure darted out from an alleyway going full pelt towards a dark car parked on the other side of the road. "Perry, look!" Bea hissed behind her. *Is it the murderer?* She found a sudden burst of energy and lurched forward. But it was too late. *Rats! They're getting away.* Sweat trickled down her temples as she skidded to a halt, her chest heaving. She squinted ahead as the figure slipped into the car and sped away. "No!" Frustration clouded her voice.

She bent slightly, her hands on her hips as she calmed her breathing. Had that been Bryan Sinclair? And how on earth would they ever prove it now?

She turned. Perry had stopped too and was leaning against a lamppost, panting, the fingers of one hand in the back of one of his shoes. In his other hand, he held his phone, the screen lit up, revealing a still of the back of a car disappearing behind a corner.

Her stomach lightened. *Did he…?*

She jogged back to join Perry. "Did you get photos?" she asked Perry hopefully. He grinned, nodding. "Better than that. I was videoing it. I'm pretty sure I got the number plate." His voice was a mixture of pride and pain.

"Good thinking. Sorry I made you run," she said, reaching out and patting him on the arm. "Are you all right?"

"I'll live," he said, tutting. "I just hope these shoes aren't ruined." He put his foot back on the floor just as a car came into view.

Fraser? "Well it looks like you won't have to walk anymore, let alone run," she said as the Bentley drew up beside them. The passenger window glided down, and Fraser's worried face peered out.

"Hello, Fraser. What are you doing here?"

"Mr Juke, my lady. I thought you might need some help."

Bea smiled. "Well, thank you, Fraser." She grabbed Perry's arm. "Come on, Hop-along. Let's go back and find out what's happened to the others." She looked around. *Oh no!* "Hold on. Where's Daisy?" Her heart lurched in her chest as she rapidly scanned their surroundings, her eyes darting between the shadows cast by the streetlights. "Daisy? Where are you?"

———

Rich knelt beside Julian's unconscious form, his fingers trembling slightly as he pressed his balled-up shirt to the man's bleeding head wound, having successfully stemmed the other smaller bleeding at his temple. Daisy suddenly appeared at his side, her eyes wide and alert. "Daisy? Where did you…?" Rich stammered, his thoughts racing. He looked around wildly. *Where's Bea?* She should be with Daisy. He glanced over at Simon, who was still on the phone as he monitored Julian's breathing. *Where are the paramedics?*

As if on cue, red and blue flashing lights illuminated the night, casting eerie shadows all around him. "Thank goodness," he muttered under his breath, the pounding in his chest relenting for a moment. Daisy whined and softly nuzzled his hand. Was Bea okay, or did she need him? The pounding started again.

A vehicle screeched to a halt not far away. Rich heard Simon tell the person on the other end, "They're here." Doors banged. The sound of running footsteps echoed around the dark alley. *Be quick. I need to get to Bea!*

45

A FEW MINUTES LATER, FRIDAY
25 JUNE

The red and blue lights danced violently in Bea's vision, sending waves of panic coursing through her veins. *Rich! Daisy! Simon!* Her heart pounded like a bass drum. She grabbed Perry's arm just as he was about to get into the back of the car and motioned frantically. "Come on. This way!"

She sprinted towards the open alley, her breath coming out in short, ragged bursts. She could hear Perry protesting behind her, but she ignored him. *Please let them be okay.*

She reached the entrance to the alley and skidded to a stop, her eyes widening as she peered into the dimly lit space.

"Oh no," she choked out, her heart in her mouth. She stared at the crumpled figure sprawled on the concrete. The body was obscured by moving shadows, making it impossible for her to discern any identifying features. Her chest tightened as she fought back the urge to scream. *Rich!*

"Who is it?" Perry breathed heavily beside her, his own blue eyes filled with fear. They exchanged a look of dread. Then Perry limped past her, his voice strained with urgency. "Simon!" he yelled as he surged towards the body.

Bea squinted into the darkness, trying to make sense of

the scene before her. Then she began to run. As she got closer and overtook Perry, she could make out a figure in green hunched over the body on the ground as another person slowly rose to their feet. It was Simon. Perry let out a yelp behind her.

But where's Rich? Her heart still hammering in her chest, she carried on running. *Is that him on the floor? And where's Daisy?*

As if summoned by her thoughts, Daisy emerged from the shadows, her tail wagging wildly. Following close behind was a familiar figure, tall and broad-shouldered. Relief washed over Bea like a tidal wave, and the knot in her stomach loosened. *They're safe.*

"Rich!" she exclaimed, sprinting towards him. She wanted to throw her arms around him. And then she wanted him to hold her and never let her go again. *But there are strangers around and...* She slowed down, and their eyes met, relief mirrored in both their gazes.

"Hey, you," Bea said, not taking her eyes from his.

"Hey, trouble," he replied.

"I was worried about—" they said simultaneously, then laughed.

"Are you okay?" he asked

She dipped her chin and gave a half smile. Then she looked over to where another paramedic had joined the first one. "Julian?"

He nodded.

"Will he be all right?"

Rich's expression was sombre. "It's touch and go."

"Did you see who it was?"

He shook his head. "No. They fled."

"We saw them," she said. "They got in a car. Perry has some of it on video." She shrugged. "It might help."

The sound of a police car arriving added to the general hubbub. She glanced over and recognised CID Steve as he hurried towards Simon and Perry.

Returning her attention back to Rich, she noticed for the first time he was missing his shirt. *What happened?* Then she saw his T-shirt had red patches on it. Her legs went weak. She staggered closer, reaching her hand out towards him. "Are you hurt?"

He looked confused for a second, then glanced down at where her hand hovered a few inches away from his chest. "No." He shook his head. "I'm fine. I took my shirt off to try to stem the blood. Julian landed on the corner of a brick. I must have got..." He trailed off. Their eyes locked as he took her outstretched hand. His hand was warm as he wrapped it around hers. The heat spread from his touch and took over her whole body. Her shoulders dropped, and she sighed. *I could stay like this for—*

The wail of an ambulance siren pierced the air, cutting through their moment. They turned and watched as two more paramedics rushed into the alley, pushing a trolley, then expertly manoeuvred Julian onto a stretcher. CID Steve stood nearby, then accompanied them to the ambulance.

"I wonder if Julian will remember who attacked him," Bea said softly. *Will he confirm it was Bryan?*

"Hopefully," Rich responded as he gently dropped her hand.

46

MEANWHILE WITH THE KILLER, FRIDAY 25 JUNE

The door to the flat slammed shut behind me with a satisfying thud that echoed through the dimly lit hallway. Leaning against the door, my heart pounding in my chest like a jackhammer, my arms and legs tingling. I took a deep breath in, then slowly let it out. My mind was a whirlpool of questions. Who were the two men who'd appeared from nowhere? Passersby, maybe, who'd heard Julian shouting? I clenched my teeth. I'd tried so hard to calm Julian down. But the man had panicked and become unreasonable. Yet again, I'd been forced to do something I'd not wanted to do because of someone else's poor choices. I took another deep breath. It was done now.

Okay. Now I need a plan.

I glanced down at my clothes. Although I'd worn gloves and used a cosh, there could still be traces of blood on my sweatshirt, joggers, or even the gloves themselves. Just as well I'd had the foresight to take the weapon and gloves with me. I hadn't wanted to use them, of course. *This is all Julian's fault!*

"Another idiot," I whispered, grinding my teeth. I was so

close to getting away with it all! *The investigation is closed, for goodness' sake!* I smirked. The late Bryan Sinclair was conveniently taking the blame for Vic's murder. Everyone was content with the outcome.

Was Julian still alive? Would he be able to talk and identify me as his attacker? Would anyone believe him? I shook my head. It would seem so fantastical to anyone else. But then, I couldn't afford to take the risk. *What's most important right now is covering my tracks and figuring out how badly Julian is hurt.*

"Stupid man!" I muttered as I stripped off my outer clothes and made my way along the hall and into the kitchen. I hurriedly shoved the soiled clothes into a bag. *I'll get rid of it later.* I threw it in the cupboard under the sink and slammed the door shut. There were bigger priorities right now.

Five minutes later, washed, scrubbed, and dressed in fresh clothes, I sat down at my laptop and began typing. Time was of the essence. Could Julian talk? Depending on that information, I would need to decide if to fleeing or finishing what I'd started.

I'll do whatever it takes to protect myself. I'm not going to jail, that's for sure. A shiver ran down my spine. Someone like me wouldn't last five minutes in prison.

47

BACK OVER HERE, FRIDAY 25 JUNE

Bea stood apart from the others, Daisy by her feet, her eyes locked onto the spot in the alley where Julian had been attacked. Blood stained the gravelled area. A chill travelled down her spine. *He didn't deserve this…*

To her left, Rich was deep in conversation with Perry and Simon. Perry was explaining something passionately to them, his hands animatedly punctuating his words. Bea overheard Perry mention Bryan Sinclair's name. *He's telling them my theory.*

She looked away and winced at the throbbing pain in her temple. Had Bryan really come back from the dead to tie up loose ends? Did it make sense that he would?

They were sure, at least, that he'd been cooking the books at the restaurant, perhaps some or even all of Julian's other businesses too. It was even possible he'd been the mastermind behind the whole thing. Had he got wind that Vic's remains had been found, so he'd come out of hiding to…do what? This was where she was stuck. Why would he risk it all to come back? He was dead as far as everyone knew. A dead man couldn't be prosecuted for murder. What would he care even if the police named him as Vic's killer?

She raised a hand and scratched at the back of her head. Unless, of course, it wasn't about Vic's death... If the authorities found out about the money laundering, could they seize his wife's assets? Did he care about her that much? Or was she in on it too? Could she be the other accomplice, allowing him to have killed Vic on Friday?

Bea looked down, intending to pick Daisy up. *Where is she?*

She heard sniffing coming from near the wall to their left. She moved over to where her little dog had her face buried in a pile of rubbish. "Daisy!" Goodness knows what was down there.

Bea bent down and swooped the terrier into her arms. As she did so, she got a whiff of a familiar smell. *Isn't that...* She spotted it — a small, discarded vape cartridge nestled in the detritus. Bea's heart skipped a beat. A gnawing uncertainty crept into her mind, casting doubt on everything she thought she knew. *This changes everything...*

48

STILL OVER HERE, FRIDAY 25 JUNE

"Bea!" Simon called, beckoning her over to join him, Perry, and Rich huddle together by a graffiti-covered wall to the side of her.

Startled, she adjusted Daisy in her arms, then stood up. She moved slowly to join them, unsure if she wanted to have this conversation or not, now lacking the conviction she'd got it right about Bryan.

She stopped when she reached Rich's side and lowered Daisy to the ground. She took a deep breath as she straightened, the chilly air filling her lungs.

"Perry mentioned your theory about Bryan Sinclair possibly being the one who did this to Julian," Simon said, his brown eyes shining. "Rich says it's true his body was never found. I think you're onto something." He tilted his head towards where CID Steve was standing on the other side of the alley, talking to a uniformed police officer. "We need to tell Steve right away."

Bea's stomach dropped. *Really? But now I'm not so sure—*

"Exactly!" Perry chimed in, his blue eyes filled with determination. "Sinclair could be making plans to flee the country as we speak!"

As Perry and Simon set off to get CID Steve, Bea sighed. *I just hope I'm not leading us further from the truth.*

A gust of wind tousled her hair. As she turned her head to tuck a stray wisp behind her ear she caught Rich's gaze. As they looked at each other, a silent understanding passed between them.

"It's not Bryan, is it?" he asked softly, his gaze steady on hers.

She shook her head. "No, I don't think it is," she admitted, her voice barely above a whisper. "I think I know who killed Vic. It's even more out there than Bryan coming back from the dead."

Just then CID Steve approached, a determined expression on his face. "Your theory about it being Bryan Sinclair is an interesting one, my lady," he said. "We'll get on it right away."

"Wait," Bea interjected, her heart racing. *Come on, Bea. Tell him.* What was the worst that could happen? *You'll look like a fool.*

She glanced at Rich. His eyes crinkled, and he winked. *But he'll still be here.* "I'm sorry, Steve, but I think I got it wrong."

Steve raised an eyebrow. "Oh? What do you mean?"

"About Bryan," she stammered. "I've been thinking, and I don't believe he would come out of hiding if he was still alive. I don't think he's the one responsible for all this."

Simon stared at her. Perry's mouth fell open.

"But—"

"But you think you know who it is?" Steve interrupted.

She dipped her chin.

"All right," Steve said, his tone serious. "Let's hear your new theory then."

"Indeed," she said, her voice steady and resolute. "Here's what I think…"

49

MEANWHILE BACK WITH THE KILLER, FRIDAY 25 JUNE

Squinting against the brightness of my laptop screen as I flipped it open in the dimly lit flat I scanned the report. *Okay, so Julian's still alive.* I curse under my breath, then carried on scrolling. *Fifty-fifty chance of survival. Good. He's unconscious, and they'll keep him in a coma until the swelling on his brain reduces.* Luck is on my side. I still had time to do something about it.

Slamming the laptop closed, I walked through in my head what I needed to do to kill Julian at the hospital. I inhaled deep on my electronic cigarette and let the smoke slowly out of my nose. *Okay!* Access wouldn't be a problem, but what about method? I looked over to the kitchen sink where the cosh was soaking in bleach. *No. I need something subtle. Something that will look like a natural death. Um… A pillow will do the trick — readily available, simple, and yet effective.* I just needed to figure out how I could be alone with him, timing it perfectly to avoid any unwanted attention. I'd only need, what, five minutes max? I sighed deeply. *I'll have to work that out when I get there. I'll have time.*

My heart was racing. Can I really do this? *But I have to.* I can't go to prison. *I won't stand a chance in there!*

I balled my fist and thumped it on the table. *I can do this!* Dropping my vape pen back on the table, I quickly typed out a message on my phone. I hit send, knowing every second counted.

Rising, I took a deep calming breath and slowly let it out. *Have I covered everything?* My confidence felt like it was draining away with every beat of my heart. What if things went south? I needed to be ready to run...

I hurried to the bedroom. *Better safe than sorry.* Quickly grabbing my overnight bag, I stuffed a change of clothes and some essentials in it. That would have to do for now. *Just in case...*

What's that? I rushed back into the living room at the unmistakable sound of a car pulling up outside. That was quick! Swiping my vape off the table, I rushed into the hall where I snatched my jacket from the coatrack. With a last deep breath, I gripped the bag's handle and flung open the door.

The light sensor flicked on, casting a wide beam of light on the path ahead. *Is that my driver?* My stomach plummeted to the floor. I was staring into the steely-grey eyes of a man blocking my way.

My gaze darted from the man's stubbled jaw highlighted in the artificial light to the car idling behind him by the side of the road where two uniformed officers stood, their arms folded over their chests. *What's going on?*

My chest tightened. I looked back at the man. The cold glint in his eyes sent a shiver up my spine. Then a smirk crossed his face.

Oh no! No. This can't be it. Not now. Not when I'm so

close. No... A wave of nausea rose in my throat as he opened his mouth.

"Albert Finch," Detective Inspector Steve Cox said, his voice barely above a whisper, yet carrying a weight that left me in no doubt about what he was going to say next. "I'm arresting you..."

50

LATER THAT SAME EVENING, FRIDAY 25 JUNE

The Bentley came to a gentle halt in front of The Dower House. Bea let out a sigh of relief as she looked at the familiar façade, its warm lights spilling out onto the sweeping driveway. *It's good to be home*, she thought as the weight of the evening finally lifted.

She, Perry, and Simon clambered out from the back, their footsteps crunching on the gravel as they straightened up. "Thanks, Fraser," Rich called as he stepped out of the front of the car, a fidgeting Daisy in his arms. He gently dropped her on the ground as he moved to join Bea.

A sudden wave of exhaustion washed over her as they walked towards the house. She knew it was partly because of the adrenaline leaving her system. Rich casually draped his arm around her shoulders as they approached the front door. She snuggled into his side. *This is nice…*

"I'm done in," Perry remarked, limping towards the front door as Daisy dashed ahead, her tail wagging eagerly.

"Indeed," Bea said, her voice weary. The door opened, and Mrs Fraser appeared in the doorway, her eyes twinkling with warmth. "Come on in. It's cold out there." She waved them in. "I thought you might need something after your…er, adventure," she said, glancing pointedly at Perry. "I've got hot drinks and crumpets laid out in the drawing room for you and some broth and chicken for Daisy."

Perfect. "Thank you, Mrs Fraser," Bea replied, touched by her thoughtfulness.

"Mrs Fraser, you're an angel," Perry said, grinning as he and Simon followed the housekeeper towards the drawing room.

As Bea walked through the hallway, it all felt comforting and familiar to her. It suddenly struck her how much this house truly felt like home now. And watching Rich talking animatedly to Mrs Fraser ahead of her, thanking her for having stayed up so late to greet them, Bea's heart swelled in her chest. Rich being here had a lot to do with making The Dower House a home.

As they entered the drawing room, the smell of warm crumpets and hot chocolate wafted through the room, making Bea's mouth water. She headed for the sideboard where Mrs Fraser poured her a drink while she added a couple of crumpets dripping with butter onto a plate. As Bea walked away to sit on the sofa with Rich, Mrs Fraser placed a bowl in front of Daisy and patted her on the head.

"So what made you think it was Finch, Bea?" Simon asked through a mouthful of food.

She took a sip of her chocolatey drink, then put her cup on the large coffee table between them. "It was the vape that made me think of him initially. I recognised the smell of cherries." Perry went to open his mouth, but she held up a hand. "I know. Lots of people vape, and anyone could have left it there. Finch can't be the only person in Windstanton that uses that particular flavour. But —" She turned and smiled at Rich. "We don't like coincidences, do we?"

He grinned back. "No, we don't."

"And then it hit me," she continued. "What a brilliant plan it would be to pin everything on a dead man and close the case."

Perry raised his eyebrows. "But what about Julian? How did he fit in?"

Bea shrugged. "I don't quite know. Maybe he was also involved in the money laundering with Finch and Bryan, and Finch had to shut him up. A loose end, as it were."

"So you think Finch was part of it all?" Perry asked, then took a huge bite of crumpet, the butter bursting over the top and running down his fingers.

"Windstanton was Finch's patch back in the day," Simon chimed in. "He could have been involved in covering up the money laundering. He could even have masterminded the whole thing. After all, who would suspect a respected senior police officer?" He shook his head vehemently. "I don't want to believe we had a bent copper in our midst, but it fits with everything we know."

Perry wiped his mouth and hands with a napkin, placed his plate on the table, then leaned back in his armchair. "Think about how easy it would have been for Finch to get Vic to let him in on that Friday evening."

Bea took another sip of her hot chocolate. She stifled a yawn. *I need my bed.*

"You know," Perry mused, his eyes narrowing. "Finch must have been thrilled when he'd heard about Bryan's death. He had the perfect scapegoat ready and waiting."

Bea winced at the thought. But Perry was right. It had been serendipitous for Finch.

"So Julian was the only thorn in his side," Rich said, rubbing his chin. "It's fortunate he said Finch's name to Steve before losing consciousness again," he added. "That, combined with your theory, Bea, was his downfall."

Simon nodded. "Steve told me he initially thought Julian was trying to tell him to let Finch know what had happened," Simon admitted, his eyebrows raised. "But then Daisy found the used vape cartridge, and as you say, Bea's idea tied everything together." He started slightly as his phone buzzed. "It's from Steve," he told them as he skimmed the text. He looked up at a sea of expectant faces. "So they've arrested Finch and taken him to the station. But he's refusing to talk without a lawyer," he said with a sigh. "They won't get anything more out of him tonight."

The room fell silent for a moment as they absorbed the news. Then Simon said, "Without sufficient evidence or Julian's testimony, they might find it hard to make a murder charge stick."

"What about the vape cartridge?" Bea asked as she clenched her mug. Surely their efforts wouldn't have been in vain?

"It's possible. If it has his DNA on it, that will place him at the scene where Julian was attacked," Simon told her. "As will Perry's video. But none of it links him to Vic's death."

Bea's heart plummeted to her feet. *Will Finch get away with murder?* Rich reached over and patted her arm. "There's a chance Julian will regain consciousness," he said. "It's early days yet."

Perry stretched out his long legs and let out a yawn. "I don't know about you lot, but I'm exhausted. It's been a long day. Let's see what tomorrow brings." He stood up, pulling Simon to his feet with him.

Bea hugged them both while Daisy danced around at their feet. Rich offered to see them out as Daisy jumped up onto the sofa and curled up next to Bea.

She was stroking the little terrier's head and staring at the table when Rich returned a few minutes later. His voice broke into her trance as he collapsed on the other side of her. "You did an amazing job today. I'm really proud of you."

She turned to meet his smile. Her heart did a little jig. "Thank you," she said, placing her hand on his knee. She looked up into his brown eyes. "He won't get away with it, will he, Rich?"

"Steve and his team know what they're doing," Rich replied, his hand covering hers with a warm, comforting touch. "Now," he said, taking her hand in his. "How about we try to get some sleep? It's been a busy day."

"Indeed," Bea said, stifling a yawn. They rose as one, his hand still holding hers tightly. Daisy lept off the sofa and landed beside them. *If we're lucky, Julian will pull through and answer all our questions.*

51

EARLY LUNCHTIME, SATURDAY
26 JUNE

By the open French doors of Rose Cottage, Daisy was curled up in her favourite chair fast asleep, her surprising lack of interest in food just going to show how tired she was from their adventures the previous night. Hunched over the wooden dining table, laden with cold cuts, salad, and fresh bread, Bea distractedly pushed a cherry tomato around her plate with her finger. *What happens now?* The excitement of last night had worn off, leaving one question lodged in her mind. Was there enough evidence to charge Finch? She pinched her lips together. *If he gets away with it, then—*

"Bea? Hello?" Perry's voice cut through her catastrophising. She looked over at her best friend. "I said, are you excited about Sam's prize giving later?" he asked her, placing a thick slice of cheese on a piece of sourdough and smearing it with sweet onion chutney.

Bea took a deep breath. *Stop worrying about something you can't control.* She smiled to herself. *Ah, Sam.* She couldn't wait to see him later. "Absolutely," she replied, her eyes sparkling. "He's worked so hard all year, and I can't wait to see him receive his MVP award for cricket." James would have been so proud that his son had made the first team for cricket. *He's following in his father's footsteps.*

"It will be good to have him back for the summer," Simon said, taking a bite of his salmon quiche. Simon and Sam had bonded over their love of food. She knew Sam couldn't wait to hang out at SaltAir with him and Ryan. *He'll be in heaven!*

"Indeed. And hopefully he'll have time to really settle into The Dower House now." She recalled how excited her son had been to be allocated his own set of rooms on the first floor over the other side of the house from her. She'd left him to liaise with Perry about what style he wanted, and now that was complete, she was pleased her business partner had compromised with her son enough that it looked tasteful and stylish, not just functional and all painted dark blue, which would have been Sam's preference. He would now get to enjoy some time in his new space without the pressure of studying.

Bea checked her watch. She'd need to leave in the next forty minutes so she would have time to get back to the house, get changed, and be ready for Fraser to drive her to Wilton College. She popped the tomato in her mouth. *I can't wait to see Sam, so why do I feel so…so flat?* Next to her, Rich leaned over to grab a slice of ham from the middle of the table. His arm brushed hers. A tingle went down her spine. She turned her head, and their eyes met. He winked. She grinned.

You! He was the problem. Going to get Sam meant leaving Rich. And she didn't want to. She looked back at her plate as heat prickled in her cheeks. They'd spent so much time together over the last week that just the thought of not being with him filled her with an emptiness she'd never felt before.

She stifled a groan. *Come on, Bea. Get a grip!* She'd be back later this evening. *It's only a few hours. Surely you can live without him for that long?* Of course she could. It was more than that. *He should be coming with me.* Her stomach hardened. *But the press will be there.* Her presence at Wilton, combined with that of several celebrity parents, guaranteed the paparazzi would be out in full force this afternoon. Her hands felt clammy, and she rubbed them together. *If only...*

The sound of footsteps crunching on gravel caught her attention. She glanced towards the garden gate and saw the stocky figure of CID Steve striding purposefully towards them.

"Steve, mate," Simon called out, waving his hand at his friend. "You're just in time for lunch."

"Really?" Steve replied, feigning innocence as he stepped onto the patio and in through the French doors. Daisy raised her head, then returned it to the cushion and closed her eyes again. "That's handy." Steve grinned as he joined them at the table. He pulled out a chair and plonked himself down, sighing. "I was passing by after checking on how the search of Finch's flat was going and thought I'd drop in to give you an update. But now you mention it, I wouldn't say no to a sandwich."

"Shocker," Simon said with a grin, passing him a plate. "Help yourself." He poured him a glass of water.

"Thanks, mucker." Steve grabbed some cheese and bread and made himself a sandwich. *He looks tired,* Bea thought as he took a bite of food. A serious expression settled on his face as he chewed. *Is it bad news?*

"Any fresh developments?" she asked, unable to hide her curiosity.

"Actually, yes," Steve said, placing his half-eaten sand-

wich on the plate in front of him. "Julian regained consciousness early this morning."

"Really?" Perry's eyes widened. "That's great news!"

"Yes. It was quicker than we'd expected," Steve said,
looking from Rich to Simon and back. "And it's thanks to
your quick thinking and ability to stop the bleeding that he
survived according to the doctor. You two did an incredible
job."

Bea reached under the table and squeezed Rich's hand,
her heart swelling with pride. He held on to it as she asked,
"So has he told you what happened? Was it Finch?"

She held her breath while Steve took a sip of water. The
room was filled with an electric anticipation that prickled the
skin on the back of her neck.

"Julian was obviously tired, and the doctor wasn't keen
for us to interview him yet, but Julian insisted he wanted to
tell us everything."

And? Was it Finch? She fidgeted in her chair, then leaned
forward.

"He confirmed it was Finch who he met last night and
who attacked him."

Bea let out her breath with a whoosh. *They had him!*

"Yay!" Perry mumbled under his breath.

"Julian admitted to taking bribes in exchange for using his
position on the Windstanton Rejuvenation Council to award
contracts to certain building contractors and material suppliers," Steve continued. "He was also running a drug operation
in town — mainly dealing in weed and cocaine."

Bea shook her head. No wonder he'd been so worried
when they'd found out about the money laundering.

"And Finch knew about all this?" Simon asked, his
eyebrows raised in disbelief.

"I'm afraid so," Steve replied. "He turned a blind eye to it all for a cut of the money. Bryan was in on it too. Apparently, it was his idea to use Julian's businesses to launder the money."

Bea couldn't help but feel a little smug at having guessed right about Finch's involvement.

"Anyway, according to Julian, Vic started asking questions about the financial records of the restaurant," Steve said before taking a bite of his sandwich.

"Wait," Perry interjected, holding up a hand. "I've been thinking about this. I have a theory about why Vic would've been interested in the first place."

Bea gave him an encouraging smile from across the table.

"We know Vic was planning to jump ship and open his own restaurant with Rob," Perry said slowly. "So it makes sense he'd want to know how things worked financially with a restaurant. You know, what his expected sales and costs would be."

Bea raised an eyebrow, smiling. *Good job, Perry!*

"Good thinking!" Rich chimed in, nodding in agreement. "He must have been surprised to see how high the costs were and started asking questions."

"I think that's a likely scenario, Perry," Steve said, nodding at him. "So Bryan was getting increasingly nervous, and he informed Julian about Vic's interest. Not long after, Vic asked to meet with Julian. It was the Thursday before he died." He took another bite of his sandwich, seemingly unfazed by the others staring at him in anticipation.

Bea shifted in her chair. *Come on, Steve. Get on with it.* Rich squeezed her hand. *I know he needs to eat, but really!* She took a deep breath.

Steve wiped his mouth on a napkin. "I needed that!" He took a sip of water. Perry coughed. "Right. Well, Vic told Julian he'd been looking at the books and noticed some discrepancies. There were temporary staff whose names he didn't recognise and suppliers he hadn't ordered from. He told Julian he thought Bryan was cooking the books and suggested he should report everything to the police."

Bea's heart skipped a beat. *Poor Vic. Little did he know that at that moment, he'd signed his own death warrant.*

"Julian promised Vic he would handle it," Steve went on. "Then he arranged to meet Finch and Bryan. They met behind the bingo hall just like last night." Steve raised an eyebrow.

So that had been their meeting place.

Steve continued, "Finch advised both Julian and Bryan to leave town for a while and let him deal with the situation. So Julian left for his holiday the next day, and Bryan flew to Spain shortly after. Julian said when he returned and found the email from Vic, he assumed Finch had paid him off to keep quiet and disappear."

"But in reality, Finch had killed him," Bea said, her voice trembling slightly, still shocked that the man who'd been investigating Vic's case had been the one responsible for his death all along.

"Exactly," Steve confirmed, nodding. "Julian says he read the last line in Vic's email and took that as him saying he had no choice but to accept Finch's bribe."

Bea remembered that last line. *'I had no choice but to act on this.'* She could see why it would make sense to Julian, but now they knew the truth: had it really been Finch's way of apologising for what he'd done?

Rich dropped Bea's hand as he reached over and poured himself a coffee from the pot on the table. "Do we know how Finch disposed of Vic's body?"

Steve shook his head. "Julian doesn't know, and Finch is refusing to say anything at the moment. His lawyer's with him now. I'm due to interview him again later today." A smile of satisfaction crossed Steve's face.

Rich's brow furrowed, then he said, "When Finch came to tell us the case was closed, we asked him how Bryan had disposed of Vic's body. He told us his theory of what Bryan had done. Was he actually describing what he himself had done?"

Brilliant!

"It's possible," Steve huffed. "Finch *is* that cocky."

Simon smirked. "Too right! And didn't you say he renovated his marital home?" Steve nodded. "So he has the skills to redo the wall."

Perfect!

"Did Julian explain why he didn't reopen the restaurant after Vic left? We thought it might be because he knew Vic was in the wall, but if he didn't…" Simon trailed off, stroking his beard.

"Actually, he did say something about that," Steve replied. "He said Finch, with Bryan's support, convinced him that he needed to close the restaurant to bury the money laundering history. They were concerned that a new chef would ask too many questions."

Ah. That makes sense…

"And of course that way the body could rot in an empty restaurant," Rich said to Simon.

"Will Finch talk, do you think?" Simon asked his friend.

Steve shrugged. "We have evidence mounting up against him. From Perry's video, we've been able to confirm it was Finch and his car. We found clothes in a bag with blood on them when we searched his flat. Hopefully, it will match Julian's."

"So you can at least make the assault charge stick?" Rich said.

"We can," Steve agreed. "And we have Julian's statement, so we can prove motive—"

"But no evidence he actually killed Vic?" Simon said, clenching his jaw.

"Well…" Steve hesitated. "We have a couple of things that might help. We found a cosh we believe was used to assault Julian. It could also be the original murder weapon that killed Vic. It would fit with the postmortem description of the wound."

That's brilliant! If—

"But it's been washed in bleach, so it's unlikely to hold either Julian's or Vic's DNA."

Oh…

Just then, Rich's phone rang. Bea glanced over at the screen. The name Elise flashed up. Rich sprung up, grabbing his phone at the same time. He lightly rested his hand on Bea's shoulder as he said, "Excuse me. I need to take this," then stepped out through the French doors. Daisy opened an eye, then seeing Rich, she jumped down and trotted outside after him. Bea's tummy turned. *I hope everything's all right.*

"We're also reviewing the investigation Finch did into Vic's death. We hope to show how Finch was set on making Bryan the scapegoat." Steve rose from his seat. "I really should get going. I'll keep you all updated."

"Good luck with interviewing Finch. When he knows Julian has confessed to everything and you have enough evidence to charge him with assault, perhaps he'll give up the ghost and come clean," Simon said as he rose too.

As Simon saw Steve out, Bea's gaze shot to the garden where Rich had come back into sight, Daisy stopping to sit by his legs. He ran his free hand through his hair as he shook his head.

Oh no, this doesn't look good.

52

A SHORT WHILE LATER, SATURDAY 26 JUNE

The rattling of dishes and glasses punctuated the silence as Simon stacked the used ones in the dishwasher, and Perry fiddled with the coffee machine. Seconds later, the bitter aroma of dark-roasted coffee beans wafted across the room to Bea, who was still sitting at the table, her chin resting in her hand as she watched Rich pace up and down outside the French doors. *What does Rich's sister want?* Bea could tell it was serious. Normally, he and Elise laughed a lot during their conversations.

The French doors creaked slightly as Rich re-entered the room, Daisy stuck to his side like a plaster. Bea was struck by the way his face seemed to have aged in the few minutes he'd been outside. She knew that look; something was definitely wrong.

"Rich?" she asked softly as he came to join her at the table. "Is everything all right?"

He hesitated before answering, the lines on his forehead deepening. "Not exactly," he murmured.

Oh my goodness, what is it? Is Elise ill? Or her husband,

Rhys? Or one of Rich's nephews? Her stomach fell. *Or his mother?*

He rubbed the back of his neck as he sat down beside her. A second later, Daisy jumped up on his lap and sat down, her back resting on his chest.

"That was Elise," he said, swallowing hard. "Desperate Dougie died an hour ago."

Bea instinctively reached out to clasp his hand. *His poor mother.* "I'm so sorry, Rich," she whispered. Her heart ached as she watched his features twist with concern.

Perry and Simon appeared, cradling steaming mugs of coffee in their hands. "We're sorry to hear that, Rich," Simon said, a genuine note of sympathy in his voice. "Here, this might help," he said softly, handing a mug to Rich while Perry gave another to Bea. She took it in one hand, not wanting to let go of Rich.

"This is your mother's partner, who you call Double D?" Perry asked as he and Simon took seats opposite them.

"Yeah." Rich took a slow sip of his coffee. "Desperate Dougie isn't much of a loss to the world, to be honest. But Mum… Well, she's devastated."

Of course she is. Despite what Elise and Rich thought of the man, their mother had been with him for over sixteen years. Bea, having been through losing a partner herself, knew Rich's mum would feel rudderless right now.

"I had no idea he was *that* ill." He shook his head slowly, then took another sip of coffee. "Elise is on her way to be with Mum now," he continued. "She'll try to convince her to come back and stay at her place for a break before the funeral. If not, I'll go up tomorrow to see what I can do." Rich paused, then added, "*And* I need to make sure none of Double D's family tries to take anything from the house. It belongs to Mum, but I doubt it will stop them."

Bea squeezed his hand tighter, wishing she could take some of the burden from him. Her phone vibrated in front of her. A reminder flashed up. She needed to go. She couldn't be late for Sam. *But how can I leave Rich like this?* She bit her lip, feeling the pressure of her family's circumstances bearing down on her. It wasn't fair to Rich. It wasn't fair to her either.

She let out a slow breath, leaning into Rich's arm. *I won't have to if Rich came with me...* They were supposed to be a team, weren't they? Facing life's challenges together. Wasn't that what Perry and Simon had? *Yet, there's this invisible barrier separating us.*

Daisy leaned over and licked Bea's nose. She started backwards at the unexpected gesture, but Rich pulled her closer, a deep chuckle coming from his throat. Their eyes met. She looked into his deep-brown eyes and felt as if she was floating. *Is it me? Have I created the barrier because of my fear of the press and what they will say? I love him, so what am I so afraid of?* But did he love her? A slow smile spread across his face. She could hear Perry's voice in her head. *"Of course he loves you, you idiot!"* She smiled back. *Of course he does...*

"Give this—give Rich, everything you've got." Her sister's words echoed in her mind, followed by her mother's promise. *"When you're ready, we'll orchestrate Richard's debut into the public eye."*

Is now the right time? Should she finally take a leap of faith and let the world see them as they truly were — a couple, united and strong?

Bea's heart swelled with determination as she held his gaze. "I need to get back to get ready for Sam's prize giving, but can we talk?" she asked softly.

"Of course," he replied, curiosity etched on his face.

"Let's walk back to Francis Court now. We can talk on the way."

She let go of his hand while he gently lifted Daisy off his lap and stood. Grabbing her phone, Bea rose too. "Sorry," she said to Simon and Perry. "But we have to—" The phone vibrated in her hand. She looked down at the message.

Fred: *"Where are you? I have some news…"*

Bea's stomach flipped. *No more bad news, please…* She quickly replied, informing him that they were on their way back to The Dower House.

"Is something up?" Rich asked as he took her hand, and they headed to the door.

"Fred has news," Bea explained. "I'm not sure what yet."

Beep! She looked behind her as Perry picked up his phone. "It's Ellie," he told Simon. "Oh, she has news."

53

EARLY MORNING, SUNDAY 27 JUNE

T*he Society Page* online article:

Francis Court has confirmed Lord Frederick Astley, the Earl of Tilling and future Duke of Arnwall, and Summer York are engaged to be married.

'Charles, Duke of Arnwall, and his wife, Her Royal Highness Princess Helen, are delighted to announce the engagement of their only son, Lord Fred, and Ms Summer York,' the statement read. 'Lord Fred has informed the King and other members of the royal family. The wedding will take place later in the year. Further details will be released in due course. Lord Fred and Ms York will appear for a photo call at Francis Court tomorrow morning.'

Fred (39) and Summer (34) have been inseparable over the last few months, and speculation in the popular press about a possible engagement has already been growing, fuelled by a visit by the pair to Fenn House early this week, where King James and Queen Olivia have been staying for a short break. The pair made their first official appearance together in May at the royal wedding of Lady Sophie Clifford to actress and model Jessica Hines.

A statement from Summer's parents, Mark and Julia York, said, 'We are thrilled for Fred and Summer. Summer is a smart, kind, and loving person, and in Fred, she has found someone who shares the same qualities. We are excited about their future together, and we wish them all our hopes for a lifetime of happiness.'

From everyone at TSP — Congratulations Lord Fred and Summer!

In other royal news, Lady Beatrice (37), the Countess of Rossex, attended her son's end of term prize giving event at Wilton College in Derbyshire yesterday. Samuel (15), the future Earl of Durrland and son of the late Earl of Rossex, James Wiltshire, was presented with the Most Valuable Player award for his efforts as part of the first XI cricket team. Lady Beatrice, who has recently moved with her son into The Dower House on the Francis Court estate belonging to her parents, was accompanied by Superintendent Richard Fitzwilliam (45) of City Police. It is believed the couple has been quietly dating for several months.

In other Francis Court news, Pete Cowley (47), head gardener, and Ellie Gunn (46), catering manager, are to be married. The couple, described by Lady Sarah Rosdale as "well-liked and highly valued members of the Francis Court team", got engaged in Paris yesterday. The wedding will take place in December at the famous Francis Court Orangery and will be attended by members of the Astley family.

54

MID-MORNING, SUNDAY 27 JUNE

"Should I wake Sam?" Bea asked as she glanced up at the kitchen clock above the doorway in the basement of The Dower House. "He's usually up by now."

"Let him sleep," Rich replied with a warm smile, reaching for another piece of toast. "It's his first proper lie-in for ages. He deserves it."

Bea's gaze lingered on the door for a moment longer before turning back to her food. *Rich's right. Sam's been working so hard lately. He needs the rest.* Besides, when she'd popped in fifteen minutes ago to tell him Perry and Simon were here, he'd looked so peaceful fast asleep with Daisy curled up beside him, she hadn't wanted to disturb them.

"How's your mother doing, Rich?" Simon asked, slicing into his eggs Benedict with gusto.

"Holding up," Rich replied, picking up his coffee. "I had a long chat with her last night, and she's agreed to come back with Elise tomorrow. Apparently, Double D had been seriously ill for a few weeks, so in the end, she says it was a happy release."

"She must be feeling so lost without him," Perry said.

Rich nodded. "She's worried about what she'll do now she doesn't have him to look after."

"Perhaps we should invite her to stay with us for a few days," Bea suggested.

Rich's face lit up. "I'd love that — if you think Sam wouldn't mind."

"Sam's going to be too busy helping me and Ryan at SaltAir to worry about additional guests," Simon chimed in.

"Don't worry; we'll make her feel right at home," Perry said, taking a huge bite of a bacon bap. "Talking of mothers," he continued through a mouthful of food. "Your mother surpassed herself this time, Bea. She managed to bury that you and Richard are dating in the news of Fred and Summer's engagement and even added Pete's proposal to Ellie to boot."

Bea grinned. She'd already thanked her mother for orchestrating such a low-key introduction of her and Rich as a couple. Fred's announcement had been great timing!

Bea thought back to the day before and how surprisingly easy it had been to face the world with Rich by her side. As they'd driven through the gates of Wilton College, the car having been lit up by the flash of cameras coming from the rabble of press outside the school, she'd felt a calmness wash over her she hadn't expected. And Sam's reaction to seeing Rich had been a great relief. He'd excitedly introduced Rich to his friends as "the detective who got shot" and had even insisted Rich show off his scar to Sam's cricket teammates.

She suppressed a smile as she recalled the conversation she and Rich had had with Sam in the car on their way back from Wilton. With much trepidation on her part, she'd told him they were dating. "Oh, that? I already knew," Sam said, rolling his eyes and adding, "I'm not stupid, Mum!" As he and Rich had then spent the rest of the journey home talking about the men's Cricket World Cup qualification rounds coming up soon, Bea had relaxed back in her seat, letting the voices of the two men she loved the most wash over her, glad they had successfully cleared their first hurdle together.

Perry grinned mischievously at Bea. "And was I right about Paris? Or was I right?" he said gleefully, his blue eyes dancing.

"Fine, fine," Bea conceded, rolling her eyes but smiling nonetheless. "You were right, Perry." She kept to herself the fact that she'd discreetly nudged Pete in that direction a few days ago, warning him of Ellie's expectations. He'd been more than happy to oblige, telling Bea the only thing that had been holding him back was that he hadn't been sure if Ellie would say yes.

Before Perry could gloat any further, Simon's phone rang. Simon accepted the call and put it on speaker. "Steve, mucker. Don't tell me — you're just passing, and you wondered if we're having breakfast?"

"Ha!" Steve chuckled. "I wish. I'm at the station in King's Town, and all that's on offer on a Sunday morning is stale doughnuts."

"Sorry to hear that, mate."

"Anyway, I called to tell you some interesting news. Is Lady Beatrice with you?"

Bea raised an eyebrow at Rich.

"Yes, she is."

"Well, I just want to say congratulations, my lady. Your hunch was correct."

Bea blinked rapidly. "What hunch?"

Steve chuckled at the other end of the line. "Bryan Sinclair is still alive."

Bea's stomach flipped. *What!?* Rich grinned at her.

"Alive?" Perry cried, nearly choking on his toast.

"Yep," Steve continued. "He's been living in Spain all this time with his wife, disguised as her live-in groundsman."

Perry's eyes widened. "No way!"

"How did you find out?" Simon asked.

"After Lady Beatrice highlighted that Bryan's body had never been found, we made a few enquiries. The local Spanish police went to Ann Sinclair's villa. Obviously, she's still over here at the moment. They encountered a man at the property who said he was the caretaker. He spoke Spanish, but they reported they didn't think it was his first language. They came back with a description, and although he'd clearly had some work done to his face, he is the same build and height as Bryan. They sent over a picture, and just on the off chance, I showed it to Julian Thornton. He spilled the beans. He said he found out Bryan was still alive and living in Spain with his wife a year ago when he turned up to visit her unannounced while in the area and had come face to face with Bryan when he'd opened the door. Apparently, Bryan was worried about the money laundering being discovered after Vic found out, so a year later, he staged the boating accident, disappeared for six months to Mexico, then returned to Spain and supposedly was hired by his wife as the groundsman and caretaker at their villa."

Oh my goodness! And he'd got away with it until now. She almost felt sorry for him. *Almost...*

"Unbelievable!" Simon shook his head. "What now?"

"We're working on an extradition request," Steve replied. "That will take some time, so we're going to talk to his wife and see if she can persuade him to come back and face the music."

"Good luck with that," Perry quipped, raising an eyebrow.

"Yeah. A bit of a long shot, I know. But now he knows the game is up, he might cooperate for a deal."

"How's Finch?" Rich asked. "Is he talking yet?"

"We're working on it. We had some luck this morning. Going through Finch's Amazon account, we found a large order for silica gel packs from a few days after Vic's murder."

"That's great news," Simon said. "That will be difficult for him to explain away."

"Exactly. His lawyer has now said they will consider a guilty plea if it will avoid Finch going to court, mostly to spare his son and ex-wife the attention." He breathed out noisily. "No doubt they'll work something out by the end of the day."

"Thanks for letting us know, mate, we really appreciate it," Simon said while Rich, Bea, and Perry mumbled, "Thanks," as well.

As Simon cut the call, Perry turned to Bea. "Bryan alive! Can you believe that?" he said, his eyes dancing.

Bea touched her neck, then shook her head.

"Well, now that's finally over, we can focus on more important things, like the grand opening of SaltAir!" he continued.

Bea smiled, the heavy feeling in her stomach replaced by a lightness in her chest. "Indeed. Only twelve days to go. I hope we can get it all done in time."

Rich reached over and squeezed her hand. "Don't worry, you'll be fine. It's just a question of putting up a bit of wallpaper, isn't it?"

What! Snatching her hand from his, she spun around to face him. He was grinning as he raised his arm as if to fend off a slap. "Oh, ha ha," she said, trying unsuccessfully not to laugh.

55

TWELVE DAYS LATER. GRAND OPENING OF SALTAIR, THURSDAY 8 JULY

H er heart pounding, Bea clutched her phone tightly as the Bentley purred along the coastal road in Windstanton. She slowly took a deep breath in through her nose. This was it — her and Rich's first official outing together. The moment when they would present themselves to the scrutinising gaze of the press that would inevitably then thrust them into the public eye.

"Relax, Bea," Perry whispered beside her as he reached out and put his hand over hers. "We're all here to support you and Rich."

A tingling warmth spread up from her hand. She turned and smiled at her best friend. *What would I do without you?* She let the air out of her lungs in a rush.

"Your mother knows what she's doing, Bea," he continued in a low voice. "Arriving as a group is — Well, safety in numbers or, at the very least, a diffused spotlight."

"Thank you," she said, squeezing his fingers before dropping his hand. She hoped her mother's suggestion to arrive with Sam, Archie, Perry, and Isla would help dilute the attention she and Rich were bound to receive.

Her eyes drifted to the front of the Bentley where Rich sat chatting amiably with Fraser, who was driving. Rich seemed so at ease; his relaxed posture and easy laughter clearly indicated that he felt right at home. It was a talent of his, this seamless blending into new surroundings, mirroring the way he'd slipped into her life and reshaped it without any visible seams. Ever since the investigation into Vic's death had led him to stay at The Dower House, her world had become infinitely brighter with him in it. She smiled to herself. She could never have imagined just over a year ago that the man who had made her blood boil in frustration would now have integrated himself into every aspect of her life – her family and friends. And, of course, the Frasers loved him. He simply belonged now.

Her thoughts drifted back to the weekend, a smile playing on her lips as she remembered the vet visiting Francis Court for Daisy's six-month check-up. Perry, who was supposed to have been there to take some responsibility for the little terrier's weight issues, had conveniently scheduled a trip to London with Simon and Isla to see a West End show. Rich, ever supportive, had offered to be there with her instead. After Daisy had been given a clean bill of health, the vet had turned apologetically to Bea and said, "She's still a little on the chubby side, I'm afraid, my lady."

Before Bea had had the chance to explain that she had been trying but was in a constant battle with everyone around her to not overfeed Daisy treats, Rich had stepped in, assuring the vet he would make sure that they upped Daisy's exercise and cut down on the titbits. When the vet had gone, Bea had smirked as she'd wished Rich good luck with fulfilling his promise, but at the same time, her heart had soared, knowing that he was happily making commitments that would see him continue to be a part of her life far into the future.

"Wow, there are so many cameras," Sam said, his voice betraying his excitement as his words snapped Bea back to the present. The car was approaching the turn-off that led to SaltAir, and the glimmer of camera flashes lit up the sky. Sam, Archie, and Isla craned their necks to look down the street.

Bea looked over at Sam's best friend. "Are you sure you're okay with this, Archie?" Bea asked, her stomach churning.

"Don't worry, Lady B. My mother taught me a technique that makes it all kind of fun," Archie told her, beaming.

Really? Bea couldn't imagine anything that would make stepping out in front of hundreds of flashing cameras fun.

"What is it?" Isla asked, her eye's wide.

"You imagine all the press as dogs."

What?

Rich turned around and popped his head over the seat. "I think you'll need to explain that to us in a little more detail, please, Archie."

They all turned to stare at the boy.

"Okay, so you know how if someone asked you what dog they were, you would instinctively be able to tell them based on what they look like?"

Bea tilted her head to one side. *Is he saying we all look like dogs?*

"Let me give you an example," Archie continued. "So you, Isla, would be a red setter. Your hair is that colour, and you're so sleek in that green outfit."

The corners of Bea's mouth twitched. She and Perry had had so much fun taking Isla late night shopping to find her something to wear after their spa day. Isla had protested at first, insisting she didn't do dresses and that a new pair of black jeans and a white shirt would be fine. But Perry had insisted, pointing out she was the co-owner's daughter and, more importantly, *his* stepdaughter, and as he'd put it, waving his arms in the air, "We have to look fabulous, my dear." Once she'd started trying outfits on and got lots of *oohs* and *ahs* from Bea and Perry, she'd relaxed and had begun to enjoy it. Eventually, they'd settled on a flowing green jump-suit made of silk that hung beautifully on her slender frame. A pair of gold sandals completed the look, and as Perry declared, she looked like a model. As he'd paid, Perry had whispered to Bea, "It's fun having a stepdaughter."

Isla giggled.

Archie turned to Perry. "Mr Juke, you would be a chihuahua."

Bea snorted.

"You've got spiky hair, and you're smart and fierce at the same time."

"I'll take that!" Perry replied, chuckling.

Sam laughed. Archie turned to his best pal and pulled a face. "Sam is definitely a poodle! You should see how long it takes for him to get his hair right in the mornings."

"Oi!" Sam nudged Archie, still laughing. "It takes ages to look this good!"

"You, Lady B, would be a black Afghan Hound. You're elegant and a little aloof."

"Ha!" Perry barked a laugh.

Bea smoothed down the skirt of her long black dress, feeling a little smug. *Elegant, heh?*

They all looked at Rich. He straightened his features and cocked his head at Archie. "Be careful what you say, young man."

"You're a rottweiler, sir. You look really tough, but with people you know, you're actually really nice."

Rich dipped his chin. "Fair."

"And what are you, Archie?" Bea asked, wiping away a tear of laughter.

"Oh, mum says I'm a Yorkshire terrier because I get excited about the smallest little thing."

As their laughter filled the air, and the bright light of the flashing cameras filled the car, Bea leaned back, her shoulders relaxed.

"We're here, my lady," Fraser announced as the Bentley pulled up to the entrance of SaltAir.

Bea glanced out at the red carpet with gold roped barriers that had been erected to create a walkway leading to the main entrance. It had been Perry's idea. All around the area, the press jostled for the best position while uniformed policemen kept them in check.

Bea took a deep breath, steeling herself for the onslaught of flashbulbs and questions from the press as Fraser got out of the car.

Click! Click! Click!

The barrage of noise and flashing lights was almost overwhelming as Fraser opened the door, and Sam, Archie, Isla, and Perry scrambled out onto the scarlet carpet. Bea shuffled along the back seat, her pulse quickening.

"Ready?" Rich extended his hand to help her out of the car, his voice calm and reassuring.

"Let's do this," she replied, placing her hand in his and stepping out of the vehicle.

Flashbulbs popped like electric raindrops, and a barrage of voices called out from behind velvet ropes.

"This way, my lady!"

"Sam, Sam, over here!"

"Lady Rossex, over here, please!"

Bea's heart thrummed in her chest, but then there was Rich beside her, his hand finding its place on the small of her back, gently nudging her forward—a silent anchor amidst the storm of noise and light.

"Can we have a picture, please?"

"Everyone, this way!"

Bea glanced at the others, knowing that the best way to bring an end to this was to give the press what they wanted. She nodded, signalling for the group to gather together and turn for the cameras.

As they posed, Archie cried, "Dogs," over the uproar. They all looked directly at the mass of press before them, and Bea began to chuckle as she spotted a big German shepherd, a grumpy looking bull dog, and a corgi with large sticking up ears. As laughter spread through the group, a surge of warmth radiated through her body, stemming from Rich's fingers resting on the base of her spine and melting away her anxiety. *This isn't so bad, after all.*

Just as her cheeks began to ache, the arrival of another car turned the tide of attention. Fred and Summer stepped out as the cameras swung towards them.

Click! Click! Click!

"Looks like the cavalry has arrived," Rich mumbled in her ear as their gaze followed the frenzy.

Her brother, with his charismatic smile, and his fiancée, ever the picture of cool, strode over to them, their arms wide. As they merged into the group with handshakes and warm embraces, Fred grabbed her. "We'll take it from here, little sis," he whispered into Bea's ear as he gave her a hug. "See you in there."

"Thanks, big brother," Bea breathed, kissing him on the cheek. A sudden lightness invaded her body as she turned and followed the others into SaltAir, the chorus of, "Lord Fred, Summer, over here!" fading as they greeted a beaming Ryan and Simon just inside the door.

Sam and Archie immediately ran off to the kitchen to fulfil their promise to help serve the canapés, and after giving her father a hug, Isla asked if she could help too. An enormous smile spread over Simon's face as he said,"Yes.".

Bea glanced at Rich beside her.

"See? That wasn't so bad, now was it?" Rich asked, his eyes searching her face.

"Actually, no," she said. It had been much easier than she'd thought it would be. Because of him. As she looked into his deep-brown eyes, she knew that she needn't have had any doubts about their feelings for each other. She took a deep breath and then smiled slowly. "With you by my side, I think I can face anything."

56

LATER, THURSDAY 8 JULY

Bea swirled her Tia Maria, the ice cubes tinkling gently against the side of the glass as she looked across the drawing room of The Dower House at Perry and Simon. They sat on the sofa on the other side of the low coffee table. "It feels like tonight went great, doesn't it?" she said, a hint of uncertainty in her voice.

"Of course it did!" Perry said before taking another sip of his gin and tonic. "Everyone we invited showed up looking fabulous. It was the hottest ticket in town, according to social media."

Bea looked from Perry to Simon. *Is he happy with his guests' response to SaltAir?* He caught her eye and beamed, raising his glass in a silent toast. "I had a text from Ryan while we were on our way back. He said the first supper club is already sold out, and we've a full waiting list for the next one."

"That's brilliant news," Bea said, her heart swelling with pride. Simon and Ryan had put their everything into this restaurant. *They deserve for it to be a tremendous success.*

Next to her on the sofa, Daisy gave a sigh and snuggled

closer into her side. Bea looked over the snoozing body of her little terrier and smiled at Rich. He winked at her. Her heart fluttered as heat prickled her cheeks. *How does he do that?*

Simon coughed. "I'd just like to say a big thank you on behalf of myself and Ryan for all your support. We couldn't have done it without you." He raised his glass, and they all leaned over the table to meet in the middle for the toast. "Oh, and I must add that Sam, Archie, and Isla did a fantastic job handing out canapés to the guests. They really made an impression."

"I think that's because they were so knowledgeable about the food," Perry said, leaning back on the couch. "They really did us proud."

"Indeed," Bea agreed, smiling at the thought of the trio upstairs playing video games in Sam's games room. "I'm so pleased they're getting on well, even though Sam and Archie are four years younger than Isla."

"Sometimes we forget," Simon said, his voice a little shaky. "Isla has had to grow up quickly since her mother fell ill. It's good to see her having fun and being young again."

Perry reached over and placed his hand on his husband's knee. He patted it, saying, "She was a real credit to you tonight, love.

"*And* Clary House looked amazing," Rich said, raising his glass again. "Especially the restaurant. You two have done an incredible job." He looked from Bea to Perry and back.

"Hear, hear!" Simon said, clinking glasses with Rich. "Everyone was talking about the Victorian conservatory mural."

"Thank you," Bea and Perry replied, both beaming with pride. Their decision to take vintage to the next level and go full-on Victoriana in the restaurant downstairs seemed to have paid off.

As a comfortable silence descended on the foursome, Perry pulled out his phone. After a few minutes of scrolling, he looked up at the others, his eyes sparkling. "The opening is already all over social media. They're talking about how amazing the food was and saying the decor made it feel like an immersive experience. And they're describing the guest list as a who's who of food royalty interspersed with real royalty," he told them. "Oh, and listen to this. 'The red carpet for tonight's opening of SaltAir in Windstanton, Ryan Hawley's new restaurant in Fenshire' —" He paused and patted Simon on the arm, saying, "Sorry, love," before continuing, "Rivalled last month's Met Gala for glamour and famous faces." A huge smile split his face as he murmured, "I can't believe they compared us to the Met Gala."

Rich nudged Bea with his elbow and mouthed, "The what?" She grinned as she leaned towards him and said in a low voice, "It's a big annual fundraiser in New York that's become the most prestigious and glamorous event probably in the world. It's invitation only, and tables cost over three hundred thousand pounds each." Rich's eyes opened wide as his mouth fell open. "Indeed." Bea laughed.

"I hope there will be some wonderful photos of us in the papers tomorrow," Perry said, his blue eyes glinting in the low lights.

For once, Bea shared Perry's excitement. Her mother had been right (*of course — her mother was always right!*) about them arriving all together being a great idea. Some photos had already been posted on social media, showing the seven of them standing together, capturing the moment when they'd all laughed at Archie's shout of, "Dogs." The pictures had given Bea a warm and fuzzy feeling. *I'm so lucky to share my life with these amazing people.*

"Talking of tomorrow," Simon said, now addressing Rich. "Is everything set for Dougie's funeral?"

"Yep, all sorted," Rich replied, taking a sip of his rum. "In fairness, Double D's children have actually stepped up and arranged it all. Although Mum's paying, of course." He reached out and took Bea's hand, their fingers intertwining over a snoring Daisy. She was going with him to the funeral tomorrow afternoon, and she knew he was glad she would be there.

"Dawn seemed to have a lovely time staying here last week," Perry commented before finishing his drink.

"She really did," Rich agreed, his face softening at the mention of his mother. "She's made firm friends with Mrs Fraser and has promised to come back again soon."

Rich's mother had been surprisingly chirpy when she'd arrived to stay with them at The Dower House and had been clearly excited to spend some time with her son. It hadn't taken long for Bea to work out where Rich had got his dry sense of humour from, and the two women had soon hit it off. It had taken a little while for Dawn to adjust to being away from the city, but after a day or so, she'd relaxed and had enjoyed walking in the grounds with Rich or going with Sam to take Daisy for a walk along the beach. Bea's son and Rich's mother had formed an instant bond, and when Archie had joined them a few days later, Dawn had taken the two youngsters under her wing. She'd taught them card games, and they'd showed her how to play Minecraft. It was clear, though, that she didn't like to sit around and be idle for long, so Mrs Fraser had allowed her to join her in the kitchen. Soon the house had been full of the aroma of freshly baked bread, cakes, and biscuits, much to the boy delight. They'd all been sorry to see her return to Leeds earlier in the week and were looking forward to her coming back to them later in the year.

"Actually, she's away with Elise and her family after the funeral. They're going to Scotland for a month," Rich continued. "She's loving finally getting to know her grandsons better."

Elise's two sons were also enjoying getting to know 'Nanny Leeds', as they knew her. Even Sam and Archie had started calling her that by the end of her stay.

"It was good to see CID Steve and his wife, Julia, tonight," Rich said, changing the subject. "He was telling me Finch is likely to be sentenced in the next few weeks."

They'd all been relieved when Finch had finally pleaded guilty to the murder of Victor Blackwell in return for the charge of attempted murder of Julian Thornton being reduced to grievous bodily harm with Julian's agreement. The local businessman had in turn pleaded guilty to money laundering but drug trafficking charges had been dropped. Bryan Sinclair was still in Spain but under house arrest while the authorities tried to get the extradition order cleared in court. He, unlike Finch and Julian, was determined not to come quietly.

"I still think it's amazing how so much of Finch's confession matched up with our own deductions." Perry pulled a face.

"Finch thought he was bulletproof," Simon pointed out, shrugging. "He always was a bit too sure of himself. He probably believed he could get away with anything."

"Well, he *had*. For over three years. Just as well Finch had those corrupt councillors in his pocket to block Julian's planning permission for so long," Rich said, dropping Bea's hand to pour them all another drink. Daisy jumped off the sofa with a huff and sprawled out under the table.

"I bet he had a bit of a shock though when he found out you were planning to knock down the wall. How *did* he find out, by the way?" Bea asked.

"He heard it from someone in the pub who works for Charles," Simon told him.

"No wonder he tried to break in to remove Vic's remains. If it hadn't have been for Ryan's state-of-the-art new security system, then he might've been successful," Rich said. "The damage would have been put down to vandals, and we'd have been none the wiser."

Bea's stomach flipped. *Finch would have got away with it.*

Simon shook his head. "And then, of course, he had his contingency plan — blame Bryan."

"You realise that if Julian hadn't panicked when he'd worked out Finch was the killer and forced the meeting, then we would have had to accept Finch's conclusion that Bryan was the murderer, and he'd still be free and unpunished," Perry said, accepting a fresh glass from Rich.

"And Bryan would still be living it up in the sun without a care in the world," Simon said, a wry smile on his face.

57

A FEW MINUTES LATER, THURSDAY
8 JULY

"Talking of living it up in the sun," Rich said, leaning back and wrapping an arm around Bea's shoulders. "How would you feel about taking a holiday?" he asked her. "I'd like to take you and Sam away for a couple of weeks later this month."

"Really?" Bea's eyes lit up. "That sounds amazing. I wonder if we could borrow Lady Grace's villa in Portugal if it's free?"

"Perfect." Rich grinned, pressing a kiss to her temple. "Although, I think you'd better ask her rather than me." Bea grinned. Rich and Lady Grace had butted heads during an investigation at her ladyship's country home in Fawstead last year, and although Bea had had a message from her recently saying how pleased she was that Bea had found love again, she no doubt having been brought up to date on the news by her close friend, Bea's mother, she hadn't mentioned Rich by name. He was, therefore, convinced she still disapproved of him.

"That's a good idea," Simon said, giving Perry a gentle nudge. "I don't know about you, but I could do with a holiday. We should do something like that too, don't you think? Just the three of us before Isla goes back to Barcelona. Maybe we could hire a camper van and explore the south coast. Isla's never really seen how beautiful it is down there."

Perry's eyes widened in sheer panic. Bea stifled a laugh. *Poor Perry.* Was it the idea of roughing it in campsites full of over-excited children on their school holidays or the idea of being alone with just Simon and Isla that had made him go so pale? He swallowed and glanced longingly towards the door like he was planning his escape. Bea looked at Rich. *Can I?* He dipped his chin. *This is why I love this man!* "Why don't we all go together? Lady Grace's villa is huge, and it will be nice for Sam and Isla to have someone nearer their own age to hang out with."

"What a fantastic idea, Bea!" Perry cried, his blue eyes shining as he let out a deep breath. He shot her a grateful look. She tilted her head to one side in acknowledgement.

They chatted about their new holiday plans, and not long after, Bea received a text message from Lady Grace confirming the villa was available. The sound of footsteps descending the stairs signalled the arrival of Isla, Sam, and Archie. Daisy, jumping up from the floor, bounded towards them, wagging her tail wildly.

"Sam, Isla, guess what?" Perry cried, scrambling out of his seat, unable to hide his excitement. "We're planning a holiday together later this month! How does Portugal sound?"

"Awesome!" Sam and Isla chorused. Isla gave a little hop as she joined Perry and Simon on the sofa, a huge grin on her face.

Bea watched her son as a beaming smile split his face, brightening his brown eyes. *He deserves a nice holiday.* Then his face clouded as he looked at his best friend beside him.

"Can Archie come too?" he stared into her eyes, a pleading tone in his voice.

Rich's hand squeezed her shoulder. "Of course," Rich said. "As long as his parents are okay with it."

"Brilliant!" Archie chimed in, grinning from ear to ear. "I'm sure they will be."

The boys were buzzing with anticipation, though Bea could see signs of their growing exhaustion. "Right," she said, rising. "You two should head up to bed. You can talk more about the holiday while you pack for your weekend with Sam's grandparents."

"But, Mum…" Sam protested, trying to stifle a yawn.

"I'll bring you up a hot chocolate," she told him as he rubbed his eyes.

"Okay…" He and Archie bid everyone goodnight, then calling Daisy to follow them, they left the room.

Simon rose, placing his now empty drink on the table. "We'd better get going too. We're off to visit my parents tomorrow, so we have an early start."

"Thanks for everything, Lady…I mean, Bea." Isla jumped up, flashing a warm smile. "I can't wait for the holiday!"

"Neither can I," Bea assured her as she gave the young girl a hug. After they finished all their goodbyes, Perry, Simon, and Isla departed, leaving Bea and Rich alone in the now peaceful drawing room.

Rich pulled Bea to him, wrapping his powerful arms around her. The warmth of his embrace enveloped her, and she breathed in his comforting spicy scent. "Right, let's go make those boys their hot chocolate," he said, giving her a gentle squeeze before moving to release her.

"Are you really okay with Archie, Perry, Simon, and Isla all coming on the holiday too?" she asked tentatively as she held on to him and looked up into his handsome face.

"Absolutely," he replied, dipping his head and kissing her softly. "As long as this place is big enough for you and I to have some time alone," he whispered as his lips left hers.

She smiled coyly, her heart swelling with affection for this man, who always seemed to know what she needed. "Don't worry. I'll make sure of it."

58

THE NEXT DAY, FRIDAY 9 JULY

T*he Society Page* online article:

<u>*Newly Engaged Royal Couple Attends Restaurant Opening*</u>

Lord Frederick Astley and his future wife, Summer York, last night attended the hot-ticket event, the opening of SaltAir, the restaurant jointly owned by Ryan Hawley, renowned chef and Bake Off War*s judge, and crime writer and celebrity chef, Simon Lattimore. Summer, looking radiant in a long pale-yellow maxi dress, stopped for pictures on the steps of Clary House in Windstanton, Fenshire, on the arm of Lord Fred, who looked dapper in a black dinner suit and a matching pale-yellow bow tie. The couple, who announced their engagement twelve days ago, are currently staying at nearby Francis Court, having made a surprise visit to Fenswich Children's Hospital this afternoon, where they spent time with children and staff in the burns unit.*

The restaurant opening was also attended by other royals: Lord Fred's twin sister, Lady Sarah; her husband,

John Rosdale; and Lord Fred's younger sister, Lady Beatrice, the Countess of Rossex. Lady Beatrice was accompanied by: her son, Samual Wiltshire; his school friend, Archie Tellis, son of film director and producer Hal Tellis and his wife, acclaimed actress Andrea Tellis; Simon Lattimore's daughter, Isla Scott; and his husband, Perry Juke. Also by Lady Beatrice's side was her boyfriend, Richard Fitzwilliam, a superintendent in City Police.

Other celebrities seen at the opening included: Ryan Hawley's girlfriend, the renowned food critic, Fay Mayer; Finn Gilligan, Ryan's co-presenter on the TV show Two Chefs in a Camper; *and the popular chef and* Bake Off Wars *judge, Mike Jacob. Rob Rivers, the local TV and radio personality and chef-patron of the bistro Rivers by the Sea in Windstanton, also attended, along with the social media influencer and* Love Resort *contestant, Bella DeMarco.*

Guests were treated to an assortment of bite-size tasters made using seasonal, locally sourced ingredients, with food bloggers raving about the exquisite presentation and the luscious flavours. Pictures of the Victorian-inspired SaltAir restaurant on the downstairs level have been appearing online since the event, with the posts describing the style as elegant modern-Victoriana. On the first floor is the supper room, where the monthly SaltAir Fine will be hosted. Guests were given a tour of the room, although no pictures were allowed, with one guest reporting the room as classic, stylish, and enchanting. Membership for the supper club is full, and so is the waiting list, according to a SaltAir spokesperson.

One local dignitary who was missing from the opening was Windstanton businessman and previous owner of Clary House, Julian Thornton. The Windstanton Gazette *reports Thornton, who had hoped to be a future mayoral candidate, recently pleaded guilty to charges of money laun-*

dering and is keeping a low profile while on bail pending sentencing. The local newspaper also reported a man was recently charged in connection with the death of Victor Blackwell, a chef whose remains were discovered in Windstanton three weeks ago, three years after he had supposedly left the country. No further details are available at this time.

––––––

I hope you enjoyed *A Death Of Fresh Air*. If you did then please consider writing a review on Amazon or Goodreads, or even both. It helps me a lot if you let people know that you recommend it.

Will Bea, Rich, and the others get to enjoy a relaxing holiday in Portugal? I fear not! Find out in the next book in the *A Right Royal Cozy Investigation* series *I Kill Always Love You*. Pre-order it on Amazon now.

Want to know how Perry and Simon solved their first crime together? Then join my readers' club and receive a FREE ebook short story Tick, Tock, Mystery Clock at https://www.subscribepage.com/helengoldenauthor_nls   or buy it in the Amazon store.

For other books by me, take a look at the back pages.

If you want to find out more about what I'm up to you can

find me on Facebook at *helengoldenauthor* or on Instagram at *helengolden_author*.

Be the first to know when my next book is available. Follow Helen Golden on Amazon, BookBub, and Goodreads to get alerts whenever I have a new release, preorder, or a discount on any of my books.

CHARACTERS IN ORDER OF APPEARANCE
A DEATH OF FRESH AIR

Ryan Hawley — Executive chef at *Nonnina* in Knightsbridge, judge on *Bake Off Wars*, and joint owner of SaltAir with Simon Lattimore.

Simon Lattimore — Perry Juke's husband. Bestselling crime writer. Ex-Fenshire CID. Winner of cooking competition *Celebrity Elitechef.* Joint owner of SaltAir with Ryan Hawley.

Lady Beatrice — The Countess of Rossex. Seventeenth in line to the British throne. Daughter of Charles Astley, the Duke of Arnwall and Her Royal Highness Princess Helen. Niece of the current king.

Perry Juke — Lady Beatrice's business partner and BFF. Married to Simon Lattimore

Charles Hallshall — Local building contractor and owner of Hallshall Building Renovations (HBR)

Julian Thornton — Local businessman. Previous owner of Clary House. Chair of the Windstanton Rejuvenation Council.

Daisy — Lady Beatrice's adorable West Highland Terrier.

Finn Gilligan — TV chef and co-presenter of *Two Chefs in a Camper* along with Ryan Hawley.

Mark Jacob — renowned TV chef and judge on *Bake Off Wars.*

Lord Frederick (Fred) Astley — Earl of Tilling. Lady Beatrice's elder brother and twin of Lady Sarah Rosdale. Ex-Intelligence Army Officer. Future Duke of Arnwall.

Summer York — comedian and TV presenter. One of presenting duo on *Bake Off Wars.*

Lady Sarah Rosdale — Lady Beatrice's elder sister. Twin of Fred Astley. Manages events at Francis Court.

John Rosdale — Lady Sarah's husband.

Sam Wiltshire — son of Lady Beatrice and the late James Wiltshire, the Earl of Rossex. Future Earl of Durrland.

Archie Tellis - Sam's best friend from school.

Richard Fitzwilliam — Former Detective Chief Inspector at *PaIRS (Protection and Investigation (Royal) Service)* an organisation that provides protection and security to the royal family and who investigate any threats against them. Now a Superintendent at *City Police*, a police organisation based in the capital, London, heading up the Capital Security Liaison team.

Isla Scott — Simon Lattimore's recently surfaced daughter.

Robin 'Rob' Rivers — Owner of bistro Rivers By The Sea. Local TV and radio personality. Former senior sous chef at The Seaside Lounge.

Marco Rossi — Fenshire food critic and wine expert. Former maitre d at The Seaside Lounge.

Isabella 'Bella' DeMarco — Fenshire based social media influencer and food blogger. Former sous chef at The Seaside Lounge.

Olivia 'Liv' Belmont — Manager of the Winstanton Theatre and ex-girlfriend of Vic Blackwell.

Ellie Gunn — Francis Court's catering manager.

Claire Beck — Francis Court's human resources manager.

Maisey Dixon — Claire Beck's sister. Former server at *The Seaside Lounge*. (Reader suggestion by Maggie Allen)

Victor 'Vic' Blackwell — Chef at The Seaside Lounge in Windstanton who disappeared 3 years prior.

Fraser (William) — driver/butler/handyman The Dower House.

Mike Ainsley — Detective Inspector at Fenshire CID.

Hayden Saunders — Detective Chief Inspector, investigations team PaIRS.

Albert 'Bert' Finch — Detective Inspector Fenshire CID Cold Case Unit.

Fay Mayer — Ryan's girlfriend and food journalist.

Steve Cox/CID Steve — ex-colleague of Simon Lattimore at Fenshire CID.

Eamon Hines— Detective Sergeant at Fenshire CID.

Roisin — Simon Lattimore's friend who works in Forensics at Fenshire Police.

James Wiltshire — The Earl of Rossex. Lady Beatrice's late husband killed in a car accident fourteen years ago. Sam's dad.

Mrs (Maggie) Fraser — cook/housekeeper The Dower House.

Nicky — server in the Breakfast Room restaurant at Francis Court.

Dorothy 'Dot' Thoms — Owner of *Dot Dusts* and local gossip.

Mrs Carol Hall — lives opposite Clary House. (Reader suggestion from Gwen Desselle)

Sonia — Front of house manager at Rivers By The Sea.

Bryan Sinclair — Julian Thornton's accountant, deceased.

Mr Cartwright — General Manager of The Fawstead Inn

HRH Princess Helen — Duchess of Arnwall. Mother of Lady Beatrice. Sister of the current king.

Queen Mary The Queen Mother — wife of the late King, mother of HRH Princess Helen and grandmother of Lady Beatrice.

Pete Cowley — gardener at Francis Court. Ex-marine. Boyfriend of Ellie Gunn.

Angelia (Ange) — Dot's sister-in-law. Cleaner.

Dawn Fitzwilliam — Richards Fitzwilliam's mother.

Desperate Dougie (Double D) — Dawn Fitzwilliam's long-term partner.

Elise Boyce — Richard Fitzwilliam's sister

Charles Astley — Duke of Arnwall. Lady Beatrice's father.

Ann Sinclair — Bryan Sinclair's widow.

A BIG THANK YOU TO…

…everyone who continues to offer encouragement and support. It means so much to me.

To my editor Marina Grout. I worry about you living on a boat during hurricane season, as I couldn't do this without you!

To Ann, Ray, Lissie, and Carolyn for being my beta readers and/or additional set of eyes before I push the final button. Your support is pivotal to making this all happen.

To my ARC Team. Your reviews and feedback are invaluable, and I appreciate everything you do for me.

To you, my readers. Thank you for encouraging me to keep writing. Us writers are an insecure bunch who never think we're good enough. Your feedback keeps me from going too far down that rabbit hole of self-doubt. I must mention two readers in particular, Gwen Desselle from Georgia, USA and Maggie Allen from Yorkshire, UK who won a competition to name a character each in this book. Thank you for taking part, and I hope you enjoy seeing your name in print.

My final thank you goes to my lovely soon-to-be nephew-in-law, Rob, who came up with the title of this book. It is so much better than my original idea!

As always, I may have taken a little dramatic license when it comes to police procedures, so any mistakes or misinterpretations, unintentional or otherwise, are my own.

ALSO BY HELEN GOLDEN

A short prequal in the series A Right Royal Cozy Investigation. Can Perry Juke and Simon Lattimore work together to solve the mystery of the missing clock before the thief disappears? FREE novelette when you sign up to my readers' club. See end of final chapter for details. Ebook only.

First book in the A Right Royal Cozy Investigation series. Amateur sleuth, Lady Beatrice, must pit her wits against Detective Chief Inspector Richard Fitzwilliam to prove her sister innocent of murder. With the help of her clever dog, her flamboyant co-interior designer and his ex-police partner, can she find the killer before him, or will she make a fool of herself?

Second book in the A Right Royal Cozy Investigation series. Amateur sleuth, Lady Beatrice, must once again go up against DCI Fitzwilliam to find a killer. With the help of Daisy, her clever companion, and her two best friends, Perry and Simon, can she catch the culprit before her childhood friend's wedding is ruined?

The third book in the A Right Royal Cozy Investigation series. When DCI Richard Fitzwilliam gets it into his head that Lady Beatrice's new beau Seb is guilty of murder, can the amateur sleuth, along with the help of Daisy, her clever westie, and her best friends Perry and Simon, find the real killer before Fitzwilliam goes ahead and arrests Seb?

A Prequel in the A Right Royal Cozy Investigation series. When Lady Beatrice's husband James Wiltshire dies in a car crash along with the wife of a member of staff, there are questions to be answered. Why haven't the occupants of two cars seen in the accident area come forward? And what is the secret James had been keeping from her?

When the dead body of the event's planner is found at the staff ball that Lady Beatrice is hosting at Francis Court, the amateur sleuth, with help from her clever dog Daisy and best friend Perry, must catch the killer before the partygoers find out and New Year's Eve is ruined.

Snow descends on Drew Castle in Scotland cutting the castle off and forcing Lady Beatrice along with Daisy her clever dog, and her best friends Perry and Simon to cooperate with boorish DCI Fitzwilliam to catch a killer before they strike again.

A murder at Gollingham Palace sparks a hunt to find the killer. For once, Lady Beatrice is happy to let DCI Richard Fitzwilliam get on with it. But when information comes to light that indicates it could be linked to her husband's car accident fifteen years ago, she is compelled to get involved. Will she finally find out the truth behind James's tragic death?

An unforgettable bachelor weekend for Perry filled with luxury, laughter, and an unexpected death.
Can Bea, Perry, and his hen's catch the killer before the weekend is over?

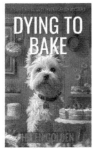

Bake Off Wars is being filmed on site at Francis Court and everyone is buzzing. But when much-loved pastry chef and judge, Vera Bolt, is found dead on set, can Bea, with the help of her best friend Perry, his husband Simon, and her cute little terrier, Daisy, expose the killer before the show is over?

Lady Beatrice's peaceful holiday in Portugal is shattered when a Hollywood star's husband is found dead. What appears to be an accident soon reveals itself as murder. Tasked with clearing an innocent woman's name, Bea and Rich must untangle a web of lies to uncover the truth before it's too late.

ALL EBOOKS AVAILABLE IN THE AMAZON STORE.

PAPERBACKS AVAILABLE FROM WHEREVER YOU BUY YOUR BOOKS.

Made in the USA
Columbia, SC
12 February 2025

53770856R00202